D1603648

Frontispiece: Oliver La Farge. Photograph courtesy of the *New Mexican*.

YELLOW SUN, BRIGHT SKY

The Indian Country Stories of Oliver La Farge

YELLOW SUN, BRIGHT SKY

The Indian Country Stories of Oliver La Farge

Edited and with an introduction by
David L. Caffey

UNIVERSITY OF NEW MEXICO PRESS
Albuquerque

Library of Congress Cataloging-in-Publication Data

La Farge, Oliver, 1901–1963.
    Yellow sun, bright sky : the Indian country stories of Oliver
LaFarge / edited and with an introduction by David L. Caffey.
      p. cm.
    Contents: North is black—Harder winter—Higher education—
Women at Yellow Wells—All the young men—Country boy—
Policeman follow order—The happy indian laughter—The bride at
Dead Soldier Spring—A pause in the desert—The little stone man
—The ancient strength.
    ISBN 0-8263-1101-6.   ISBN (invalid) 0-8263-1933-8 (pbk.)
    1. Indians of North America—Fiction.   2. Southwestern States—
Fiction. I. Caffey, David L., 1947– . II. Title.
PS3523.A2663A6   1988
813'.52—dc19   88-17193
                 CIP

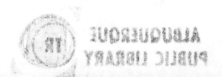

Contents

INTRODUCTION
David L. Caffey

He was not a happy young man, riding over the harsh high desert of the Navajo reservation, looking without relief at a searing landscape that repelled him and fulfilled his worst imaginings. Oliver La Farge, a nineteen-year-old Harvard anthropology student, had not wanted to spend the summer—1921—in Arizona. He was there at the urging of Dr. Alfred Tozzer, director of the Division of Anthropology, who thought La Farge should experience life and work in the field before cementing his interest in anthropology as a career. If his destiny was at hand, La Farge could hardly appreciate that.

La Farge would have preferred exploring Stone Age caves in France, but Harvard's current projects were in the desolate canyonlands of the Southwest. He looked upon his new environs from the back of a plodding horse, and was not impressed. "The damn country was a howling ash-heap," he recalled, "and this kind of riding was a pain in the neck."[1] La Farge did not expect to learn anything worthwhile from the ragged Indians he saw—pitiable wards of the American government. "So this was Arizona," he concluded; "The hell with it."

His resistance to the country began to break down with an overnight visit at Kayenta, in the home of John and Louisa Wetherill.[2] "No one could be even that short a time in the Wetherills' house, hearing them talk, seeing the beautiful things hanging on their walls, without catching some sense of the riches to be found among the Navajos and being stimulated to some desire to learn for himself," La Farge wrote. He started to see the country through new eyes—to wonder

1

at the qualities required to live in such a land, and to look more intently for the cultural riches he had glimpsed. He was soon won to an enduring love of the Navajo people and their barren, hostile, beautiful land. Back at Harvard, he dug into materials available in the Peabody Museum. As he came to know the people and learned more about their beliefs and ceremonial legends, his appreciation grew. "Above all," he said, "I was hit where I lived by their remarkable literature."

"The Indians had got me," he admitted. Indians became the dominant theme of his life. They engaged his intellect as a scientist, his imagination as a writer, and his passion as a man of social responsibility. Indian religion provided the key to his own spiritual liberation, Indian issues the substance of his political agenda. His strong public identity as an "Indian expert" was a distinction La Farge would come to regard with some dismay, but there was no denying the importance of the affinity he had discovered.

Born to an Eastern family of achievement, La Farge suffered through his prep school years, then flourished as an undergraduate at Harvard. He worked on the school's literary and humor magazines, manned an oar on the one-hundred-and-fifty-pound crew, and took part in student council. He returned to the Navajo reservation in 1922, and he led a field team there in 1924, just after graduation. Significantly, his own academic interest shifted from archeology to ethnology, as the living matter of language, literature, and custom took precedence over objects of material culture.

La Farge continued his training as an anthropologist, starting work toward a masters degree at Harvard, then accepting the invitation of Professor Frans Blom to join Tulane University's studies of indigenous cultures in Guatemala and southern Mexico. He took part in two field expeditions and coauthored, with Blom, one major report, *Tribes and Temples* (1927).

The association with Tulane meant spending a good deal of time in New Orleans. In a time he came to recall fondly, La Farge spent many hours in New Orleans turning out reams of short fiction. The atmosphere was agreeable, the society of other artists invigorating, and words came easily. He placed almost none of the material initially, but he was at least giving vent to the long held conviction that he could write successfully.

2

Introduction

One short story, "North is Black," was published in *The Dial* in 1927. The significant result of that minor victory was that it brought an inquiry from Ferris Greenslet, editor at Houghton Mifflin, who wanted to know whether La Farge might have some idea of doing a novel along the same lines—about the Navajos. The break could not have come at a better time. Suddenly dismissed at Tulane, beginning to doubt his future as a writer, La Farge was back at Harvard taking up the graduate studies suspended earlier. He returned to New Orleans to complete *Laughing Boy,* which was published in 1929, the same year La Farge completed his second degree. The Literary Guild did a book club edition, and publication in England followed in short order. To the author's surprise, the book was awarded the Pulitzer Prize for Literature, and La Farge found himself a celebrated figure with a comfortable income. "And at last," he could exult, "*I was a writer.*"[3]

Being *a writer* meant something to La Farge. He had aspired to write professionally for many years, and he bought most of the conventional expectations of the craft. He moved to New York to live as he thought a writer should live. He married, took an uptown apartment, and tried to enjoy the social life of other writers and their admirers. The Pulitzer opened the way to a certain level of success; publishers in a half dozen European countries snapped up foreign rights to *Laughing Boy,* and Houghton Mifflin was eager for new material. Short stories rejected earlier now found their way into respected periodicals.

More to the point, La Farge cared what editors and critics thought. He was attuned to conventional tastes, sensitive to critical judgments on his own work. Alarmed at the prospect of being forever labeled a writer of romantic Indian tales, frustrated at his lack of accomplishment in writing about white people from his own experience, he abruptly backed away from Indian subjects. He wrote about nineteenth-century New England privateers, about prep school boys, about the life of a struggling artist in New Orleans. For his biographer, D'Arcy McNickle, these efforts "only proved that he wrote best when he dealt with an Indian subject and with Indian characters."[4] La Farge never abandoned his pursuit of a wider canvas, but fortunately, he did return to Indian material from time to time in nonfiction and in short fiction pieces. Though he wrote no more novels about Indians after *The Enemy Gods* (1937) and no long fiction at all after *The Copper Pot* (1942), he continued to write and publish short stories to the end of his life.

Even as he fled the stereotype of an "Indian writer," La Farge took on activities that bound him more closely to the Indians he admired. As a result of the notoriety arising from *Laughing Boy,* and of his own active social conscience, he became President of the Eastern Association on Indian Affairs in 1932. With time out during the war years, he continued to head the association or one of its successors for the remainder of his life. La Farge took his association duties seriously, devoting substantial time and energy in pursuit of a more enlightened Indian policy. He also broadened his familiarity with American Indians, forming close relationships with the Hopis and Jicarilla Apaches. Following his divorce, marriage to Consuelo Baca, wartime service in the Army Air Transport Command, and relocation in Santa Fe, he also became better acquainted with the Pueblo Indians of the middle Rio Grande.

The stories collected here were written and published between 1927 and 1963, the year of La Farge's death. Like other writers of Southwest fiction, La Farge found engaging plots in the disparities among the region's varied cultural groups. Each of these stories turns on such a conflict. The element of contrast allows the author to show, in sharp focus, the assumptions, attitudes, and ways that characterize each culture. In some cases, especially in early stories of the Navajos, the story ends not in reconciliation, but in tragedy. In other stories, white and Indian characters sometimes find their way to the common values that unite, rather than divide them.

The contrast of cultures serves to illuminate differences, questions of relationship, and social issues. Like other good "regional" materials, these stories reveal the distinctive features of an area and its peoples. La Farge brings to his writing the point of view of a trained observer of wide learning and experience. He is able to grant access to an exotic culture, while applying the broad perspective that enables readers to relate to the characters as people not entirely unlike themselves. "What doubtless was his most significant contribution," McNickle wrote in appreciation, "was that he brought Indians into the consciousness of Americans as something other than casual savages without tradition or style."[5]

Introduction

La Farge is never condescending or patronizing, and he does not play favorites. His Indians are people as his whites are people— some admirable, some contemptible, some pathetic, some who are not especially remarkable in any of these ways.

Like Tony Hillerman in his later mystery novels of the Navajo country, La Farge delivers a wealth of reliable ethnological material through a literary form, the major purpose of which is to entertain. It is likely that such "teaching" was entirely incidental to the editors for whom La Farge was writing. They meant to intrigue and amuse, but so did La Farge; he placed a high value on readability, even embellishing or rearranging non-fiction materials to enhance their appeal to readers.[6] At the same time, the scientist in La Farge demanded that portrayals of culture and character be true to his data. Never hortative or didactic, La Farge simply moves through those items of ethnographic material that lie in the path of his story. Though he knew his stories had to be entertaining above all else if they were to sell, La Farge was not unaware of the potential for influencing attitudes toward Indians through his writing.[7]

With the exception of the delightful "Women at Yellow Wells," La Farge's early (1927 to 1935) stories speak of the tragedy he saw in the deterioration of traditional Navajo society—a deterioration accelerated by malevolent or ill-conceived intervention on the part of white missionaries and bureaucrats, and accompanied by much suffering on the part of individual Navajos. In "All the Young Men," the breakdown of Navajo society has reached the point that some Navajos, like whiskey runner Homer Wesley, have crossed over to become predators, rather than victims of outside influences. And in "Higher Education," La Farge shows how an effort to educate young Navajos has resulted in the complete and irremediable alienation of a school-girl from her family and her people.

Later stories of the Jicarilla Apaches and the Pueblos reflect a more optimistic view on the author's part. The change may be attributable in part to real differences in circumstances, as observed by La Farge, and in part to his increasing sense of effectiveness as his political role in Indian affairs increased. In any event, two stories about the Pueblos published near the end of La Farge's career, "The Little Stone Man" (1960) and "The Ancient Strength" (published shortly after the author's death) depict Indians who are far from helpless victims. Proud, strong, protective of their insular religion and society, the Pueblo people of San Leandro deal with outsiders on their own terms.

La Farge usually did not use actual place names for the central locations of his stories, though he freely referred to nearby towns like Santa Fe, Shiprock, and Farmington. He created numerous place names for stories set on the Navajo reservation and apparently patterned his San Leandro Pueblo after pueblos with which he was familiar. A possible curiosity for readers is the Gohlquain Apache Indian Reservation, the fictitious location of several stories published in the 1950s. Gohlquain (or Gohlkahin or Gohlkakin) is an obscure term for a division of the Jicarillas; it means "prairie people."

Two other notes about the stories: Mabel Dodge Luhan was a flamboyant public figure, inscrutable in her affinity for people and places with which, by background, she seemed to have little in common. Even in her own time, she was fictionalized, often satirized, by writers who knew her. Something of her life and legend is strongly suggested in "Hard Winter" (1933). As in other stories of that early period, La Farge's strong sense of the destructive influence of whites comes through as he shows two wealthy Eastern women pursuing Indian men, seemingly to escape their own boredom.

"Country Boy" (1938) is not about Indians, but it is of the Indian country, and La Farge takes care to convey the flavor of the spacious Southwest, because it is key to the story's pivotal conflict. In this case the contrast is not between Indians and outsiders, but between a naive, hard-working Westerner and a sophisticated, well-to-do Eastern girl. Despite a very real attraction, the barrier between them based on ingrained values and experiences proves quite as formidable as any cultural difference. A western dude ranch provides a natural venue for the encounter.

La Farge wrote in an era in which there were ready markets for good short stories. Like others who made a living from their writing, he found magazine sales a significant part of his income. After 1950 La Farge had a standing agreement with the *New Yorker,* giving its editors "first reading" rights to all of his short fiction. More than twenty pieces appeared in the magazine while the agreement was in force, including the popularized and partly fictionalized tales of

Consuelo Baca's childhood in a northern New Mexico mountain village, subsequently incorporated in *Behind the Mountains* (1956).

La Farge had definite ideas about the short story as a literary form. His column in the Santa Fe *New Mexican,* 1950 to 1963, permitted him to pontificate freely on a wide range of subjects. On one occasion he took the opportunity to denounce Guy de Maupassant as the recognized inventor of the short story, nominating instead his own candidate, Edgar Allan Poe. La Farge thus claimed the short story as an American contribution to literature.[8] According to La Farge, a novel may be almost formless, but a short story must have a plot, an increasing intensity of drama, and end in some sort of resolution.

La Farge's best writing is characterized by *skill, grace,* and *clarity.* The style appears natural, but it is the result of exacting effort. With ever a view to the reader's interest, and the editor's, La Farge professed to apply constant judgment as he wrote, examining each sentence, phrase, and word, checking frequently to ensure consistency in his characters and in relations among them.

La Farge was something of a stickler concerning use of the English language, defending it against alleged mutilation at the hands of bureaucrats and educationists.[9] He also took on Margaret Mead and the editors of the Merriam-Webster dictionary, prompting even admirers to observe that he was perhaps being overrigid about a matter "as evolutionary as any other human practice."[10] La Farge likewise deplored the use of polysyllables in an attempt to make prose sound more "literary."

Whatever the merits of his indictments against others, his regard for correct and balanced use of language endowed his own finest prose with a style that appears ageless. Stories written in the thirties are as readable today as when they were published, and though they speak of their own times, they often anticipate questions that may occur to visitors to Indian communities today.

Frank Waters and Oliver La Farge were contemporaries, born only about a year apart, but they were not close friends, despite their proximity and a shared interest in Southwest Indians. In many ways they were opposites. One was East and one was West. One was Harvard, the other Colorado College. One knew instant success and one struggled. La Farge was part scientist, Waters a divergent thinker.

If they sometimes clashed in print over their varying points of view, they shared the bane of writers who chose to write about Indians and the West. Both felt keenly the bias of Eastern critics and editors who could not regard Indians as fit subjects for serious literature. Meritorious works were as likely as not to be lumped with pulp westerns and misrepresented by publishers who themselves did not understand the works.

La Farge died prematurely, a victim of emphysema. But it was Waters's good fortune to live many years longer, witnessing a surge of new and more sober interest in materials about Indians—a seeming consequence of the Civil Rights movement and the environmental movement. Waters saw his early "failures" revived and circulated to wide and appreciative audiences.

Though La Farge did not live to enjoy the new respectability of works about Indians, his books and stories remain a source of rare insight. *Laughing Boy* had become a popular classic before his death, and *The Enemy Gods,* which he favored in some ways, has since found new readers in a reprint edition. With them, the stories published here are the literary legacy of a remarkable forty year friendship between La Farge and the native peoples of the Southwest. The stories embody a style that graced virtually all of the author's published works, and they demonstrate his considerable skill as an observer. They reflect the concern that motivated his many efforts in pursuit of Indian causes, and they express the boundless good will which was characteristic of La Farge in his dealings with Indians, whether as friend, political ally, or writer.

Notes

1. Much of the information and all quotes for this section are from "Indians," in La Farge, *Raw Material* (Boston: Houghton Mifflin, 1945), 148–63.
2. The Wetherills were early day traders and explorers of the canyonlands and the Navajo reservation. Their trading post at Kayenta was established in 1910–1911. Their story is told in Gillmor and Wetherill, *Traders to the Navajos: The Story of the Wetherills of Kayenta* (Albuquerque: The University of New Mexico Press, 1953).
3. *Raw Material,* 206.
4. D'Arcy McNickle, *Indian Man: A Life of Oliver La Farge* (Bloomington: Indiana University Press, 1971), 97.
5. *ibid.*, 236.

6. La Farge explains himself in this regard in the Foreword to *Behind the Mountains* (Boston: Houghton Mifflin, 1956).

7. Invited to write a book about Cochise for children, La Farge wrote Elliott Arnold, "I see in this a marvelous opportunity to insert into young minds a great number of concepts concerning Indians and white men which are exactly the reverse of those which they are generally fed." La Farge to Arnold, 12 February 1952. Harry Ransom Humanities Research Center, The University of Texas at Austin.

8. La Farge, "Return to de Maupassant," in *The Man With the Calabash Pipe,* Winfield Townley Scott (Boston: Houghton Mifflin, 1966), 107–9.

9. See "The Ways of Words," in *The Man With the Calabash Pipe,* 110–22.

10. T. M. Pearce, *Oliver La Farge* (New York: Twayne Publishers, 1972), 125.

NORTH IS BLACK

It is true that we say that North is black, and cold, and bad because of the stories of our old men, but those are good stories. They had them from the old men before them, from the time that there were no Americans. The Navajo have been here ever since the land was made, the Americans are new.

It is no use to show me that picture of mountains in the North again. I know it is white because it is all snow. I know those mountains. I have seen them. Yes, why do you suppose they call me North Wanderer? I went there, I came back with many horses. Ask my people about the horses Nahokonss Naga brought with him. Yes, that is why I went, to steal horses. I stood on a high place, praying, and my prayers fell away from me, down into the valleys. My prayers got lost, they would not fly up to the Four Quarters. It is bad there.

Give me more coffee.

I speak with one tongue, I went to steal horses. I was always brave. When I was a boy they took me to San Carlos, where the Apaches are. They taught me to talk American. I ran away, and lived all alone until my hair grew. When my hair was long again, I had made myself a bow and arrows, moccasins, a skin blanket. I had stolen two horses. I was always like that.

It is true there are good horses nearer than there. I was three moons going, and three moons coming, but I wanted to see.

Then I will tell you the truth. I am old, it is good someone should

*Originally published in *The Dial,* January 1927.

11

know. But you must not tell. I know you, you will not tell; no one would believe.

You see that fire? If you try to shut it up in a box, it will burn the box. I was like that. The soldiers would not let us go on the war-path. There was no work for us. Sometimes we went down to raid the Mo-qui a little bit, to steal sheep, but not enough. We young men were looking for trouble.

A man with a big red beard came and made a trading post near the railroad, a few miles from my mother's hogahn. I lived there, be-cause I did not think of marriage; all the time I was studying to be a singer, learning about the Gods, and the Medicine. I was like the Black Robed Preachers at Chin Lee, I did not think about women.

Red Beard was not like other traders, he was the other kind of American. They don't have that kind out here, I got to know about them later. They are different. Red Beard was sick, that was why he came out here. He did not care about the trading. He was honest with us and we made money off him. He never understood us. He was a good man.

He had a lot of friends coming to see him, from the East. They, too, were different. They liked to wear little pistols. At this time, Ameri-cans only carried pistols when they thought there would be trouble, then they had big pistols, not like the ones most of Red Beard's friends carried. And Red Beard's friends never shot anything. Most of them did not know how to shoot. They had bad manners, like the people at Grand Cañon. We were not used to that then, two or three times we were going to kill them.

Their women came out with them. There was one who was tall, and straight, and had black hair, like an Indian's, and brown eyes. She pulled her hair tight, tying it behind, like a Navajo. I fell in love with her.

I was digging holes to plant corn one day, and I saw She-Rain com-ing up the valley, with a rainbow behind it. I thought, "That looks like that American Girl." Then I was frightened, for I knew I must be in love. How could any man think that the rainbow, which is the Way of the Gods, looked like a woman, unless his eyes were twisted with love?

The next time I was with Mountain Singer, learning Medicine, I sang the Hozoji. When I said, "I walk with beauty all around me," my mind wandered to her, I forgot about the Gods and the Holy Things. I said to Mountain Singer, "My mind is bad." He told me to fast.

When I had fasted for four days, I returned to my mother's hogahn. When I came in, she said, "What is the matter with you?" I said, "Nothing."

She asked me again, "What is the matter?" Again I told her, "Nothing."

She asked me four times, and the fourth time she said, "Warrior-with-Gods, tell me what is the matter with you."

When she called me by that name, I had to answer true. I said, "I am sick inside, I am bad inside; I must cleanse myself."

My mother said, "You will not wash out your sickness, not pray it out. That is man's talk."

I had already fasted. Now I let down my hair, praying. I went into a sweat bath. All the time that I was there I sang. When I came out and jumped into the creek, I felt all well again. I ran, singing and leaping.

Then I saw mother-of-pearl dawn in the East, all-colour rain, and the rainbow. I heard the Four Singers on the Four Mountains. But it was midday, and clear, and the desert was silent. I had seen that American Girl come out of the post to watch me running. So I went back to my hogahn, and sat down, covering my face with my blanket.

My mother said, "By and by she will go away, then you will get well."

After that I tried to keep away from the post, but I was like a horse on rope. She used to hire me to guide her to places. When I had been with her and she was friendly to me, I used to feel weak, so that after I went away I sat down and groaned. Sometimes, though, I would want to leap and run, because I had foolish thoughts. When the corn began to sprout, I was like that all the time. She should not have been so friendly to me.

One day she said to me, "I will give you this bracelet if you will let me ride your pinto horse."

He was the best horse anybody had around there. I answered, "You do not need to pay me to ride my horse; but if you will give me the bracelet, I should like it."

13

Her face was strange when she gave me the bracelet. I was afraid she would laugh at me, but she did not. My heart sang. I did not understand them, those people.

She wanted to go up to the top of Blue Rock Mesa, where the shrine is, where you can see for many days' ride all around. So I took her up there. She was not like most Americans, the way they act. They talk fast, and shout, and spit over the edge. She was quiet, and looked, and thought about it, like an Indian. Then she made me tell her the names of all the places we could see. I showed her the mountains where the Utes are, you could just see them, like a low line of smoke in the north.

She said, "Tomorrow I go up there."

I told her, "It is far."

"I am going in the iron-fire-drives. I am going to my brother's house, far beyond there. He lives there because there is good hunting. You can come there."

When she began, my heart was sick; when she ended, my heart was high with joy, that she should want me to follow her. I thought I would make sure. I said, "I do not know that trail."

She told me she would show me on the map when we got back to the post. I did not know about maps, then; I thought it was strong medicine. She told me about the trail, then she told me about one of the mountains you have in that picture. You see it a week before you come to it, and it is marked so that you can tell it. She showed me a picture of it. While she was talking, her expression was strange; again I thought she was going to laugh at me, but she did not, so I read those signs another way, and was glad.

I did not watch her go, there was no use. I went on learning to be a singer, to make myself strong. My heart was happy, and I learned well. I traded close with Red Beard, to get money. I had Mountain Singer make me a fire drill, with turquoise and abalone-shell and mother-of-pearl and black stone on it, because it would be dark in the North, and I knew I would need it. I made more arrows, with fine points to them. A man came to the post who had a rifle, the best I had ever seen, and lots of cartridges for it. It took me three weeks to steal that rifle. Every day, I drew the North Trail in the sand. I gave that girl a name, Nahokonss Atat—that is, in American, Northern Maiden.

A lot of time went by this way. When I was ready, I went and gambled with my money. I knew that I could not lose, my medicine was sure. I gambled with some Americans, with their cards; that was easy. Then I gambled with Indians. I won very much, so that I was rich.

At the moon of tall corn there was a squaw dance in Blue Cañon. I told my mother I would go there, and see if I could find a girl I liked to marry. She saw me gathering all the jewelry I had won.

"That is well, if you do not lose your way." She said, "Have you good medicine, lots of corn pollen?"

My face was ashamed when I heard that, but no one could have stopped me then.

I painted my pinto horse, so that he was an ugly dun colour, and I tied a horsehair around his hock to make him lame. I packed my jewelry and buckskin on him, and my good blankets, and dressed myself in old American clothes, with an old blanket. I had much jewelry for her, and a silver bridle to give her with the pinto horse, I did not want it stolen. I tied turquoise to my gun to make it strong.

It was a long trip. When I was far enough North, I took my hair down and braided it, saying I was a Pah-Ute carrying a message for some Mormons. The Pah-Utes are always poor, and they are friends of the Mormons; they let me pass. I passed beyond the Ute country, through tribes I did not know. I talked signs with them, asking for this mountain. Once I had a fight with some Indians, and two times with Americans. Those Indians scalp everyone they kill, like the Utes.

I was three moons on the trail. Then I came to where snow was. It was the end of harvest moon, too early for snow, I knew I was coming to the North. I hoped to meet some of the Frozen Navajo, who live up there, but I did not. By and by it got to be all snow and colder than it ever is here. That was not like winter snow, but deep like all-year snow that you see on the north side of Dokosli, high up. Then I saw the mountain.

I had not seen Indians for a week, it was all ranches and cattle. There was a railroad, and a big town. I made camp where there were some woods, away from the town. I had stolen a hat from a ranch I passed near, leaving a lot of fine horses, because I was afraid to make trouble. Now I wound my hair up around my head, so that the hat covered it. I took off my headband. With my old American clothes,

I looked like a Mexican. I talk a little Mexican. So I went into town.

That town was big. It did not look as though I could ever find Northern Maiden there. And I could not ask for her, I did not know her name. All I could do was walk around and look. I saw places where they sold bitter-water, and thought I would buy some. I had tasted it before, but never enough. The first place I went into the man said, "Hey, Injun, get the hell out of here."

Then I went into another, and I spoke in Mexican before the man noticed me. So he sold me drinks. I bought a lot. They cost ten cents, and I spent a dollar for them. Then I felt so good I began to dance a little bit. One of the men said, "Hey, that Greaser's drunk, throw him out."

They threw me out. One of them kicked me hard when I went through the door. I fell down in the snow. My sight was red with anger. I walked away, out of town, to the woods where my things were. There I made ready for the war-path—let my hair down, and took off my American clothes. I thought, none of the people in that town carry guns. Now I shall take my very good gun and shoot them, all those people. I shall burn their houses. While I am doing this, I shall find Northern Maiden; her I shall take away, and go back to my own country, with many horses, and much plunder. That way I thought.

I began making war medicine, praying to the Twin Gods. I held my gun across my knees, that my medicine should be strong for it, too. Praying like that, I fell asleep there in the middle. That is a bad thing.

When I woke up, it was night, and I was cold. I was shivering. The fire was out. My head hurt. When I thought how I had gone to sleep in the middle of my prayer, I was afraid. I put on my clothes, and made a fire with my fire drill. Then I prayed, for a long time I was praying. But my prayer would not go up; it fell down where I said it. All of a sudden I was sick for my own country, for the smell of dust on the trail when the sun is on it, for the sound of my horse's hoofs in the sand. My heart was sick for the blue South, where the rainbow is, and tall corn growing by red rocks. I remembered the smoke of my mother's fire, and the thumping as she pounded the warp down in the loom.

Then I thought how far I had come, and how I was near to Northern Maiden, and how she was waiting for me. My medicine was strong, it was the bitter-water that had made me feel like that. I thought that I would be ashamed to go back now, and I was a brave who did not run away from things. So I rolled up in my blanket and went to sleep again. I was like that, we were warriors in those days.

There was game in the hills behind those woods, so that I had enough to eat. When I was not hunting, I stayed in the town. I stayed eight days, until I began to lose hope. Then I saw her. She was in a wagon with a man. They had two good horses with it; they were not as good as my pinto. I followed them out of town, and saw their tracks in the snow, along a road. Then I ran to my camp.

I threw away my American clothes then. I sang, and while I sang I tied up my hair like a Navajo. My headband was good, my shirt was worked with porcupine quills, my leggings had many silver buttons. My belt was of silver, my necklaces and bow-guard were heavy with silver and turquoise. I put the silver bridle on my horse, to make him look well, and so that when I gave it to her, with the pinto, she should know it was my own. Then I rode out, still singing.

I looked all around me. I said, the North is not black. The ground is white; where the sun strikes it, it is all-colour. The sky is blue as turquoise. Our old men do not know. I galloped along the trail. I sang the song about the wildcat, that keeps time with a horse galloping and makes him go faster. That way I felt.

I started in the morning, I got in just after noon. It was a big ranch, there were many horses in the corral, but no sign of cattle. That is not like an American ranch. They were just getting out of the carriage when I rode in. When they saw me, they cried out. She was surprised, she did not think I would come. I sat still and rolled a cigarette. Inside I was not still. I looked at her, and my heart kept on saying, "beautiful, beautiful," like in a prayer.

She came forward to shake hands with me. Some more men and a woman came out. She told them who I was. One of the men kept saying, "George, George!" I thought he was calling someone. Later I found out it was his way of swearing. They were different, those people.

She told me to put my horses in the corral. She went with me

17

while I unsaddled my pony. Her face was flushed, she was glad to see me. I could not speak, I was afraid all those people would see what I was thinking. When we were alone in the corral, I gave her the pinto horse, and the bridle. At first she would not take them. She gave me a room to sleep and keep my things in. Then she took me into the big room where the people were.

There were her brother and his wife. They were good people. There were two other men who were good. One of them knew Indians, he could talk American so that I could understand everything he said. There was another man who was not good. His mouth was not good. He had yellow hair, but there was a dark cloud around his head. I could see that, especially when he was thinking bad things. I did not like him, that one. There were other people who stayed with them and went away again, but these people were there all the time.

They were nice to me. I stayed there a long time. Those men were always going hunting, they took me with them. I was a good hunter, so they thought well of me. They liked a man who could do something better than they could. They thought well of me because I had come so far. They asked me to play cards with them. They did not play cards the way the Americans here taught us, except the man I did not like. I won from them, but never very much. I did not think it was good to win too much from them. They were my friends.

The man I did not like was called Charlie. He, too, wanted Northern Maiden. He was not like those others. Sometimes when they had friends and drank bitter-water, one of the women would tell them they had too much, or one of the other men would. Then they would go out and walk around until they were all right. I did not take anything. Sometimes, when there was another woman staying with them there, one of the men would be making love to her. If she told him to stop, he always stopped. This I saw, different times, when people came to stay with them. But Charlie was the only one who made love to Northern Maiden. He did not stop when she told him to. One day I was coming down the long room they had that ran between the other rooms. He was out there, trying to kiss her, the way Americans do. I walked up. He got red in the face and went away. I made talk to her as if I had not seen anything.

I stayed there a long time. I thought, when it was time for spring in my own country, I should ask Northern Maiden to come with me, and I thought she would say yes.

One day I was walking into the door of the big room, when I heard someone inside say my name. Horse-Tamer they said, that was my name, that people used. The man's voice was angry, so I listened. I could not understand everything that they said, they were talking fast in American. But I understood that Charlie was telling them that I cheated at cards. This made them angry. They said that if they caught me, they would run me out. They called me a damn Indian. I was angry; because I knew that Charlie cheated, too, as I have said. I did not understand this, so I went to Northern Maiden.

I told her that the cowpunchers taught us to cheat at cards, that we thought it was part of that game. An Indian is better at it than an American. I did not say anything about Charlie. She said that her kind of American did not cheat at cards, any more than they told lies. They were always honest. So they trusted everyone who played in a game, that was why they were so angry. They would run out anyone who cheated when they trusted him. Then I understood.

I took my money and went in where they were. I said: "Here is your money, that I have won at cards. I did not know you did not cheat, until I heard you talking. The Americans who played with us always cheated. Now I will not cheat. That is my word. It is strong."

Northern Maiden's brother said, "The Indian's all right."

The other one, who knew about Indians said: "Yes, what he says is true. He will not cheat any more. Let him play."

Charlie was angry, but he was afraid to say anything.

So then I played with them some more, and I watched Charlie. I knew what I wanted to do, and I took my time, like a good hunter. Finally my chance came, it was like this—We were playing poker. Charlie used to hide a good card from the pack. When he thought he could use it, he put it in the palm of his hand. Then when he reached down to pick up his draw cards, he mixed it with them. He discarded one more card than he should. Sometimes he slipped it in with the other discards; sometimes, if it was a good card, he kept it out. I knew it would be no good to find the card in his clothes, they would think I had put it there. I had to catch it in his hand, and he was quick.

This time there were a lot of people there, some men from other ranches, cowpunchers. There was a lot of money, and Charlie got excited. I was sitting next him. He did not like to see me next him. I waited till I saw he was about to use his card. I got my knife ready. When his hand was sliding along the table, before he got to the draw, I put my knife through it. He screamed, and everyone jumped up. I took out my knife. There was the ace of diamonds, and he held two other aces.

Charlie went out of the room. He was white in the face. The cow-punchers stood around for a little while, then they went away, too. I said nothing, waiting for them to thank me. These three men, the ones who lived in the house, went off into a corner and talked. I could not hear what they said. Something was wrong.

The man who understood about Indians came over to me. The rest went out.

"Now," he said, "you must go away. It is not your fault. Charlie is one of us. You were right to show that he cheated, but not in front of all those cowpunchers. Now we have lost face with them. We are all made ashamed. You should have told us, and we should have caught him when no one else was here. When we see you, you will make us remember that you, an Indian, showed up our friend in front of those people. When you are here, we shall be ashamed. If a white man caught a friend of yours in front of a lot of Moqui, would you like it?"

I said, "I see. Now I go."

He shook hands with me. "You are a good man," he said, "I want to be friends with you. I shall come and see you on your reservation. We shall hunt together."

I said: "Your talk is straight. It is good. Now I want meat and coffee and sugar to take on the trail."

He brought me what I needed while I was saddling my horse. He gave me the money Charlie had won from me. He wanted to give me more.

"He will go to the train tomorrow," he said. "he is too weak now, you made him bleed a lot."

It was in the middle of the afternoon that I rode away. I went up to a high hill behind the ranch-house. There I made camp. When I had a fire lighted, a little one that would not make smoke, I began my medicine. It was not good. My prayers fell away, down into the valley. I saw that a man could not pray there, where there was only one direction, North, the Black One. I wanted to go back to where there was East, and South, and West, Mother-of-Pearl dawn, Blue Turquoise, and Red Shell. I prayed the best I could. I used the last of my corn pollen. When the sun set, I made black paint with ashes. I drew the Bows of the Twin Gods on my chest. I put a black line on my forehead. I stripped to my breechclout, moccasins, and headband. I took off all my jewelry except my bow-guard. I took my bow, because a gun makes too much noise. Long after it was black night I went back to the ranch.

They were all in the big room, except Charlie, sitting round the fire. I came in quietly. I hid in a corner behind a chair. All the time I had my bow ready. They did not say much, but sat, not talking. One by one, they got up to go to bed. I was hoping that Northern Maiden would be the last, but if she was not, I had enough arrows. I could not have come so well to her bedroom, it was upstairs. That house was built like a Moqui house, with two floors.

My medicine was good. She stayed sitting and looking at the fire. I could see that she was sad. That did my heart good. In the firelight she was beautiful. I stood up.

Then Charlie came into the room. I was in the corner. I did not move. He never saw me. I made ready to shoot him. He walked over until he stood in front of Northern Maiden. For a little while they looked at each other. I waited. Then he spoke.

"I'm sorry."

She said nothing.

"Can't you forgive me?"

Then she spoke to him. She got up and stood very straight. I could not understand all those things that they said. They were talking in American, and using words I did not know. They used words we have not got. But this I understood. She loved him. Now she sent him away, for the thing he had done. She said she was very angry. But I saw that she loved him. She gave him a ring, a ring that Americans give when they are going to marry a woman. Now she gave it back to him. I saw she was that kind, that she sent him away, although she loved him, because his heart was bad. She told him that he was like a snake. She meant he was all bad.

21

He went away again, holding his face down. His hand was bandaged. He looked like a sick man. I let him go.

Northern Maiden sat down in the chair. She began to cry, like an American, hard, so that it hurts, and does no good. I came, then, and stood in front of her. She looked up. She did not start. She was not afraid of me.

I said: "I did not know, now I do; I would not have done this. Here is the bracelet you gave me. I should not have it."

She said, "I understand."

Then I went away. I rode all night.

I came home at the time of short corn. I had twelve good horses with me. I met a man prospecting in Chiz-Na-Zolchi. I got a good mule from him. These I showed to the people who asked me why I went away. It was good to see the cañons again, with the washes full of water from the snow. It was good to hear my horse's hoofs in the sand, and smell the dust of the trail.

I sat down by my mother's fire. The smoke was rising up straight. She was weaving a man's blanket. She said: "This is for you, your blanket is worn out. You must choose yourself a wife, you are too much alone. That is the best medicine for you, to have a house and children. When the corn is green, tell me the one you want. I shall ask for her."

I saw that she was right. I said. "It is good. You will ask for one."

But I did not care if she were old or young, beautiful or ugly.

HARD WINTER

He saw his wife start backing her horse out of the packed circle of mounted Indians and wagons, and without ceasing to sing, he turned his head slightly to watch her. The horse, nervous from the crowd, answered uncertainly, with shifting forefeet and resistant tossings of the head which made the bells on his bridle ring together. She forced the animal back with a firm hand, turning in the saddle to speak laughingly to those behind her; then getting clear of the narrowest press, she wheeled sharply, heading toward her tipi.

The song ended. Tall Walker looked around to watch her pass along the skyline of the first rise, a satisfaction in him at the sight of her, the very type of a young Jicarilla Apache wife. She sat her horse firmly, easily, riding with high bridle hand and slack rein. Her heavy, black hair hung in two braids intertwined with ribbon; above the meeting of the braids was a red celluloid comb. A circular design was painted on each cheek, and three red lines drawn on her chin. Across her shoulders she wore the yoke of gold-coloured buckskin with wide, curving bands of beadwork and the long fringe hanging down each arm to her wrists. Her dress, under the yoke, was made of blue cotton; about her waist, covering her saddle and skirts, were draped gay blankets of strong design, beneath which her feet showed in gaily beaded moccasins. Her horse moved easily at the jog trot, with tinkling bells. She was going to prepare food. Tall

*Originally published in the *Saturday Evening Post,* December 30, 1933.

23

Walker, considering himself, found that he was moderately hungry and would soon be more so.

The drums began again, he returned to singing. His uncle, an elderly man, and another slightly younger one were drumming; Tall Walker and six others made up the chorus. As many more danced, according to their mood—all *Llaneros,* plainsmen, celebrating their victory in the sacred race that morning. There was a chief, tall, slender, straight, white-haired, incredibly old, on his face the impress of a culture and a way of thought far removed from reservations and Government officials. He wore all white buckskin, from head to foot, fringed and beaded, with downy eagle feathers in the otter fur around his braids, and he danced in a quiet, happy manner, holding an eagle-feather fan, like an ancestral voice which even the middle-aged men there could scarcely comprehend.

A young man danced gracefully, stripped to the waist. He wore a horsehair roach and a feather on his head, blue work pants, moccasins. Another sported a brilliant flannel shirt; another a buckskin jacket, cloth leggings and big hat. A boy from the mission school, short-haired, had been given moccasins and leggings by his father. He danced energetically, with gusto, knowing that he must return to classes and Christian influences the next day. Older men joked, laughed and urged him on. Sweat made channels in his face paint; he danced hard and well, smiling, strutting a little.

They danced all together or by turns, without fixed order. Laughter came readily. Around the performers were ranked mounted Indians, Indians afoot and in wagons, and a few intrusive, alien-seeming motors. The people crowded together, the Apache tribe and their guests—Navajos, Tewas, Keres, Taos, a couple of Utes, Mexicans, and a few Anglo-Americans. The spectators formed a mass with jingling bridles, fretting hoofs, men, women, children, dark faces, big hats, bright blankets, a constant uprising of thin dust clouds to make a blur in the noon sunshine. It was the Apache *fiesta.*

A slender young man with a white blanket wrapped about himself and over his head sat down beside Tall Walker. The Apache turned and saw a handsome, aquiline face, cut off at the line of the ear by a neatly wrapped braid. There was yellow paint on the forehead, yellow and red on each cheek. He stopped singing and extended his hand. Their hands touched, clasped lightly, and remained so while they smiled.

"*Como 'stamos?*" the man asked.

"*Bueno. Y tu?*"

"*Bueno.*"

They used the simplified Spanish which is the intertribal language of New Mexico.

"When I didn't see you this morning, I thought you would not come at all. What kept you?"

"Too much mud by Horse Lake; it held us up. We came in a motor. Are there many others here from Taos?"

"Three or four, I think. There's one over there. Will you sing?"

"All right."

While they talked, Tall Walker had noticed changes about his friend; a fat look, though he was not fat; something curious in his expression. The man wore blue-flannel leggings with beadwork strips, and fine moccasins, unusually showy for one who was travelling, even a Taos Indian.

Tall Walker reached over and touched the old drummer's elbow.

"My uncle," he said, "here is Juan from Taos. He will sing, he says."

The old man turned, smiling. "Good. Do you know the song?"

Juan nodded. "Surely."

"Good, then. You will sing with us?"

"*Vamos.*"

The singers shifted their places slightly to make room for the visitor. The drums intoned a few beats, establishing the feel of the rhythm. Juan sang the introduction alone, a phrase of music carried on pure vowel sounds; the clear voice of a first-rate Taos singer rang out sweetly, holding attention, inspiring the dancers' feet to move. At the end of the phrase, the chorus took up the body of the song, liver, less slurred under his leadership. The drums beat on, the dancers advanced, dust rose, pleasure increased. Tall Walker, singing, remembered Indian-school days, and thought how far they had travelled from the two unhappy children who made friends there.

At the next pause, he said: "My tipi is right over there. Come eat with us in a little while."

Juan answered: "I shall visit you, but I am camped on that side. There is a white woman with us; I eat with her."

His hesitation over the last sentence caught the Apache's attention, causing him to want to ask a question, then decide not to.

"This is our *fiesta,*" he said; "we have plenty. Let her come too."

"Perhaps. She might like it. She wants to know about Indians, all kinds of Indians."

The insistent drums broke in upon them, and their talk ceased.

The sun had moved to the middle of the western sky; the crowd had thinned and some of the dancers dropped out when Tall Walker stood up.

"I am hungry, and I know where food is. Are you coming?"

"All right."

They went together to the Apache's tipi, standing on the ridge overlooking all the eastern part of the encampment and the quiet, blue-shining lake about the muddy shores of which many horses drifted. The baby slept in its cradle board; his young daughter staggered about holding onto a puppy's tail and shouting amiably; his wife lifted a pot off the fire and set goat's ribs to broil. Although she, too, had been to school, she greeted Juan modestly in Spanish and went on cooking. The two men reclined in the shade of the tipi's entrance.

Juan said, "It seems to be a good *fiesta.*"

Tall Walker paused a moment before replying. He heard the drums and singing softly, like a central *motif* about which cohered the sounds of the encampment—a horse neighing, voices, laughter, a child crying, dogs, the tinkle of sleigh bells on bridles, and jerky clangour of cowbells on grazing horses. He saw the tents and tall, white lodges, wagons, the smoke of hundreds of fires, the patched-together shelters of brush and cloth that the Navajos put up, the medicine-men's enclosure of green branches, a white tourist's elaborate motor tent, dotted without form or arrangement on the grey-green slopes and ridges about the north end of the lake, and yet achieving complete satisfaction of form to the eye. In and out of the camps wove a pattern of moving people, afoot or mounted, singly or in groups, bright blankets, brilliant dresses of women, the varying splendours of men of different tribes. The smell of food smote his nostrils sweetly.

"It is a good *fiesta;* everybody is happy and many people have come. But we don't get any whiskey this year; the new agent, he has men watching all around."

26

"Yes, some men searched our car when we came in. We had just a little flask, but they took it."

Tall Walker's wife served food. Juan threw back the fine, white blanket he had worn wrapped about himself, Taos fashion, and during the silence of serious eating the Apache could take the full measure of his friend's prosperity. Juan wore a shirt of green silk, cut in the Indian manner, a silk scarf at his throat, a coral necklace and several rings. The shirt, like his blue-flannel leggings, was new and clean. At his waist he had a belt studded with brass and varicoloured glass knobs, on it two cartridge clips and an automatic with mother-of-pearl handle. His countenance agreed with his dress; though he was not fat, and his profile was aquiline, his face had filled out; under the painted decoration his skin was sleek.

His host was in striking contrast. For finery he had only a beaded waistcoat, worn over a red-and-black-checked flannel shirt, and a couple of feathers stuck into the band of his huge, floppy old black felt hat. His blue work trousers were worn and faded, his feet encased in old, brown shoes. Characteristically, the Taos Indian's hair was neat and shiny, the braids in perfect order, while the Apache's had a shaggy look. Tall Walker's face showed the tribal expression of hunger and capacity for war. His wife was well dressed, even expensively so, but Juan wore solid money, the value of sheep and horses, upon his person.

They consumed meat, chile, bread, melons and black coffee; then relaxed digestively over cigarettes.

Tall Walker said, "You are rich."

"I shall be, perhaps. She gives me these things, that white woman."

"Who is she? Why does she do it?"

"Oh, I'm just working for her. Guiding—that is, I take her places like here, and drive her car, and explain things to her. It's a good job, and besides these things, I have earned a gun and a saddle."

He spoke like a man withholding something.

Tall Walker said, "You know how to drive a car?"

"Yes, I learned that last year."

"I should like to know that."

Juan changed the subject. They exchanged news of other friends, particularly those with whom they had gone through the misery of school, referring to them, as they did to each other, by their Spanish names. Juan called Tall Walker "Celestino"; he, in turn, did not know what Juan's Taos name was. They spoke of the sheep and crops and the hunting season. At length Juan rose, gathering his blanket round him.

"I must go back to our camp now."

"All right."

"Come along. There may be something good to eat, and there will be people."

"Good." The Apache rose. "Let us go over."

The car, with an olive-green tent attached to it, was parked in a place well chosen to give a view while yet standing withdrawn from the smells, noises and dogs of the encampment. Around an almost dead fire were sprawled three Taos Indians, an elderly Navajo, and a white woman, eating grapes which they had purchased from a Zía peddler, who sat with them, his unsold fruit in a box behind him. He smiled blandly, as was his manner, and also, as was his manner, accepted gracefully of the grapes he had just sold; he was a commercial, overshrewd, dubious individual whose good nature and humour made him widely popular.

Tall Walker knew everyone there at least slightly, save the woman. Her he studied in the intervals of a desultory conversation in which he took little part, since it was conducted in English—a language he used but seldom nowadays. He was struck first by the fact that she was wearing moccasins and the particoloured red-and-blue blanket which the Kiowas and some Taos affect. This was incongruous. Her voice was clear and high, but attractive. She spoke English with a strange accent. She was older than he or Juan, and yet immature. Clearly there had been no childbearing to spread her figure or mark her face, no hard work, nothing to age her. She was girlish, and at the same time she was older than broad-hipped, drudging Apache mothers of the same years—she was battered. Plainly, she thought that Indians were very important, and she was enjoying herself playing Indian. She had welcomed him, Celestino, in a fluttery, excited manner, with some joking remark about Apaches spoken too quickly for him to understand. He was amused and curious.

A young man joined them from a neighbouring motor camp. He was blond, tall, and dressed ostentatiously in part Indian costume, like the woman. Those Indians he knew he hailed by name, making a great point of shared jokes and common interests, displaying an eager familiarity which they met politely, from the lips.

28

He had seen such white people fussing around Taos when he visited there; they seemed to be a special tribe. The Taos people treated them with forbearance, keeping them outside of everything important and bearing with their stupidities. Now, for the first time, he had a chance to observe some of them at close range.

Navajos and Apaches understand each other's languages. The elderly Navajo said to him: "What is this *Bellicana* in the Taos clothes? Is he a half man, or what is he?"

"Just a little crazy, I think," Tall Walker answered. "They say there are many of them around Taos. That woman too. They are very fond of Indians, it seems."

The Navajo spat. "Very fond. That woman is so fond she's likely to have a baby, I think."

Tall Walker smiled. It was true. Juan was not just working for her. She was in love with him, and she was satisfied. It was plain to see. So the women give you presents to do that.

The Zía peddler spoke Navajo. He broke into their talk:

"You can plant corn in a waterless field, but will it sprout?"

"Oh, well, it always might rain," the Navajo said nonsensically, and the three of them laughed.

She was in love with Juan, but what about him? He liked her well enough, one could see, but it was not love, nor yet the attitude of any man settled in marriage. There was a hidden shame present, a watchfulness of people. Juan had glanced around quickly when they laughed, but he understood neither Navajo nor Apache. Tall Walker spat out a grapeskin. Those other Taos, they had mockery hidden under their blankets for the white man and woman; but for the man of their own tribe—One could not be sure; they would not display themselves before strangers.

The woman spoke to him. "Are you coming to the Taos *fiesta* next month, Celestino?"

"I don't know. I got to take care of my sheep."

Juan said in English: "You better come. We got a big house, you know, and plenty hay for your horse. You come and stay with us. We can have a drink, maybe."

He greatly desired to see more of these strange people. "All right. I'll come that time. I see you there." He rose. "I got to go to my house now."

To the Navajo, he said: "I am camped over yonder; come if you

29

want. There is food. I shall be there until the dancing starts again."

The man grunted. "Good, I shall come, perhaps. I may want somewhere to lie down and laugh."

The sun was down; fires began to count as golden spots in the blue dusk; where there were fires inside the lodges, the great cones glowed softly at the base, their peaks shadowy. At his camp, his wife was rocking the baby, his daughter slept on a sheepskin. As he sat down beside her, he thought, "Juan has nothing."

The round dance lasted from an hour after dark until midnight. About halfway between then and dawn the last stubborn celebrants gave over their singing and left the bonfires to die away. The *fiesta* was ended.

People arose lazily, relaxed by enjoyment, and short of sleep. The tipis began to be struck a few hours after sunrise, and piecemeal the encampment dissolved into two streams of wagons and mounted men along the dusty road north and south from the lake. Tall Walker turned his wagon aside at a dim cart track up which they drove, arriving at their small log cabin in the mid-afternoon. Finery was laid aside; they re-entered normal life. Long uneventful days with the sheep on the thinly wooded mountain slopes; evenings of well-fed fatigue, a little talk, a little playing with the children; nights of deep sleep; and always, first and central, the sheep. Later the sale of the lamb crop would bring them in to the post trader at Dulce, and later still there would be camp life again, when they moved to the winter range.

Two days beforehand, Tall Walker announced that he was going to the Taos *fiesta*. His wife said she would not go; there was no relative near who could be trusted with the sheep, and besides, the baby was so young, it ought not to be always travelling. He agreed, although he had been inclined to argue that in olden days women and babies travelled all the time, and without wagons; but she was right about the sheep, and to him, too, the welfare of his little son was of the first importance. He had been disappointed when his first child was a girl, and he wanted the boy to grow well, to reach the crawling stage, to begin to talk and stagger as soon as possible. Besides, his wife was a person who knew her own mind and had plenty of sense. Now that girls went to school, it was different from the old times when they just took orders; though a man would not admit that before other men.

He made the ride to Taos in a day and a half, starting one afternoon and arriving the next day just before sunset. Had a white man covered the ground in the same time, it would have been a record; had he arrived feeling as fresh as the Apache did, he would have become famous for his endurance. Save for some great need, a white man would have been ashamed to arrive with his horse so jaded. Tall Walker was an Indian; he just came right along.

Even from a distance, as he rode between the two piled-up masses of Taos Pueblo, one could tell that he was not a native of the place. Slouching comfortably in the saddle, his wide shoulders and heavy-boned frame dwarfed his pony. The big, shapeless hat proclaimed his tribe from afar; near to, one noticed his dark, broad face, and felt forcefulness, that effect of fitness for war which was not an individual characteristic but an emanation from the personality of his tribe. For this visit he had wrapped his braids with otter fur trimmed with beads, and borrowed a showy pair of moccasins. Added to his handsome waistcoat, the effect was good, although his trousers still plainly indicated a poor man. Most Apaches are poor.

He kept his eye out for acquaintances, having an unexpected feeling that he did not want to ask a stranger the way to that woman's house. Shortly he encountered a man he knew well, who had played football beside him for two seasons on the Santa Fe team. He reined in his horse and raised a hand.

"*Como 'stamos?*" It passed through his mind that he ought to practise speaking English, but he was reluctant to do so. Spanish came easily.

"*Bueno. Y tu?*"

"*Bueno.*"

They shook hands and chatted. The Taos, whose Spanish name was Fulgencio Mirabal, invited him to stay at his house.

"I promised Juan I would stay with him. For that I came."

"Which Juan?"

"Juan Sota. Where does he live now?"

"Oh, that one." Fulgencio paused. "Go right on, then take a road to the right by two cottonwoods, and pretty soon you see a Mexican house with an arched gateway, so"—he moved his hands descriptively. "He is staying there, I think."

Tall Walker said: "*Bueno.* I want to see."

Ten years ago they had known each other as intimately as tribal differences and the harsh restrictions of the school would allow. They esteemed each other's opinion. Fulgencio said, pulling his blanket up over his shoulders:

"We feel badly about Juan, the people here." He paused. "Well, I'll see you tomorrow. You know where my house is."

"*Bueno. Hasta luego.*"

Perhaps Fulgencio was right. But then, a man takes what he can get; and if the white woman is rich and a fool, why not? One would not want to go on like that, of course. He found the place, surveyed it from the saddle as if scouting hostile territory, then tied his horse at the gate and entered the yard, which was pleasantly shaded by cottonwoods, their leaves beginning to turn yellow. A good place, with water and flowers and a big house; though, if he were rich, he would have put on a corrugated-iron roof. He saw no one. The door was big, carved and painted. He liked that, although he thought the paint too faded. Behind this door was a strange life; something to see, examine, perhaps enjoy, perhaps laugh at, and to tell about afterward. Life is monotonous, novelty a pleasure. He knocked.

A Mexican woman let him in and left him standing, hat in hand, in the hall. The stolid, rather stupid expression of his face disguised embarrassment, a certain awkwardness arising from the elegance of the place. He heard voices speaking English in the high, clear tones which are so unlike Indian conversation, laughter, a pause as the maid entered the room, and someone's exclamation, "An Apache!" Juan came into the hall, saying cordially, "*Llega 'migo.*"

Following his friend, he stepped over the threshold of a doorway the frame of which he filled for a moment as he paused, looking about him before he entered a place, and a period, of so much novelty and so many impressions that not until long after did he sort them out. Right at the outset he encountered numbers of people gathered together, women similar to Juan's, too rapid talk, a drink of whiskey with which began a long-continuing sense of unreality.

It was a tribe of white people, with its own strange manners and incomprehensible customs. Some of them had a remarkable knowledge of and sympathy for Indians. Others were abysmally ignorant. Some worked—many at painting—some seemed to have no occupation at all. In two things they were all alike—that much of their conversation seemed to be made for its own sake, without need, and that they all set tremendous store by Indians. All Indians were important; any man with his hair in braids was treated as something special.

The Taos people were tolerant of them; indebted to some for real services to their Pueblo, fond of some, forbearing with others. But Tall Walker had relatively little time for talking with the Taos, save when they came to visit. The *fiesta* passed as a mere background to his new explorations; he stayed on one day and another, a third and a fourth. A painter gave him good money to pose. People wanted to hear him sing, to ask about the customs of his tribe. They tickled his vanity, and from time to time some of them gave him drinks. He observed, he laughed within himself, he enjoyed, and he was confused.

Many people stayed late at one woman's house, and he, Juan, and Juan's woman stayed till the last. These two women were so similar in expression that at first he had taken them for sisters, although their features were quite unlike. He had heard that his hostess had had an affair with a Taos man once, but his family had talked him out of it. She had been making up to Tall Walker for the last few days.

As they, the last of the visitors, got ready to go, he was tipsy. When she came up to him, he saw her through a warm glow, and it occurred to him that a white woman might be desirable.

She said, "Why don't you stay here?"

He stood facing her for some time before he answered, while through his mind ran summations of what he had been vaguely thinking these last days: I'm not going to be like Juan. . . . One time, why not? . . . I am a man. . . . It doesn't matter. . . . I feel like it. . . . Why not?

He said, "All right."

She called loudly to the others, "Celestino isn't going with you."

That shamelessness caused him a wave of embarrassed anger, and he did not hear what was answered.

He thought, If I go now, it will look as if I were afraid to sleep with a woman. The outer door shut, and she handed him another drink, saying, "Sit down."

He took the drink, but remained stolid with annoyance. Perplexed, she made conversation which fell flat. She suggested that he sing some more, pointing to the fine drum she had—an instrument which he had been enjoying. He refused with a brusque "No." Then she was angry and turned sharp, scolding. He rose to his feet, silent, dangerous, and stepped toward her. Restrictions which had guarded her all her life were non-existent to this half-intoxicated Apache. She drew in her breath sharply and became meek. Even confused as he was, he could feel that he had taken her prisoner.

He stayed on at that house. She gave him Indian finery, more than he desired, and a rifle, and she surrounded him with unimagined luxury. Within a few days his eyes were opened to a scale of spending money which, even when he saw it, he could hardly believe. I shall stay a few days, he thought; I shall observe and gather goods and money, which will be useful. After that, I shall go home.

Dressed in Indian perfection to the last detail, save for the huge hat, with which he refused to part, she took him, a slightly bewildered clothes horse, to Santa Fe. He enjoyed the motor ride, and seeing that city again, and the novelty of the huge hotel, in which he twice got lost. He found that people's attitude toward him was equivocal, but he drew plenty of attention, which pleased him, and the rest he ignored. After about a week, they returned to Taos. He thought it was about time to go home, but two more artists wanted to paint him. That was easy money, and flattering. He was beginning to feel very important. It was a pleasant, easy, luxurious life; the woman was much in love with him, it seemed. Once or twice he remembered the elderly Navajo saying ridiculously, "It always might rain," and the way they had laughed together, but he put such thoughts from him. In early November he was still there, and the woman was talking of taking him to New York. He would like to see that place.

He went over to visit Juan one day, to plan a hunting trip, and the Taos handed him a letter, saying, "This came for you." It was addressed to "Celestino Roman, % Juan Sota, Taos P.O., New Mexico." He had never received a letter before, it made him uneasy. The stamp was red and had Washington on it. He wondered if that meant it came from the Indian Office. A sense of guilt stole over him. Back at the house he opened it and read it slowly, with difficulty:

> Jicarilla, Dulce P.O.
> New Mexico
> November 8
>
> *Dear Friend Husband:* I take my pen to say I am well an hope You are the Same. Agent say we got to move ship to Winter Range rigt now or he men will move them ship for us those Men is rough if they move

34

our ship we might lose some. I think good you come back now an move ship you been gone long time I not know where are you Please come back rigt now. Little girl is well baby sick a little I come into Doctor he give me some Medcin an I write this. Come back and move ship. I send this to Juan get you. Trader write it address for me. I will close now wit best regards

yours loving wife
Antonia Mariano

A letter is a strange thing; it has power. This one found its way to Taos and to Juan, told Juan to give it to him, and he opened it and his wife spoke to him. So the baby, the boy, was sick a little, but the doctor had given him medicine. The doctor was good; the baby would be all right. He went into the living-room where the white woman was.

"I got to go home," he said.

"What?"

"I got to go home."

"Why?"

A man says, "I'm going somewhere"; a woman answers, "When do you start?"

"I got a letter. I got to move my sheep onto the winter range."

"A letter? From whom?" Her voice was sharp.

"My wife, she write it."

"Your wife? I didn't know you were married."

"You didn't ask me."

The woman lit a cigarette and spoke again calmly, with a soft voice, which he liked, "You are going back to your wife?"

"I got to move my sheep and my horses. If they stay on that summer range, maybe it snow hard, maybe then they can't eat. I might lose them. If I don't move them, those Government men, they will do it. They don't care. They're rough. Some sheep might die. I got to go; I go tomorrow."

"How many sheep have you?"

"I got three hundred, and I got twenty horses."

"That's not many."

"When I start in, when they divide up the sheep that time, I got fifty head. Now I got three hundred. Pretty soon I have maybe a thousand, have cattle, plenty horses, like Agapito and them fellers. It's

35

what we eat it, sometimes, the sheep, and we sell wool and the lambs, and that way we got money to buy flour and what we need, all us Apaches. Before we didn't have no sheep, sometimes we were starving; we didn't have no money at all. Just some old clothes and a little food Washington gave us, that's all. A lot of people died then. I guess about half the Apaches died. Maybe we don't take good care of our sheep, we got to eat grass ourselves then, I guess."

He explained thus carefully, at length, knowing how deeply ignorant she was. He wanted her to know and to feel as she should. The woman listened with nervous patience.

She said: "But you don't have to count on the sheep now. Why, I could buy your whole flock. Why bother with them? You are through with all that work and trouble now. You can have anything you want. If you want to send money to your wife, I can give it to you. Let the sheep go."

He regarded her blankly. What she suggested was unnatural, incomprehensible.

"It's my sheep—I got to move them."

She rose. "Don't you like it here?"

He liked it very much; it was better than anything he had ever known or dreamed of "Yeh, it's all right here."

She spoke softly. "And I? Do you not care for me?"

Her behaviour was queer, but she could not help that. He was very fond of her; she was the symbol of comfort and great kindness, and there was no little passion shared.

"Yeh, I like you all right."

She sighed. "Why are you going?"

He felt sorry for her. She didn't understand, and she was unhappy about it. He did not want to cause her pain.

"I got to move those sheep and those horses. We go down on south half of the reservation, we get settled there. Then pretty soon I guess I come back here. I just want to move my sheep, that's all."

"Then you'll come back?"

"Yeh, I come back all right."

"All right, but don't fail. And remember, it doesn't matter how many sheep you lose; I'll make it up to you."

He disregarded the remark. She didn't know what she was talking about. He was sorry to leave her; he would return soon. After this, one would not care to live long in a drafty tent, labouring over the flocks. She put her hand on his arm, and they sat down together on the couch before the bright fire.

His horse was in fine shape, almost too fat. Although the days were short, their coolness even at noon made travelling easy, and yet he minded the journey much more than formerly, finding that long hours in the saddle irked him, and he grew tired easily. He wore good, heavy American clothes, suitable for winter work, his new rifle was under the leg, and there were dollars in his pocket. The rest of his finery he had left behind. On the second morning, the sky was clear and hard, with streaks of wind cloud in the northwest. "It's going to be a hard winter," he thought.

He arrived home at noon. His wife received him quietly, remarking, "You were away a long time." He showed her his money, rifle, and new clothes, told of sitting for the painters and said it had been worth while. He was uneasy, conscious of unasked questions, unspoken thoughts.

The little girl was well and lively, but the baby was fretful. It worried and disturbed him to see his son in poor health; he had convinced himself that the child would be well by the time he got back. During the night it cried a good deal. He was restless on the hard floor; supper had seemed coarse and unappetizing; the cabin was bleak, too small, dirty; his wife had no arts to entertain him; she was stolid, shabby, and did not give the adulation to which he was accustomed. He had found a better life elsewhere, to which he would soon return.

He overslept, waking finally to the sound of her movements about the rickety stove. They started early, she driving the wagon, he on horseback, herding the horses and sheep. It gave him plenty to do.

By mid-morning the sky was grey and lowering, with a bitter, cold winter under it. About noon the wind slackened and it began to snow; dry, heavy flakes pouring down thickly. When they made camp, the ground was already covered a couple of inches deep, the sheep had not eaten well during the day, and it was still snowing. They had both of them felt the pinch of the cold, she especially so when she sat driving. The baby was cross and fed poorly. They talked about the weather, hoping this would not last. His appetite was restored to him, he found the simple food delicious.

When he went out at sunrise, the snow was nearly a foot deep where it had not drifted, and still coming down, but less rapidly. One old ewe had died. The horses he found without difficulty, bunched under the lee of a steepish hill. They had fared moderately well, although they were stiff with cold and some of the poorer ones were gaunt.

They turned into a long, wide valley leading southward, following the faint depression in the snow which showed that others had been along the road the day before. The sky cleared, the white flakes ceased falling, the sun took effect. By noon the top of the snow was beginning to melt. Save for worrying about their son, who still did not feed well, they felt quite cheerful.

"When we get down there and stop travelling," he said, "he'll get well."

Then the wind sprang up again, driving, and with it a cold which was not a knife but a bludgeon beating upon them. They wrapped the children in everything they could, though they themselves were none too warm. With the wind came more snow, thick and blinding. One could hardly believe how fast it came. In the valley it drifted deep on top of other drifts, but even if they could have made their way along the rough ground on the ridges, they could not have faced the wind there. The string of horses became hard to manage, the sheep huddled in a dense mass, moving by inches. If the flock was to be saved, it was vital to get them over the few score miles to where the south half dipped to lower, warmer elevations and the tall grass could be reached all winter.

He drove his loose horses mercilessly into the deepening drifts to make a road. When he had it trampled down, he would go back to help his wife. She alternated between driving the wagon and herding the reluctant sheep along. When she sat on the wagon box his heart was wrung for her, since in those minutes without activity the cold went right through her. In his own discomfort, he thought bitterly of what he had abandoned to submit himself to this, and would double his efforts, impatient to get it over with and to return to luxury, once his flocks were safe.

They were exhausted by the time they reached a thick bunch of trees, in the shelter of which they pitched camp. He built huge bonfires to warm the sheep and worked long trying to clear the ground so that they could graze. Near sunset another family, Roan Horse and his wife, joined them. Roan Horse had two strong sons, but they were away at school. The two groups pitched in together, gathering fuel and clearing ground. The newcomer had some hay in his wagon, which they fed to their teams and best saddle horses. Tall Walker had lost a score or more of sheep during the afternoon.

His infant son cried and whimpered through most of the night.

His wife said: "I think my milk is no good now. I was so cold sometimes."

He spoke comfortingly and urged her to eat. Then, exhausted, he fell asleep, dimly aware that she watched late and tended the fire.

In the morning there were more sheep and one horse frozen. The wind had let up, but the snow continued, thick, soft and unmerciful.

They could not stay where they were; their animals would starve and they be snowed in. This day's drive should get them to the edge of lower country. So the two families pushed on together.

They had never seen such snow. Always it was up to the horses' bellies, sometimes they foundered in drifts saddlehigh, and in a few places it was as high as a mounted man. The hungry horses weakened, faltered and gave up; one by one they became exhausted, standing with lowered heads, already half frozen, ignoring the stinging quirts and the snow which piled fluffily on their backs. Only the teams and the mounts they rode, which had been given hay, and to which now they fed bread and anything else they could find, kept on going. The two men charged and charged at the drifts, breaking trail. The sheep followed reluctantly, leaving behind a scattering trail of frozen corpses. Tall Walker's horse, with a month of oats and alfalfa behind it, stood up remarkably well. It disturbed him to see his wife's drawn, worried expression. No complaint passed her lips, but she was visibly weary as she struggled with the flocks, and miserable with cold when she drove, urging on the team with her arm worn out from whipping. He did not like to ask after the boy.

In many places, a thin sheet of ice lay deep buried on top of the first day's snowfall. This cut the horses' chests and forequarters when they plunged through it, so that they left thin, red streaks of blood along the sides of the trail they broke.

They camped again, with huge fires for the remnant of their flocks—but little over half of the original number. For warmth, they set up but one tipi, in which they maintained a good blaze. They brought into cover with them a couple of good ewes which were particularly weak. Roan Horse's wife helped with the baby. Tall Walker was accustomed to seeing it pink, plump, and vociferous. Now its skin was tight over its face, and greenish in colour; its eyes were too large; it whimpered steadily and feebly. Roan Horse's solid wife was visibly moved, and under the wisps of disordered hair which fell over her face, Tall Walker could see that his wife wept silently. The little girl seemed hungry and cross, but well enough.

He and Roan Horse prayed long, for the sheep, for themselves, for Tall Walker's son, for other Apaches caught in the storm. During the latter part of the day they had stumbled often over the carcasses of sheep, buried under more recent snow. Even as they concentrated on their solemn chanting, the fire warmed their knees and faces, and the bitter cold pressed heavily against their backs.

There was scarcely a quarter of their flocks alive the next morning. Roan Horse's saddle pony was dead. The two men and the remaining saddle horse broke trail until the horse went down in the soft snow of a deep, hidden arroyo. They worked hard, but the animal would not help itself, and at length they abandoned it, already half asleep. They struggled on foot, leading the wagon teams over each piece of ground gained. Then the sheep stopped. Starved and half frozen, the animals simply stood still. They loaded a few of their best ewes onto the wagons, and Roan Horse took a young ram, and they went on to try to save themselves. By noon it had stopped snowing, but the cold continued. Digging and chopping in a place where wind had swept the snow thin, they got up a few armfuls of grass for the teams.

A couple of hours after that, and about five miles from their last camp, they came on a track already made, with but little fresh snow in it. Here the wagons could make reasonable speed, with much beating of the horses, although dead sheep lay under the trampled trail so thickly as to make the footing really perilous.

They smelled wood smoke in the clear air. Then, with the sun halfway across the winter sky, they saw a group of a score or more tipis and tents ahead of them under the shelter of a bluff, a bunch of about fifty sheep huddled together, some horses and, most remarkable of all, two automobiles.

Tall Walker was walking beside the wagon, whip in hand. Now he looked up at his wife.

"How is my boy?"

"He is breathing." She was crying again, single tears following one another.

"Perhaps the doctor will be there. Those are Government cars."

"Yes, perhaps." They jolted on over hard snow and frozen sheep, over the dead livelihood of the Apache tribe. Most of the people at the camp were busy around the little band of animals or at the automobiles. Something was being handed out. Near the tents, the agent came on horseback to meet them; he was haggard and unshaven.

"I'm glad to see you," he said. "There are still many people not accounted for. Have you anything left?"

"We got three ewes in the wagon. I guess they're all right."

"Are you people all right?"

Tall Walker looked at his wife. She had stopped crying and was staring hard at nothing. Slowly she turned her face toward him, then pulled her blanket over her head.

"My little boy, he's died."

"That's too bad. I'm sorry." In the last forty-eight hours, the agent had seen so much tragedy that he had lost his capacity for receiving it. The whole winter range was under six feet of snow; his Indians were destitute; many families were still to be found. He anaesthetized himself with relentless effort. "I'm sorry," he repeated. "We have feed for your stock here, put them with the bunch, and you can get food and some clothing from those cars. There is more coming. The doctor is at another camp, down below; he will be here this evening, if anyone is sick."

"All right. I think by and by he might look at my wife, maybe."

The agent glanced at her. "Yes. I'll tell him." He spurred his mount and rode over to talk to Roan Horse.

Tall Walker's wife sat without moving until he touched her arm, saying, "We must make camp, even so."

He led the team off the road and began unharnessing.

"You put up the tipi," he said. "I'll get the animals fed, and see about this food for us."

She set to work without speaking. He paused to look at her, seeing the dishevelled hair hanging all about her head, the pinched, drawn face, the self-control and the steadiness with which she went about her business. That is how Apache women are, he thought; that is why we were great warriors once.

He took the horses over and saw them fed. His wife had the lodge poles out, and, with the help of a couple of other women, was arranging the canvas. He lifted a ewe from the wagon.

More cars arrived, and he stopped to watch them—two big trucks, staggering, plunging, and throwing up snow. Taking the ewe on his shoulders, he started over to the bunch. Behind the trucks followed a big sedan which he recognized. He stopped again, midway of the camp.

The sedan turned out to pass the trucks, and then came slowly along the cluster of tents. He could see the white woman staring out of the front window beside Juan, who was driving. It was Juan who recognized him. The car stopped and she got out. He thought, inconsequently, that he had not known she owned such sensible clothing. The face of the world had been altered, but her big car remained, the token of a house with many fireplaces, of comfort and an end to effort in Taos whence it came. Aeons had passed, but she was just the same as ever. There was the contradictory appearance of being worn out and of immaturity, and the eager, blue eyes.

She said, "Celestino!"

He looked at her without answering.

She said: "You poor dear, you look done in. I was so worried about you when I heard how terrible the storm was. I came as soon as I could. I have food and clothing for you, and you must come back to my house. Are you all right?"

"I guess I'm all right."

"Did you lose your sheep?"

"I lost them, and I lost my horses. Only just three ewes we brought in the wagon. All the Apaches, they lost their sheep, I guess; only this little bunch here, that's all."

"Thank heaven, you don't need to worry. I shall take care of you."

Again he did not answer.

"Now come with me. You don't need sheep any longer."

He studied her gravely, with a blank face. From where he stood, he could see his wife carrying a bundle of blankets and a kettle into the tipi, and the little girl running after her. He shifted his ewe on his

42

shoulders, feeling its weak heartbeats against his face. For a long time he had not felt any emotion; he had just known that things had happened, and that they were bad. Since back before the sheep stopped moving he had been numb. Now suddenly he was angry—so deeply, tremendously angry that he shook and he could not speak at all. As if in a mist, he saw her step back from him with startled face. He got control of himself by an effort and, turning away, walked off to take the ewe to be fed. The woman called after him, but he gave no sign of hearing her.

HIGHER EDUCATION

T he door of the truck was hot to the touch. Even though it stood in the broken shade of poplars, the whole machine was a trap for heat more stifling than that which enveloped the sun-smitten road, the houses, the mesa. Looking northward, one saw the jumbled, garish country into which we were going, its harsh colours toned down without being softened by the over-brilliant light, its crazy shapes vibrating in the heat. The utterly silent landscape seemed to growl as one looked at it.

Joe Degler slouched over the wheel, his legs sprawling widely, his big, hairy arms lax. He was powerful, blond, unshaven; too big and hearty a man for the front seat of a truck on a June day in Arizona. He moved slightly, saying:

"Come in, Professor. We got a squaw ridin' with us. She's in seein' the agent. Soon's she turns up, we'll git goin'."

The name "Professor" is set in everyone's mind; I can't do anything about it. It annoys me, and so does the term "squaw," particularly from the lips of such as this big Texan, the aggressively *white* white men who give it always a downward intonation, by the brief word denying woman-kind a whole race of women. I stood with my foot on the running board, seeing him stupid but well intentioned, tired momentarily of his friendship, and of tolerating him.

"Thanks, Joe," I said, "I don't want to climb into that oven of yours until I have to."

*Originally published in the *Saturday Evening Post,* March 31, 1934.

45

"Suit yourself. I'd as soon roast sittin' down as standin' up. She won't be real hot till we hit the sand by T'o Haskid; then you sure will wish someone'd invent water-cooled boots."

I looked in the back of the truck—mail-bags, assorted goods for up-country trading posts, my own bedroll and duffle-bag, and a new, bright, small trunk and imitation leather valise.

"Whose luggage?" I asked.

"Hunh?"

"Whose baggage?"

"Oh." He turned his head to stare at the objects. "That's what the Great Father does for a squaw. It's hers."

"The woman who's coming?"

"Yeah. Just out o' school. Six years in California learnin' to stick her little finger out when she drinks tea, and then turned out to graze in the howlin' desert. Hell of a system, if you ask me."

I nodded. The trunk carried painted initials—L. N. L for one of the flowery names the teachers give the children when they first come to school—wild-haired, frightened things, crowding together, their true names, their pride and ancestry ignored—Lucille or Lydia or Lilith or God knows what. N might be for an English surname, or some distorted fragment of a native word, half heard, truncated, misapplied. The letter teased, forcing vain speculation, *Nakai, Nadhani, Nditligh, Niltsi*—that struck a chord. Wind Singer was expecting his daughter back from school, he had told me. This might be she.

The cheap, showy, unsuitable luggage lay tiptilted with the other freight forcing a superimposed mental vision of Wind Singer's camp, the hogahn of crude brush and sticks, the little bundles of goods and rolls of seldom-washed bedding, dogs and ashes and smoke and poverty of possessions in a home which could be moved without difficulty of packing as the grazing needs of the sheep dictated.

Joe said, "Here she is."

I noticed first the incongruous, pseudo-smart, tacky dress and the hat, already *passé* with its exaggerated angle which would not have been good even at the height of that fashion. Short skirts, and high-heeled shoes, and a stilted walk with pocket-book in one hand shocked one who was used to Navajo women moving like queens, free-striding, with a swing of long skirts cut full enough to cover their legs when they ride astride. They are more perfectly at ease

46

than most men, of any race, in the saddle, and majestic on the ground. This mincing, side-walk gait was an offence.

The face was Indian; not only the breadth of cheek-bone, fine long eyes and beautiful chiselling of a wide mouth, but the emptiness now drawn over it, the mask of absence which all Indians possess for protection in time of stress and which the school-children above all learn to use. She wore it now. One could not tell what looked through her eyes when she left school, but from then till now, on the train, re-entering the forgotten wasteland of her home, seeing the first of her own ragged people, meeting race-conscious Government employees, shunted about, disregarded, with the almost terror of her old way of life before her, she had put on the mask. She had been learning.

I knew Joe would not like it, I suspected that it was a poor idea, but there are some things one must do for his own sake. I lifted my hat, saying:

"Good morning. You'd better sit in front. I'll ride in back."

Joe was a Westerner; he could not let my gesture go without some attempt to equal it.

"Sure," he said. "Come in."

He did not move a muscle. His voice, his intonation, were hearty, but the reverse of the words ran undercurrent to them. She looked us over so quickly one could hardly detect the motion of her eyes.

"Thank you. I think I ride in back."

Joe said, "Wall let's git goin'. Hop in Professor. *Vamos.*"

That's what smugness accomplishes. I had demonstrated my high principles for my own benefit and so provided the girl with a snub, a reminder of her position, which otherwise would have remained in abeyance. Of course she had read Joe's feelings easily enough. How much better if I'd kept my trap shut and let her get in the back without that small fuss. Perhaps I was exaggerating. I didn't think so. I've known mean Indians, and stupid ones, but never one who was thick-skinned.

The car jolted and bounced and grew hotter. Dust settled upon us, little drifts of fine, grey powder and coarser, bright sand lay in the folds of the mail-sacks. The girl sat limply, resting against my bed-roll. She ought to have plenty to think about; every mile of desert, every jounce, was a warning of the completeness of this, the second shattering change in her life. The first was years ago when she received whatever name L stood for, dressed in a dowdy uniform and her young wildness was broken to the machine-like routine of an institution half penitentiary, half orphanage. How many times can the substance be shattered and yet re-create itself?

We got stuck in the sand at T'o Haskid, as per schedule, otherwise the trip was extremely dull. The road was empty. We passed a few shepherds with their flocks; altogether we saw about half a dozen hogahns at different places. The girl stared at them, and at the women. When we stopped to deliver mail at Tsaychee trading post, she stayed in the car, shrinking from the curiosity of whites and Indians alike. It was well past lunch time when we finally drew up in front of Luke's post at Kin Bukho.

Joe said: "Wall, here we are. You're lucky; I got to go on to Cheelcheen right now, or I'll lose my damn contract." He turned to the back of the truck. "All right, sister, here's your home town. I guess your folks are round here somewheres."

Bert Luke came out of the post to meet us, cordial as usual in his quiet, word-stingy way.

"Go on back," he told me, "I guess the old woman can fix you up some grub. You'll stay tonight?"

"Thanks, I'd like to. How are my animals?"

"Fat and sassy."

I took my bedroll and bag on my shoulder, and went around the corner of the post. From the front one saw a sort of low, stone barn with a door and narrow windows appearing dead black against the glaring sunlight on the wall, trampled sand and a few tin cans for foreground, a couple of lounging Indians, some tethered ponies, a wagon. It looked like a store at the tail end of nowhere, and yet, taking up Joe's phrase, I reflected that the shopping centre of that girl's home town was even bleaker and more remote. Rounding the corner, one passes through a gate onto a narrow strip of real grass which Mrs. Luke waters and tends minutely. The back porch is covered with Virginia creeper, and two big cottonwood trees cast shade upon it. It is an oasis, a credible home.

Mrs. Luke was just coming through the gate. She hailed me with "Hello, Professor, you're packed up like a mule, ain't you?"

I said, "Sure, and likely to buck."

"Well, throw down on the porch and make yourself at home. Wind Singer and his wife are here. Did their girl come?"

"I guess so. Some girl did. She's out there, kind of lost."

"I'll bring her in."

The porch was cool. I dropped my burdens, sighed, and threw my hat down before shaking hands with the medicine man and his wife. They were quiet, constrained, and anxious; their smiles as our hands touched faded again while they sat watching the gate. I seated myself in a rocking-chair and made a cigarette.

Luke came through from the kitchen to join us. A devout Mormon, he did not smoke. The four of us sat, pretending to be natural. Mrs. Luke came into view with the girl in her pathetically unsmart clothes following at her side as though the older woman's bigness had caught her up and was cradling her along. Here at last was someone of remembered kindness, unchanged, a first stable point in a quicksand world. I saw Mrs. Luke pat her arm, and the girl smiled.

Luke said, *"Kodi, sikiso,"* and gestured towards the path.

The two Indians rose, Wind Singer's Wife gathering her blanket around her shoulders, and went down onto the lawn. Mrs. Luke came past them with a brief word and a smile, and joined us on the porch. Her smile had disappeared, she looked at her husband and me gravely.

Wind Singer stopped a few yards from his daughter and her mother went forward alone. The girl stood still, her head hanging. The old woman moved slowly and we could see that her half-outstretched hands were trembling. Now they were close to each other, and Wind Singer's Wife was touching her daughter's shoulders. There was an agony of longing on her face. She said something, and the girl's head was bowed yet lower.

Mrs. Luke whispered through unmoving lips, "She don't remember any Navajo."

Wind Singer's Wife touched the girl's face lightly, fleetingly, with her hands, and the girl shrank. Then the old woman stepped back, and seemed for the first time to take in the strange clothes, the half-bare arms and neck, the short skirt. With the same slow, gentle motions she took off her blanket—it was moderately clean—and cast it about her daughter's shoulders. The girl took the edges in a curious, hypnotized fashion and drew them together. She did not shrink from

49

the heavy wool, rather it seemed as though in complete despair she had ceased to mind. The mask on her face was so perfect that it now cried out, betraying its secret. Her mother spoke to Wind Singer, the three of them turned together and walked slowly, all with bowed heads, out of the gate.

Luke said, "Damnation!" which was unusual for him.

"What does L stand for?" I asked.

"Lucille." Mrs. Luke said. "Her true name's *Zhiltnapah,* but they used to call her Running Girl because she was so lively."

Luke rose. "I got to get back to the store. Ruth, I reckon the Professor ain't had lunch." At the door he stopped, one hand on the jamb, and said, "Hooray for Uncle Sam and higher education."

"What are they going to do now?" I asked Mrs. Luke.

"Drive back with her to Lukhahutso. They came in their wagon."

"She'll sleep in the hogahn tonight, then?"

"I guess so, if she sleeps. You goin' there tomorrow?"

"Yes. I've got to stop by Show-Off's, though."

"If you started right now you could spend the night at his place."

"Thanks. Not when I can get next to your cooking."

Show-Off had the trading post nearest to Lukhahutso, a lonely place, the farthest outflung store to the north of a chain owned by a Denver firm. We called him Show-Off after the name the Navajos gave him, *Bedaylabi,* which means someone loud and too smart and annoying. I did not know his right name. Although I disliked him, I had to use his post as my base while I worked in that district, and we got on all right. He was a big man, handsome in a flashy way, with curly black hair, a quick smile, and over-hearty handshake. He was industriously two-fisted, hairy-chested, he-man, hundred per cent and all the rest of it.

Leaving Luke's in the middle of the next morning, I reached Show-Off's early in the afternoon, and went in to let him know I was back and to get supplies. There were some six or eight Indians, men and women, in the store, mostly just loafing and talking, having finished trading. He urged me to stay for dinner and spend the night, but I said I had to get back to my camp.

Just about as I had my grub together, Show-Off said, "For Gawd's sake!"

I turned towards the door. Wind Singer and his daughter were

50

coming in. She had discarded her hat, and wore a blanket loosely over her shoulders, but she still carried her pocket-book, her costume was still incongruous. I noticed that her expression seemed dazed, possibly resigned. There was nothing positive.

Her father came over and spoke to me. "Are you coming out to your camp?"

"Yes. I'll be there by sundown, I think."

"Good." He hesitated. "We have come here to buy cloth. She is going to make proper clothes, and put those things away."

I was glad to hear that, it sounded hopeful, but when I looked at the girl I was not so sure, and I wondered again, how often can the substance be shattered and re-create itself? She was dazed, there was a mechanical quality about her actions. Her father joined her at the counter, to help her pick out her materials. He was solicitous, quietly tender, and faintly proud as she talked with Show-Off in English.

He kept them waiting till he had given me the last of my grub, and rolled a cigarette, then he faced them.

"Just back from school, eh?" he said.

"Yes, sir."

"What do you want?"

"Calico. That there, and that, twelve yards of each, please." She continued, ordering the velveteen and rick-rack braid and thread, and a fringed Pendleton blanket.

Show-Off slapped the goods down before her in a tumbled pile.

"Will you pay for them, or do I put it on your old man's ticket?"

"I pay for them."

He told her the price. She gave him some bills from her pocket-book. He made change at the cash register, and threw the change towards her, the coins sliding along the counter and ending all scattered.

"Better get a necklace or some earrings, hanh?"

"No, thank you. Will you wrap the things up, please?"

He stopped still, put his hands on his hips, stared at the girl and then at me.

"My God," he said, "the airs these squaws put on nowadays!"

She winced. Most of the Indians present knew enough English to understand the general meaning of what had been said. There was a period of utter silence while she gathered up her purchases, and then a man said his name in a low voice, pronouncing each syllable with slow, mocking clarity, and not addressing anyone at all, *"Be-day-la-hi."* There was a snicker all round the store, and Show-Off flushed deep crimson. Wind Singer and the girl departed. I took my supplies and went to the corral, packed my mule and got going.

I passed by Wind Singer's hogahn where the trail crossed the wagon-road, but decided not to call there. That family might desire to be alone, it ought to be tired of white men just now. I rode up the cañon to my camp, checked over my cache of goods, threw down and turned my animals out to graze. Then I walked a few hundred yards to the cave, to make sure nothing had been disturbed. All was as I left it, a nice little ruin of the earliest period, with my test trench, half completed, running across it. I figured that I'd do another week's work on it before moving on, and that next year when the University gave me a regular expedition again—the funds were promised—I'd excavate this place thoroughly. This year I was simply scouting, enjoying the frequent changes of camp, and finding it a relief not to have any students to take care of.

The sun was low. I went back, built a fire and cooked supper. Camp again, the restful cañon, the sharpness of night air adding to my pleasure in the fire, the big sky, the irregular, jerky clanging of the bell on my lead horse as he grazed, all good things of which one does not tire.

Hearing a single, barely audible footstep, I peered out of my circle of light. Wind Singer became visible in the darkness. He stepped up to the fire and warmed his hands, then sat down, remarking, "My wife said you came by."

"Yes, I got in sooner than I expected. I came faster than you, I think."

I passed him coffee and the makings. He rolled a cigarette slowly, and juggled with a live coal to light it.

When he had taken a few puffs, he asked, "What did Show-Off say that time?"

"He was rude."

"How?"

"Well—you know, in those stores by Wide Water, where your daughter was, they wrap things for you in paper, they tie them with a string. Nobody does that here. Your daughter asked him to wrap up her goods, and he was rude about it. It's stupid, I think."

Wind Singer grunted. "That's the way he is. Now she feels badly. She was not happy anyhow; now she is worse."

"It will take a little time, you know. Everything is different here, she cannot get used to it right away. Just give her time. How long was she at that school?"

"Six years."

I nodded. She must be about seventeen; she had not seen anything remotely suggesting this country or this life for that time. Wind Singer stared at the fire, and then spoke quietly, with deep feeling behind his level voice. His lined, kindly face was grave.

"She has all but forgotten our language, just a few words have come back to her since she returned. I can talk with you more easily than I can speak to my own daughter." He paused, making a small, desperate gesture with his hand. "She turns her face from us. Her brother went a little while to the school here at T'odnesji, he speaks English to her, he does what he can, but she will not look at him, either." He shifted his position. "What is this? We are men, we People. We think well of ourselves. We want our children to have what we have. We want them to learn English and writing and those useful things, but not to forget everything white men do not know, everything that has made us strong.

"I can understand a man like Show-Off; there are plenty of bad Navajos, too. But what is this other thing? What kind of man orders it?

"We know we are poorer than white men. We are ragged and dirty, I suppose. We live simply, a hard life. But we are not ashamed. We are strong, we are men, we have beauty. There is not one of us who would lower his face before any man. But my daughter comes back from that school at T'o Ntyel, where they sent her because she was the best in the school at T'odnesji, and she is all shame and fear. At night, when she thinks we are asleep, she cries."

He stopped. I wished I could change my colour, my skin, my race.

Wind Singer said, with less tension in his voice: "Perhaps if we have a ceremony for her, it will help. We should like her to marry Strong Hand—you know him well, I think."

"Yes, a very good man." I considered. "Don't do anything about it yet, either that or singing for her. Go slowly, let her become accustomed. Right now she is upset by the strange things, she is thinking about things, so that she cannot see the trail. Give her time, that is all."

"Perhaps you are right." He glanced upward. "It is late."

He rose, tall, spare, white-haired, dignified for all the shabbiness of his costume. He was well-to-do, but like many medicine men, he didn't care much what he wore. His wife used his jewelry. He walked off, Navajo fashion, without any farewell. I finished another cigarette. Luke was right. Hooray for Uncle Sam and higher education.

I hadn't covered my grub properly. While I slept, a coyote got under the tarpaulin, and in the morning I found myself robbed of bacon, and my sugar had been spilled out of the sack into a hopeless mess of sand and ants. I tracked the beast for a mile, and lost its trail, so I breakfasted in bad humour and then saddled up to ride to Show-Off's and restock. It was still early when I reached the post, and there were no customers. Show-Off seemed pleased about my accident.

"Ain't you got a gun?" he asked.

"Sure I have, but I was asleep. Never heard him."

"That's right, you wasn't expectin' no thieves. But the coyote finally fooled you."

I let his remark pass by. He always resented the fact that the Indians, who stole from him when they could, let me wander unguarded among them without taking anything. Let it go.

When he had weighed out the sugar, he said, "Stop and have a smoke, Professor. Hell, thar ain't no hurry," and shoved tobacco towards me.

The store was still cool, and the day outside was hot. I leant against the counter and made a cigarette.

"Say, you kind o' didn't like the way I talked to Wind Singer's girl the other day, did you?"

"No, frankly, I did not."

"Wall, I guess you was right. I hadn't ought to of done it. But here she come in in them civilized clothes, and then would she give me a tumble? No, sir. Jest looked at me like I was a slot machine she was a-goin' to get gum out of, and then she tells me to wrap it up. I got kind o' stampeded."

This was more grace than I thought was in him. "It was a pity," I said. "Hard enough on the girl, coming back from school like this, without adding onto it."

"Yeah, that's right. I didn't mean to. I'm sorry, that's truth. Tough on her, being kicked back into the blanket. And she's a cute little trick, too."

I glanced at him suspiciously. "I hadn't noticed," I said, although now he spoke of it I saw what he meant.

He seemed to feel a need to justify himself. "You know what I mean. It's the way she was dressed, partly. Hell, I ain't seen a girl dressed snappy in more'n a year. Too bad she's goin' to put on them Navajo clothes. It's a kinda relief to look at something else sometimes."

"More than a year?" I asked. "Haven't you been out at all?"

"Not at all, barrin' one trip to Tuba to see the Agent. Since Buck took sick and went out I been here alone. Can't leave. They've promised to send a man in to relieve me, but they're damn slow about it. I'm achin' to get drunk and have me some fun."

I nodded. "That's a long spell. But I bet you've got whiskey here."

"Sure I have, only I don't dare get rightly stewed, nor hand any out. The Gov'ment's strict as hell. And it is lonely."

"Yes. Well, I hope you get out soon. Meantime, don't try to fix yourself up with any Navajo women; it isn't safe."

"That's right, Professor. No squaw-trouble in mine. All I meant was that girl looked cute, see, and no harm in being friendly. And it is a pity she's got to go back into them Injun clothes. Anyway, I don't want to lose her folks' trade, so if you can say anything to 'em, I wish you would."

"All right. Well, I've got to be going. So long."

"So long. Come in some evening and have a drink."

"Thanks."

I was back at camp by noon, and spent the rest of the day extending my test trench in the ruin. While I worked, I kept thinking about the girl, and her family, and Show-Off, and Strong Hand who was my particular friend. Show-Off's dangerous, because he's both stupid and smart. Hope he goes on leave soon. Well, what the devil, this isn't my affair. I can't settle it, it only makes me feel badly.

Ordinarily, I should have dropped in on Wing Singer after supper,

55

since no one came to my fire, but I thought better not to. Instead I damned the whole situation and the Great White Step-Father, turned in, and had considerable difficulty going to sleep.

I slept late, waking to find it broad daylight and the sun about to rise. Someone was near me. Rolling my eyes, as I lay still flat in my bedroll, I saw red moccasins and above them familiar leggings of blue calico, right behind my head. Looking steadfastly forward, I sat up, yawned and stretched. Then with my eyes still on the trees beyond my feet, I said,

"*Ahalani, sitsili*—hello, younger brother."

Strong Hand laughed. "Hello, sleeper."

"Light the fire," I said, pulling on my trousers.

By the time I joined him he had a good blaze going. He had breakfasted, he said, but he would take some coffee. We talked about this and that, idle remarks, bits of small news. There seemed to have been nothing much new since we last saw each other. Our unimportant conversation was merely the vehicle for our pleasure in being together.

Finally I said, "Wind Singer's daughter is back."

"Yes, I saw her last night. I went to their hogahn. I thought you would be there, too."

"I was tired, so I just went to sleep. What do you think of her?"

He looked at me keenly. "You know what they were talking about, before she came?"

"About you and her? Yes, I have heard something."

"I went to see what she was like."

He rubbed his forefinger and thumb together. I passed him tobacco and papers. When he had his cigarette lit, he spoke again.

"It made me angry, what I saw. I was angry with all white men, even you, my friend."

He was a big young man, strong, intelligent. His friendship was good, I thought I would not care to have his enmity. He must have read my face, for he smiled, a flash of even teeth in a wide mouth, saying,

"I did not stay that way."

Then the smile faded.

"What was she like before?" I asked.

"I was older than she, I was beginning to be a man and she was

56

still just a child, but one liked her. She was very lively, and she had that which pulls at people, Running girl. Everyone liked her. I was looking for that last night, and all I could see was pain in her. She was pitiful. So were her parents." He dug in the sand with his fingers. "But she was most so. Then I did see it, a little, I think. Way down inside her is some of what she was, but frightened almost to death. She would be beautiful, too, I think, if she could take the cloud off her face.

"I wanted to help her. It made me want to fight. She was afraid of me, too."

He finished. I hesitated, then said, "You like her."

"Yes. I don't know why."

"What was she wearing?"

"Navajo clothes. She had just finished making them."

"It is a matter of time," I said. "If they will go slow, let her learn again, she will be all right, I think."

I stood up, gathering my notebook and tools.

"Perhaps," he said. "I don't know. Are you going to dig in the Old People's house there?"

"Yes."

"I'll watch you, if you aren't going to bring up any bones."

"I don't think so."

He stayed till lunch, making amusing remarks about the sandals, bits of pottery and so on that I uncovered, and in general being excellent company. Then he went away without further reference to Running Girl. That's enough of that, I thought. If I get involved in the subject again I'll scream. It has a horrid fascination.

The girl herself turned up just before sunset, while I was cooking supper. I saw her coming with no pleasure, although she looked infinitely more attractive in the dignity and real style of her native costume. She had chosen her colours well. The full skirt was rather a bright blue, with two green lines of braid around it near the bottom, matching her green velveteen blouse. A new, fringed blanket lay across her shoulders, and she wore a necklace of many strands of coral, undoubtedly a present from her father.

I did not know just what etiquette to follow, so I sat like a dumb lump, stirring my stew with a big spoon, until she was right by the fire.

"I am Lucille Niltsi," she said. "I came up with you in dat car."

I rose awkwardly, took off my hat and shook hands. "Won't you sit down? Excuse me if I go on cooking."

A long and painful silence ensued. I remarked that it had been a nice day, and got no answer. More silence. Then I asked her please to look in the Dutch oven and see if my bread was baked.

She said, "I don't know how you open it."

My God, I thought, and I bet she's had every known form of Domestic Science.

"Take this stick and poke it through the handle on the lid."

She did so, and managed to raise the cover and look in without spilling more than a few coals on the bread.

"I guess it's done."

"Then will you take it off the coals, please? Thanks."

Silence again, while she twisted and untwisted the blanket fringe in her fingers.

"Will you have some supper?"

"No, thanks. I got to eat pretty soon, over dere."

"Some coffee, then? Here's sugar and canned milk."

She took that. I knew she didn't get milk at Wind Singer's.

Had she been a normal Indian, I should have made no effort to talk, knowing that in time, out of silence would emerge whatever she had on her mind. But she was not normal; maladjusted education had left her with neither the poise for talk nor the faculty of gracious quietness. She fidgeted.

"That was a long, dusty ride we had in the car," I offered.

"Yes."

More braiding of the fingers in the fringe.

"How long is it since you were home last?"

"Six years. I was ten."

"Then you're sixteen?"

"Yes."

"You went to Riverside?"

"Yes."

"Did you like it?"

"Not at first. Dey treated us pretty rough. Only since dat new Commissioner came in, it was better. I liked it pretty good, den. It ain't goin' to do me much good."

Superimposed upon her native Navajo accent was the bad English of her under-educated teachers.

"I should think you could get a lot of good out of it."

"How can I? My people—dey live like savages. I got to live like a savage. Dere ain't nothin' else for me to do. I didn't want to come back, I asked to get a job. Dey couldn't get me one. I had to come. Now I can't get away."

"With your education, you could do great things for your people."

"I can't even talk to dem."

"You'll remember that soon."

"I guess so." She said these last words in a tone of utter misery.

"Is it so bad, Lucille?"

"Yes it is—" She hesitated.

I really wished she would go away and not burden me, but I did feel sorry for her, and I saw she wanted to talk.

I said, "Tell me about it."

"My fader says you're a good man. I thought maybe you would understan'. Dey can't. My broder can't. It's everything. Dese Inyan clothes I got to wear."

"They're handsome."

"Maybe. But I want nice, pretty things like white girls have. I don't like to sleep in my same clothes on de groun', an' get up an' not wash, an' go on like dat. I like clean things, an' change dem—an' you know, like you see in de movies, pretty things underneath. De blankets an' sheepskins are dirty, an' de food ain't no good, an' my fader an' moder, dey spit an' scratch demselves—pretty soon I guess I'll be scratchin' myself, too. An' den, dere ain't nothin' I know how to do. I spent five years learnin' to cook real good, on a stove. What can I do here?"

I nodded. "Of course it's hard. But if I can learn to live and work in camp, and even get so that I love it, so can you. You're thinking about the things your people haven't got yet—fixed houses, beds, baths. You can't have those things when you run sheep in a desert. But they will come. You like the movies and lace underwear." She started when I said that. In her prim, over-religious school world men did not speak casually of underwear. I went right on. "Those things don't make life. You forget what your people have—strength, intelligence, pride, skill, beauty, character, and a magnificent religion."

She interrupted me. "Ain't you Christian?"

"Not that way. I believe in God and Our Saviour, yes, but I see more of Them in the Navajo religion than I do in any of the missions around the Indian schools." I was getting the effect I wanted, I was startling her narrowed mind into fresh thinking. "Do you remember what *bik'é hozhoni* means?"

"Well—kind of. Trail of beauty, ain't it?"

"Yes. But find out what it really means; get to understand it. Then you'll know something you never could learn at school."

She looked at me dubiously.

"I know, you're up against a tough situation. Remember this: you belong to about the only tribe of Indians that has a chance to continue and be really great. instead of being destroyed. Make them your business, become one of them, and with your education you can make yourself great through them."

"But de Inyans, dey don't think much of me because I can't do nothin'. An' de white people, dey hold it against me, some of dem, because I'm Inyan."

"Only some," I said, "they're fools. We aren't all like Show-Off, you know."

"Oh, him," she said. "He didn't mean no harm. I guess he was just feelin' cross."

It was my turn to be surprised.

"I went dere yestiddy with my broder to trade on some things. My fader he thought I could get a better price, because I can read and do arithmetic, you know."

I nodded. I had a feeling, without explanation, that this was what she really wanted to talk to me about.

"I got a good trade, too. He was real nice, Mr. McClellan, and he said he was sure sorry."

McClellan, I thought, so that's his name. *Mister* McClellan. "Well, that's good, but don't trust him. He's a bad man."

"Is he? I—I kind o' thought he looked—well, sort of like Ramon Novarro, you know."

My God, I thought, is this the Navajo country? Heaven defend us! "Maybe he does, but all the same, he's a cheap skate."

"Oh." She paused. "Well, I got to go back dere now. Thank you Mr.— I don't know your right name."

"Fayerweather."

"Mr. Fayerweader. I'll remember what you say about dat—*bik'é hozhoni,* you know."

"All right. I'll see you again."

"Yes, sir. Good night."

I poured myself some more coffee. My God! Heaven above! There can't be anything in it, but—subject for a Ph.D. thesis, "The Influence of the Cinema in Aboriginal American Life." Holy Moses!

About a week after that I packed up and moved to Nahki Tees Cañon, where there was an "open site" ruin I wanted to test. I was relieved to get well away from Wing Singer and his family's problems, although in the last days when I visited there I thought the girl seemed more at ease and almost cheerful. The old man told me that, on account of her knowledge, she was a remarkable trader and got him many bargains. He said he always knew Show-Off had cheated on those pieces of paper he used, but had never been able to do anything about it before. I said that was good, and I wondered, until, in the saddle once more and driving my mule and spare horse, I shoved the whole thing out of my mind.

Save for the two cottonwoods where I camped, from which the cañon took its name, Nahki Tees is a bare, bright expanse of sand and adobe between two low, red walls of rock, unshaded, empty, and harsh, but beautiful in its own strange way. Where I dug, it was like working on top of a stove. I prolonged the siesta hour. There were no near neighbours, but a main trail passed close by, so I seldom lacked for company at meals. The ruin I was exploring was interesting; the moon, approaching full, made the whole place a liquid silver glory at night, and I enjoyed myself.

One day Strong Hand dropped in for lunch. It was pleasant to see him. While I was cooking he made fun of me for doing a woman's work, and thence got into a direct, Rabelaisian, and very Navajo line of kidding about the disadvantages of being single.

"You, too." I said. "It is past time you left your mother's hogahn."

"I don't know. Perhaps I shall never marry."

"Why?"

"Oh, nothing. Only I may never marry."

I let that pass and dished up the grub. Something was on his mind. When we were finished, he said: "I have been seeing that girl again. I have been there two or three times."

"Yes."

61

"You were right, what you were thinking when we talked before. I like her. Very much I like her." He stopped.

"Then, in the end you will marry, I think."

"Perhaps not."

"Why?"

"She might marry Show-Off, I think."

I grunted.

"You know how she makes such good trades with him? I was there one time when they were trading. I saw them. They like each other, I think. He gives her things, he does it just for her—and she knows it, I think. That is how it seemed to me, that time."

He paused. I waited.

"Yesterday her mother finished a blanket. She said she would get a better trade at Red Mormon's." (He meant Luke.) "She said she knew the way all right, so she went alone. She would have to be gone all night—Broad Woman" (that is Mrs. Luke) "would give her a place to sleep. So she went." He fiddled with his bow-guard while he talked, not looking at me. "I followed her, a little distance behind. Her tracks went right to Show-Off's, but she did not come home last night." He picked up a handful of sand and let it fall through his fingers, watching it. "I said 'marry,' I meant just sleep with him. Then what? I don't know."

We must have sat, thinking, for about a minute.

"What do you think of Show-Off?" he asked.

"I don't like him."

He looked square at me. "My friend, by that which stands up within you, would you be sorry if he were dead?"

I'm a white man, and we were speaking about a white man, but I had to tell the truth.

"No."

"All right. Lend me your rifle."

I took time to think before I answered. "No. You are not sure. Perhaps she did go on to Red Mormon's. Perhaps he honestly wants to marry her. There is much we do not know. Besides, one must not kill people. Those days are over. No."

It was plain to see his thoughts going beyond my answer. In the last analysis, I was just like other white men. We stood together, regardless of all else. He thought he could resolve a bad situation cleanly, in an old way, but my help ended where my race began.

"Wait," I told him. "Have patience a little. Your bullet might land in Show-Off. But even if she were safe in her hogahn, it might reach her heart too—yes, and in the end, yours." I sounded pompous and unconvincing to myself.

He grunted. The idea was hostile to him, but worth considering.

"It's going to rain soon," he said. "You'll have a wet camp here."

Strong Hand was right about the rain. It came in mid-July, concentrated thunderstorms, sometimes lasting a minute or two, sometimes an hour. Grass began to show in the valley, individual, pointed spears of green scattered through the sand. Because of my feeling about Show-Off and what I suspected he was doing, I had kept postponing going after supplies until now I was clean out of grub and there was nothing for it but to saddle up and visit the post.

Travel was better with clouds in the sky to temper the sun. My animals found grass at noon. About three I reached T'o Tletsowi Wash, to find it way up, a boiling flood of brown water from bank to bank. Nothing to do but wait. The crest of the flood went by shortly, and in about an hour it looked safe to cross. Just as I was mounting, Jake Barnett arrived in his car, an old, battered Dodge.

"Howdy, Professor," he said, "where's your boys?"

"Hello, Jake. Haven't any this season, just me myself prospecting. How's Mrs. Barnett?"

"She's fine as ever. You fixin' to cross?"

"Yes."

"Well, I'll let you scout it. See if you can find hard bottom for me."

"All right."

I snubbed my mule's lead-rope around my saddle horn and started across, working my way cautiously over the new-spread, treacherous mud. The going seemed good, with only one soft place. From the farther bank, I shouted instructions to Jake. He came over slowly but steadily, the car splashing up great showers of mud and water, until where it began to climb the bank it stuck fast.

For about thirty seconds he just swore, without any special objective, then he directed the stream of his profanity more specifically, upon the Navajo country and Navajo roads, the rain, the creek, automobiles in general, and finally at me for sitting in the saddle and grinning at him like a God damn laughing jackass. Then he smiled.

"Well, hell," he said. "Come on and help me dig out."

We dug, and I put my rope on the front bumper and pulled with my horse. Finally the car struggled free.

"Thanks," he said. "It's gettin' late. Looks like I'd have to spend the night at Show-Off's. You headin' thar?"

"Yes. I'm out of grub."

"Fine. If I get stuck again you can help me. That horse pulls good. If I get thar first I'll tell him you're comin'."

"All right. Bet you stick."

"How much?"

"Four bits."

"Taken."

I caught up with him again just at sunset, bogged down in an adobe flat about a mile from the post. It took us a good hour, digging, laying brush and using all my animals to get the car out. By then we were tired, wet, and coated with mud. The day had been cool, the night was going to be cold.

"Stick your pack in the car," he said. "then you can make time. Show-Off's an ornery son-of-a-gun, but he's got a stove, anyway."

With my mule unloaded I came along fast, arriving at the post just after Jake did. A light showed in the store windows, but he was getting no answer to his knocking.

"Isn't he here?" I asked.

"Sure he's here. I seen him. He don't want to let us in, by God. Show yourself in that window, Professor, let him know we know he's thar."

I had a sudden horrid idea of why he didn't want to let us in.

"Look here," I said weakly, "if he feels that way, I don't want his hospitality. Let's camp."

"Hell, no! I'm goin' to set by his stove if I have to kick his God damn door in. Rap on that window."

I dismounted and rapped. Sure enough, Show-Off was in the store, standing well back in the shadows, away from the lamp. I shouted and nodded to him. He came forward slowly to open the door, and as he did so, tried to place himself so that he blocked the entrance, saying, "I thought you was Injuns."

Jake said "Sure, I'm Sittin' Bull in person," and brushed past him. I followed.

"Come in," Show-Off said. "Come in. I wish you'd 'a' got here earlier. I've finished supper and the stove's out. But pick yourselves some grub. Here's plenty canned stuff; what'll you have?"

He moved toward the food shelves, talking, hanging onto us with words, greatly desiring that we should stay in that room, afraid.

Jake was bristling. "We'll start a fire," he said, "and pick out our grub later. Come on, Professor."

Show-Off stepped over to the cash register where he kept his revolver handy on a shelf under the counter, but whatever wild idea he may have had of holding us up, he was too late. Jake was through the door already and I went after him automatically, not knowing if I wanted to or not. Just over the threshold of the kitchen-living-room he stopped short, and I came up alongside him.

Lucille—Running Girl—*Zhiltnapah*—sat opposite us in one armchair, frozen with terror, her eyes wide and pitiful. She wore some kind of very frilly, elaborate, négligée, pink in colour, and high-heeled slippers with big, feathery tufts on them. She had long, un-Indian earrings, and with the natural colour drained out of her face, it was plain to see that she wore make-up. I wondered what movie star she thought she looked like.

Jake took off his hat, saying, "Beg pardon, ma'am." Then we backed out and returned to the store together. Coldly and shortly, Jake told Show-Off, "Our mistake. We come to the wrong place." When he reached the door he turned to add, "You're sure playin' with fire, Show-Off. Or are you fixin to marry?"

The man stood rigid, his hands resting on the corner just above his gun, looking at us and hating us. He was sullen and afraid and dangerous. We went out.

"We can camp up by that tank on the mesa," Jake said. "Thar's plenty of wood, and I guess I got enough grub."

When we had the fire going and there was a smell of coffee in the air, we relaxed slightly.

"Who's the girl?" Jake asked.

"Wind Singer's daughter. She just came back from school."

"Damn them schools! You mean the medicine man from Luk-hahutso?"

"Yes."

"I know that family. They're fine people. Damn it all. Damn him." Jake spat. "Do you figure he give her them fancy clothes?"

"I think so. I talked with her one time; she's a movie fan. She hates dressing like an Indian. I guess he found out what she wanted and ordered it from Flagstaff, the Indian schools don't issue that stuff. She thinks he looks like Ramon Novarro."

"Who? Oh, yeah, I seen one o' his pictures once. Yeah. Ain't that hell now? It sure makes me sick to think of a Navajo gettin' full o' that stuff. I've lived with these people thirty years. The God damn, dirty—"

The coffee boiling over interrupted him.

"Well," I remarked, "as you said, he's playing with fire."

"Sure, but even if they get him, that won't help her none. The school mixed her up bad enough, but now she'll never get out o' the wire." He began dishing out food.

I thought for a while. "Jake, Wind Singer and his wife are good friends of mine. And do you know Strong Hand—*Billah Betseel?*"

"Big, handsome young feller, Tahchini clan?"

"Yes, that's the one."

"Sure. He's a particular friend of yours, ain't he?"

"He certainly is. And he's in love with her, wants to marry her. Well, now, if all those people were white, and I liked them so well, and I saw this going on, I'd do something. But now I don't feel as if I could. What is it?"

"Wall, I dunno. Or maybe I do. Thar ain't many of us on this reservation, and forty thousand Navajos, let alone how many Hopis and Pah-Utes and so on. Suppose one white man sets the Injuns against another, or like we did what we'd ought to and bend a rifle barrel over Show-Off's head on account of an Injun? Suppose we got that started once? Well, all us white folks ain't always friendly. In the end the Injuns'd get up on their own hook. Then what? Troops—fightin' and sheep killed and cornfields burned and damn fine Injuns defendin' their country and gettin' killed or goin' to jail for it. I ain't just imaginin', you know that. It ain't but a year since Scar Face was killed and his Pah-Utes rounded up, and not so damn long since the troops was into Hotevila.

"It's just like that business with Skinny McGinnis and Yucca Chief's

66

wife. We tried to warn Skinny, but he wouldn't listen, no more'n Show-Off would. That kind o' bastard thinks he ain't a man if he ever fails to make use of a woman. He don't think, he tells himself smokin'-car stories and believes 'em. Well, Yucca Chief got Skinny in the end. We all know that, but you couldn't prove it on him. Nobody holds it against him, he's a good citizen right now. But we had to keep out of it."

He stared at his plate. "It's cock-eyed. It don't make sense. But thar it is. We can't split on each other, and if we know an Injun's layin for a man, we got to warn him, even help him. We got to. Maybe that's what makes us strong, I dunno. Only sometimes it don't seem worth while."

I nodded. "I guess you're right. But I feel sort of sick of being white."

"Yeah. I often do, livin' out here. You goin' on to Luke's?"

"Yes."

"Well, you may have to pull me out of some more mud tomorrow, let's turn in."

I got back to Nahki Tees three days later, and had been there two days more when Strong Hand appeared again, just as I was washing the breakfast dishes. His face was set, his eyes seemed deeper in his head, after we had touched hands he said nothing until I was through with my chores. At length, reluctantly, I sat down opposite him, passed over tobacco, and waited.

"You know Adudjejiai?" he asked.

The question was curious. "You mean that cañon with the straight sides, where the woman threw herself over?"

"Yes."

"I know it."

"Now she has done it, too. That same place—that woman long ago, and now—now she."

I made no answer. There was nothing to say.

"I feel badly about it. I feel a pain for her and her family. I think it would do me good to go hunting. I know about a coyote that I want to kill. There is nothing to wait for now; we know it all. Lend me your rifle for a day or two."

I thought for a long time. White man, the white man's burden. To hell with white men! Anger and sorrow and shame began to move within me, and this my friend sitting before me, demanding the

67

means to do that which cried aloud to be done. I lend him my rifle, and he will go and shoot Show-Off. Fine. White man, I cannot compound with my soul for having failed to prevent tragedy, by helping my friend to a murder. I thought hard, with some difficulty, finding a whirlpool of feelings turbulent in my mind.

If Strong Hand had been white, he would have kept his eyes on me, trying to force me with the strength of his own intentness. Being Indian, he allowed me to be alone and to think for myself. There was only one conclusion, it was inevitable and I hated it, for itself, and for the opinion of this man whom I loved. I brought it all together in one piece, finally; I saw it and nerved myself to speak.

"I cannot." I heard the words unforgettably, as though someone had said them into my brain, the wretched inflection of my own voice making finality. "*Do bineishe'an,* I cannot." I dug my hands into the sand, watching my fingers bury themselves. "I cannot. I am going to pack up now, I am going to leave this country. It is not just because of what has happened, but also because of what I cannot do."

We sat for some little time. At length Strong Hand said, "I shall help you catch your horse." He took out his tobacco, and papers and tossed them over. "It is pleasant to smoke."

I bent low while I made my cigarette, to hide my face. When I passed the makings back, I said the word which is so rarely used in Navajo, "*Kehey,* thank you." It is a humble word, implying deep gratitude and the laying aside of pride.

WOMEN AT YELLOW WELLS

She pushed aside the tablet and laid down her pencil. If she were alone in the living-room, she might be able to concentrate, catching in slow, written words the piled-up thoughts and feelings that were jumbled within her. The continuing storm pounded and drummed on the iron roof, filling the store with premature dusk. As she sat behind the counter, glancing from time to time at the four Indians who loafed, storm-bound, she could not be sure whether she really wanted to set it down, even to her mother. She needed to decide how much was genuine—loneliness, boredom, disgust with a cramped, hard life, and a growing streak of fear as the light faded—how much a luxury of regret whipped up because one knew it to be vain, and annoyance was an outlet for timidity.

It had been raining, right here at the trading post, for over an hour, a driving, tearing rain with occasional, violent punctuations of lightning. Up the cañon, and in the tributary valleys, it had been going on much longer. Early in the afternoon she had heard the first flood go down Natahn Kai Wash, five miles away, as loud as an express train when one stood in the station. The wash would be running banks full now, with miles of rainsoaked territory to drain, and that meant that Pete would be stuck indefinitely on the other side of it, even if he had succeeded in crossing Tsay Tlakai. Of course this had to happen when his helper was on vacation, so she and the baby were in for a night alone. It was the first time, and now she knew she dreaded it.

*Originally published in the *Saturday Evening Post,* November 24, 1934.

Foolish, of course. In the middle of nowhere, in the middle of the Indian country. Why did Pete have to be an Indian trader?

She leant her chin on her hands, gazing moodily before her. The open door and two small windows at the far end of the store showed a washed-out blue with water streaking down them; against their paleness the unlighted central stove stood up black and bug-like, saddles and ropes against the ceiling were dusty, the corners filled with the appearance of cobwebs. The high counter running around three sides of the room took a faint gleam on its battered surface; where many hands had rubbed the edges greasy were narrow, bright lines.

Two young Navajos lounged on one side, facing the middle, el-bows on the counter. Good-looking, slightly horse-faced young men, their big hats canted forward rakishly as though to balance the heavy, untidy mass of their queues, they chewed gum and stared at nothing with expressions of utter vacuity. Opposite them, Mrs. Rope and Brown Woman sat on the floor, pulling their blankets over their faces when the lightning flashed. Mrs. Rope was a dreadnaught ma-triarch, her name translated and shortened from an original Buck-skin Rope's Wife. Her velveteen blouse and calico skirt were shabby, her blanket old, and she had about five hundred dollars' worth of turquoise around her neck. Jane Tenterden studied idly the old woman's strong jaw and nose, and the small, bright eyes deep sunk among innumerable wrinkles.

Brown Woman was even younger than herself; a big, good-looking girl, neatly dressed in new materials, but owning no jewels beyond the silver buttons and a shell charm in the fringe of her sash. She was a source of interest to Pete and Jane because she and her hus-band, newly married, were in love. That is rare enough among Nava-jos. She had a golden skin and soft, dark red flush in her cheeks, and the fine, silky hair, not quite black, which one sees among Navajo women, and from which she received her name.

Pete often said, when someone asked him if Yellow Wells wasn't a lonely place, "No, there's always plenty of Injuns around"; but it seemed to Jane that one could be lonely enough among Indians. Part of her attention was turned towards the door to the living-room, in case the baby should cry. The fire in the kitchen stove was dead, the house would soon be dark. Mrs. Rope reminded her of elderly ladies she had known along the San Juan Valley, but how could one start conversation as she sat on the floor there, withdrawn, meditating, one would guess, on some inadequacy of her subject clansmen. The girl too—occasionally Brown Woman looked towards Jane, the big, liquid eyes like those of a fine wild mare, full of fire and shyness, not fear, something at once attentive and free and unapproachable.

The two young men whispered together. They grinned and giggled. About what? About her? Memories of attacks on trading posts, murders and loot: Bill Morehouse at Kin Dotklish, Juan Gallego at Wagon Spring . . .

Of course this rain broke a long chain of insufferable days under an iron roof, too late to save the corn, but in time to make grass for the starving sheep and fill up water-holes. But now the welcome coolness was becoming a damp chill, relief from glare turning to a sad, grey dusk which foretold how lonely a trading post would be after dark. The young men still whispered and giggled. The forty-five pistol lay in the cash-drawer, a foot from her right hand. The two Indian women sat like monuments; they were a safeguard, somehow. Everything was in timeless suspension, but the baby could not stay in his pen forever, darkness would come, things must be returned to motion. The young men might go out, and return late at night. That was more foolishness, of course; she knew them both, but sometimes, as now, the persons you knew disappeared and you faced the same alien Indians you first had seen, impenetrable, impersonal.

Well, I guess this makes me a pioneer mother, she thought.

"It's about sunset," she said in Navajo, "I'm going to close up."

The two men laughed. "Here's where we get wet," one of them said. "You ought to lend us slickers," the other told her.

"I'll lend you a slicker if you'll lend me five dollars," she answered.

The men laughed again. "What you lend a Navajo you give, elder sister," the first one said. "I think your husband is sleeping in the mud."

"Yes, I think so."

"Oh, he's all right," Mrs. Rope said suddenly. "My nephew's hogahn is right there by the wash. He's eating broiled mutton right now, I think."

The men buttoned their jumpers, jammed their hats down, and plunged out. The two women rose, adjusting blankets, reluctant.

Jane remembered that Mrs. Rope's hogahn was on the far side of the wash, not far from the nephew's—surrounded by a tribe of daughters and nephews, in fact. The house was about to become empty. At least, these would be people, if not company.

"Why don't you spend the night here, Grandmother?" she asked before the impulse could fade. "You, too, little sister. You can't get home tonight."

They hesitated. Brown Woman watched Mrs. Rope, anxiously.

Once you get in the middle, you've got to go on across. "I don't like to be all alone here."

Mrs. Rope laughed. "All young women see things in the dark. Good, we'll stay."

"Good."

Jane pumped up the gasoline lamp and lit it. "Go on in back. I'll lock up, and then we'll start some supper."

"Our horses are outside."

"Put them in the corral. Here's the key to the hay-shed, get some hay out for them. Help yourselves."

If you're going to do it, you'd might as well do it right. Navajo hospitality has no strings to it.

Mrs. Rope took the key. "Come on," she told the girl.

Jane locked up and went into the living-room. With the bright lamp in it, the windows became quite dark. The boy began to cry at the sight of her. It was past his supper-time, and he was tired of the pen. All his toys were out on the floor.

"Wait a minute, honey," she told him, "till I get the stove goin'."

He cried harder. She sighed, frowned, picked him up and kissed him. He could crawl on the kitchen floor, although he was at the age which is bound to get into the garbage pail. She took him in and set him down, giving him a rubber horse that squeaked, then she lit the kitchen lamp. There was only enough wood in the box to start the fire.

Pete had built on a separate kitchen and a bedroom when they were married. He thought it the height of luxury, and she could remember the tact she used when she first saw the place. She was used to it now, and could compare it with other posts, some better and some worse, but occasionally she remembered her mother's gas stove in Farmington, the enamel and nickel and electric machines.

She laid the short logs, poured on kerosene, and touched a match to it. She pulled apple-sauce and porridge forward from the back of the stove, and filled the big coffee-pot from the bucket. One thing about a rainstorm, it puts water in the barrel by the door, and you don't have to go clear to the wells. If wool ever went high again, Pete had promised her a windmill, tap-water and a hot-water boiler.

The two women came in the kitchen door, their hair jeweled with rain, and dumped their saddles in a corner. Mrs. Rope, taking a chair, looked about her.

"I can see you're a hard worker. Well, if you have a house like this, it's worth the trouble."

Jane smiled, conscious of oilcloth on shelves and other small, hard-won improvements. Brown Woman stared over the edge of her shawl.

The baby began to cry again. "He's hungry," Jane said, "I have his food almost cooked."

"Give him a piece of mutton-bone," Mrs. Rope advised.

Jane almost shuddered. "We don't do that way." She picked him up.

"How old is he?"

"Fourteen months."

Mrs. Rope looked him over and grunted. "Let me heft him."

Jane obeyed, without thinking.

"Fat. You *Belicana* know a lot about these things that we might learn, I think." She dandled the boy, and he played with her shawl.

Jane saw that it was far from clean. "I'll take him," she said.

"You go on and cook. I don't understand those iron things, but I do know babies."

"Well———"

The matriarch looked at her keenly. "What is it?"

"Well, you see, I don't want him to have lice."

"Cha! He's too well washed for that, and, anyway, they're easy to find. You young women are full of ideas."

Jane didn't know whether to laugh or cry.

Brown Woman asked, "Don't you have lice?"

"No."

"Oh."

"The *Belicana* settle where there's lots of water, and they can wash all the time," Mrs. Rope said. "If every Navajo could camp by a

73

well, we shouldn't have lice either." The baby seized her necklace. "Where's your axe?"

"Out there, by the woodpile."

"Daughter-in-law, you'd better cut some wood. You can leave your shawl, it won't hurt you to get wet a little."

Brown Woman went out obediently.

Jane turned to her cooking. She had taken these people in, now they were established. Heaven knew what the baby might catch. Of course, Navajo lice don't generally go on white people, but still——If Pete were here, he'd know how to take the baby without giving offence. If he were here, she wouldn't have asked them in. And if she hadn't asked them in, she'd be cooking now, with the forty-five on the table, the baby crying, and herself glancing over her shoulder every minute.

She got out the baby's bib and spoon. Mrs. Rope watched the process of feeding with interest; the child, being hungry, ate fairly well. Brown Woman came back with a big armful of wood.

"It's raining less," she said.

"Watch this, daughter-in-law," the old woman said. "This is the way the *Belicana* get their children so fat and healthy."

Brown Woman sat down by them, smiling. Shyness was gone. They discussed the food, and the idea of regular sleeping and eating hours for infants.

Brown Woman said, "I've never been in a *Belicana's* kitchen before, I want to see how you do things, so I can do better for my husband."

"She's in love," Mrs. Rope said. The girl smiled.

Jane noticed how handsome she was, and how she kept her dignity, that ladylike quality as she sat on the floor, the presence of chairs conveying to her no faintest requirement to use them. The coffee came to a boil. With one single, swift movement Brown Woman rose and took up the pot.

"Where do I put it?"

"On the back there. So, to that side. Then it won't boil."

"You have both hot and not so hot on top, here?"

"Yes."

Jane decided to omit the child's bath. There was too much audience, he would become excited, and it was late. She changed him,

74

demonstrating diapers, and washed his hands and face carefully, mindful of Mrs. Rope's shawl. To her great relief, when she put him down in the bedroom, he seemed ready to sleep. The presence of strangers had not worked him up; it was that quality of quietness they had, the lack of gabble or attention over-focussed and vocalized towards the child which is so common among white women.

She said to Brown Woman, "Do you want to see how the oven works?"

The girl was delighted. Jane demonstrated the door, talked of degrees of heat, and showed her how to baste, comparing it to Dutch-oven processes with which the Navajo was familiar. Just as she finished, she heard a new sound which brought her to keen attention.

Mrs Rope said, "Motor coming."

She nodded. "Perhaps the wash has gone down."

"I don't think so, It's still raining."

Still she waited. The sound of the car became clear, driving in low gear through mud; she saw a reflection of lights, they struck full on the kitchen windows as it came to the gate, turned, and stopped. The gate was shut, she remembered. She ran out into the rain. Silhouetted against the lights, a man fumbled at the chain. He was too tall and slender for Pete. She stopped, settling her face into composure with an effort, then called "Evenin'."

"That you Jane?" The man swung the gate open.

"I guess so. Come on in."

She returned to the shelter of the kitchen door. The car drove in, stopping close by, now she recognized the man.

"Hello, Marty," she said, "you're just in time for supper."

There was a woman beside him, she seemed young. Jane stepped back to let them in.

Marty Gorton was the picture of the Easterner's cowboy—his two-inch heels exaggerated his lean tallness, he carried a very large, expensive hat, his silk scarf and his clothes all cut for riding giving an effect of the consciously picturesque, and about the whole outfit and himself, his charm, his mannerisms of the wide-open spaces, something unsound and unreal. A man for rodeos and dude ranches, but not much use on night-herd in a blizzard. The sight of him caused Jane a mixed feeling of amusement and tenderness. It was so like him, she should have known that dude-wrangling would be his natural job. It was still the unchanged Marty, entranced with himself and his own showing-off, winning, gay, colourful, not entirely adult—the man she almost married, only instead she had buried herself in this desert, for a real man.

She guessed that the girl was eighteen; dressed in accurate, working cowboy's costume. Every detail showed the Easterner who has just discovered and fallen in love with the West. A nice girl, she thought, and wondered what she and Marty were doing travelling together.

"Mrs. Tenterden," he said, "meet Miss Enderby. Miss Enderby's stayin' at Rancho de la Mesa. We was headin' for the Snake Dance, but we got caught."

"Pleased to meet you," Jane said. "You must be soaked. You're just about in time for supper."

The Eastern girl said, "How do you do? It's good of you to take us in."

"Good Lord, if you didn't take people in in this country, how'd anybody travel? Sit down." Jane waved her hand towards the Navajos. "These are two friends of mine, hope you don't mind eatin' with 'em."

The girl looked at them with grave wonder. It was another thing to write home about. "Of course not! Should I shake hands with them?"

"Yes, do."

The girl was unaffected, likable. She shook hands without fuss, saying "How do you do?" in the Eastern fashion, and smiling when Mrs. Rope laughed at her. Marty followed suit with an air of the old-timer and Indian expert, saying to each one "*yartehay*" with the vile, flat accent and offensive heartiness characteristic of whites who live near, but not next, to the Navajos. Brown Woman covered her face, Mrs. Rope all but ignored him.

The Enderby girl leapt to help Jane set the table. Jane said in Navajo, "Younger sister, you wanted to learn how to do things. Will you lend a hand here?"

Brown Woman kept the shawl across her mouth. Mrs. Rope said, "Go ahead, that man won't bite you." Brown Woman rose, embarrassment covered by dignity, without awkwardness.

"Does she speak any English?" the Easterner whispered. "Isn't she lovely?"

"Better count your spoons," Marty said, joking.

76

"Oh—would they steal?"

"No," Jane answered tartly, "these are friends of mine."

She felt things happening in her which she did not quite understand; mixed feelings about Marty, the girl, about this kitchen, Pete, and the trading post.

Mrs. Rope asked, "Are these two married?"

"No." Jane explained briefly about dude ranches and guides.

"What is she saying, Mrs. Tenterden?"

"She asked if you and Marty were married."

"Oh, no!"

The girl blushed deeply, turning her face away. Goodness, Jane thought, she's gone on him. She glanced at Marty. He was rolling a cigarette, and he looked singularly well pleased. But not in love—well . . .

The two Navajo women were completely silent during supper, sitting at one end of the table and eating with capacious competence. The others talked too eagerly, as though they were under some stimulus. Miss Enderby's first name was Anne, this was her first visit to the West, she was full of broadcast hero-worship.

Under her questioning, Jane let out some of what had been pent in her that afternoon, the loneliness of this life, months without seeing a white woman, or hardly any white man save Pete and his helper, deep snow and mud which brought on weeks of isolation, the battle to keep a decent house and raise a baby. Conscious of Marty listening, she gave her talk another twist, switching the emphasis to the unusual in her life—this girl here who had never looked in an oven before (neither had Anne, but she didn't say so), the power of the matriarch, the calls that came—to help a woman in labour, in a distant hogahn, to get a sick man sixty miles to the hospital, invitations to ceremonies no scientist had yet reported—horse-races, family troubles, tracking down a horse-thief, the games that Navajos try to put up on a trader, the kindnesses they do him. As an increasing portion of the girl's hero worship swung to her, she felt elation, and went on, with some unconscious exaggeration, to tell of the little edge of danger in a trader's life, posts burned down, narrow escapes, and the gun in the cash-drawer.

She was talking to the girl, responding to her, and she was talking at Marty, bragging about this life, and Pete.

Then she, in turn, questioned him about his past three years. He told of dude ranching, Santa Fe, dances, rodeos, hunting trips, and Hollywood. He spread out before Jane a life full of all the things she was missing, all in his casual manner, just things that happened as he drifted around, nothing at all, deprecatory and modest. From the mention of hunting he went on to detail hardships and Western experiences for Anne, like a Sioux brave putting on *coup* feathers. The force of his charm reached out, and one listened without reservations to the slow voice with its very Western intonations. He had those pleasant mannerisms of simplicity and straightforwardness which are characteristic of the cattle country.

Jane rose to stack the dishes. Mrs. Rope and Brown Woman settled themselves in a corner, withdrawing definitely from the others. Jane was sorry; she had been enjoying them, and Anne, she knew, would have appreciated some contact, but she could not see how to arrange it. It was a party made up of friendly people who should get together, and yet something made it impossible to jell.

As she washed, with Anne and Marty drying dishes, he took up his tales of hunting again, and her feelings veered in a new direction. She became aware of the unreality—he called himself a cowboy, and that he had never been. He was overdressed. His stories were too good and his modesty false. His grammar was worse, and more Western, than when they graduated from high school. A faint odour told her that he had managed to sneak a drink, and she resented it in a Mormon. She was annoyed with his self-satisfaction, and wanted to puncture it. A story of Pete's, quite unlike her, came almost of its own accord out of her mouth.

"You sure can have trouble huntin' bear," she picked up his last remark, "but I tell you, it's worse when the bear hunts you."

"Anne turned to her, wide-eyed. "Have you killed a bear?"

"Well, not exactly, but a bear nearly got me one time. I sure thought I was a dead girl."

"What happened?"

"Well, you see, when it don't rain here in summer, it's awful hot, so sometimes we go up in the mountains for a picnic, or maybe camp overnight, leavin' Harry in charge here. Well, we were in the Lukachukais this time. I was green to the country then, and I ran across some wild currant bushes, and I set to work pickin' my hat full of them. I didn't notice I'd worked into a little box cañon, you know. There was a lot of aspen, and bushes, and you couldn't see very well. So I was pickin' along and not noticin' much, when I heard an awful noise in the bushes, and, my goodness, a bear came out right on top of me, you might say."

"What did you do?"

"Me? I ran. I went right through all those bushes like a greased pig, only I ran the wrong way, and pretty soon I was backed up against the sheer cañon wall on top of a steep slope, with the bear comin' right behind. You know, when he gets goin', a bear runs awful fast. I sure wanted my husband.

"Well, the bear came at me with his great, big, red mouth open, and I thought I was gone. I was so scared I didn't know what I was doin', I guess, and when he was right on me I stuck my hand right down his mouth, and I got a-hold of his tail and turned him clean inside out. He was runnin' so fast he kept right on a-goin' the other way, and that was the last I saw of him."

Marty's laughter came in late, but hearty.

"Did you ever have any huntin' experience to beat that, Marty?"

"No, ma'm, I didn't. But I knew one tame animal would sure surprise you."

"What was that?"

"You know that hill by Ed Breitmann's house between Blanco and Aztec, where the cars are always gittin' stuck? Well, Ed does a lot of business pullin' out cars there. He used to use horses, but recently he's been usin' a tractor. Well, I was workin' for Ed two years ago, and they was a cloudburst uncovered the side of the hill, back of his house away from the road. It opened up what we had took for an old mine shaft. Well, ma'm, it warn't no mine shaft, it was a snake hole, and down in the bottom of it, jest about drowned, was the biggest bull snake you ever seen.

"I told Ed to git some dynamite and we'd kill it, but he says no, bull snakes is useful, to go fetch him a dozen cans o' milk. So I did, and Ed opened 'em up, and when the sun had warmed that snake up, Ed fed him, and the snake was sure grateful. Wagged his tail jest like a dog. So Ed brung the snake right into the house, and after that the house warn't fit to live in, because the snake got tamer and tamer, and you never could tell when it would reach down from the rafters and make a pass at you, jest to be playful, or wantin' to have its head scratched. I moved out and slept in the barn, and even so it turned up sometimes in the hay.

"Well, Ed he worked on that snake, and trained it to all sorts of tricks, and he fed him milk, and the snake hunted rats and rabbits and cats and stray dogs and things, and got even bigger and stronger. When a car got stuck on the road, Ed'd go out and make his bargain, and then he'd whistle up the snake and tell him to hitch on. That snake would curl his tail around the bumper of the car, and his head end around a stump or somethin', and pull, and out would come the car. Sometimes you couldn't find the passengers till they come out of hidin' after the snake had left, but they never refused to pay.

"Well, this was good business, savin' Ed a lot in time and new ropes and harness, and besides he was terrible proud of that snake. He jest about lived for a car to bog down and let him bring the critter out. Then he died."

Marty stopped to make a cigarette.

"How did he die?" Anne asked.

"One o' them new cars that looks jest like woggle-bugs come by this spring, and he et it."

"And that killed him?"

"Well, not exactly. He mought ha' got away with that, he was so awful big. But the driver had false teeth, and they kep' on a-workin' and a-workin', and by and by they chewed a hole clear through him, and he bled to death before we could git a doctor."

Still laughing, Jane put the last dishes on the shelf. She saw the Navajos smiling in sympathy with the general amusement.

"This man has just told a funny story," she said to them.

"That's the way to pass a night like this," Mrs. Rope answered.

Jane translated the story as best she could. The women took it gravely until the last, when they laughed hard, the pleasant, clear, delighted laughter of Indians.

"They didn't care much about a snake story, you see," she told Anne. "The Big Snake, *Tleesh Tso,* ties up with some pretty sacred things, and they were bothered a little until they were sure it was pure foolin'. But the false teeth—that fetched 'em."

Mrs. Rope was still chuckling when they moved into the living-room. Marty lingered behind the others.

"Do you want me to bring in the lamp?" he asked.

"No, thanks. The gas lamp's enough in there."

Her feelings had changed again. It was so like Marty, his good nature and sportiness, to have taken her oversharp rebuke in good part; and only his wit could have turned her action into an opening for more pleasantness. They seemed to be back in old times, intimate, knowing each other always. She noticed the faint smell of whiskey again.

"How long've you been usin' liquor, Marty?" she asked.

"About two years. I guess I ain't much of a Mormon any more. Don't Pete never use it?"

"No, nor smoke. Well, that's your business, I guess. Only you oughtn't to bring it on the Reservation."

"Jest a flask, that's all. And it does strengthen a man after a spell like drivin' through this mud, you know."

"I guess so. I figure to supply my own strength, though."

Marty nodded gravely. "That's how you always was, Jane. You can supply your own, and other people's, too, I reckon."

He stood aside to let her pass through the door. What he said was true-seeming, she thought, and yet she drew so much from Pete. She saw his big, heavy shoulders and the homely face with the block of a chin under a wide mouth, and felt the surplus vitality, strength spilling out for a woman to use. But Marty, here, needed a prop. He was a maverick; if someone took and branded him, he could be a fine man. Anne now—Jane looked at her sharply. She couldn't do it, she was too green herself. Her feelings were still mixed, with a tinge of elation now from Marty's last words. A tall, attractive man, so much fun, so unformed; someone should take him in hand.

The living-room was very plainly furnished, saved from being bleak by the generous colour of Navajo rugs on the floor, and a magnificent, fringed, beaded Ute scabbard in which the 30–30 rifle hung by the door. Jane wished it were cool enough to light the stove, that would have made the room more cheerful. This was a funny place to be calling home; only a couple of hundred miles from Farmington, but another world. They used to be gay in high school, and just after. You couldn't call this gay. She went in to look at the baby.

Everyone was tired. The chain of talk broken by moving from the kitchen, they sat awkwardly, letting fall a few remarks without force. Anne commented on the rifle hanging ready. Such furniture was still a novelty to her, possible in a camp, but not where one lived.

Jane, hearing a new noise, asked, "Is that thunder, or is something loose?"

They listened. Mrs. Rope said, "Someone is pounding at your door. He's pounding hard." She listened again. "He's a Navajo, and he's shouting something."

Jane opened the door into the dark store. A gleam of distant lightning made the barred windows at the far end flash blue-white, dramatically. She could hear the pounding clearly, and a voice calling.

"It's some Indian," she said.

There had been too much talk of old-time troubles at supper. Anne drew in her breath, Marty cleared his throat. Why must I be silly-feminine, Jane wondered. I know it's nothing. Somebody wants shelter.

Marty said: "Better not open. They got no business comin' round a post this time o' night."

Jane hesitated.

Mrs. Rope rose, pulling her shawl about her. "It's only Navajos," she said firmly. "I can manage them. Come along."

Jane smiled. "All right, I'll get a light."

She fetched the kitchen lamp, and she and Mrs. Rope entered the store together.

Marty said, "I'd better come with you." He pulled the rifle from its scabbard, threw a shell into the breech and followed, the protective male, slightly belated.

Jane drew back the heavy bolts, letting the door swing open. The light fell on a youngish man, drenched, who held a wrapped-up blanket in his arms. His eyes were at once big and sunken, his mouth quivered towards hysteria. Behind him his horse's head glistened, with white, rolling eyes.

"My baby," he said, "my baby," thrusting the bundle at them.

Mrs. Rope asked, "What is it?"

"My wife—my wife is dead. This baby—"

She gasped and took the bundle. "It's a new baby," she told Jane in a sharp commanding voice. "Just born. We must take care of it."

Jane said: "Come in. Better tie your horse up in the shelter of the

82

house, there, and then come in." In English she said, "Marty, wait here and lock up after him."

Mrs. Rope was already in the living-room. Jane arrived in time to hear her tell Brown Woman to build up the fire in the stove, whether she knew how or not, and to warm a blanket there.

Jane told Anne, "Get the salad oil off the shelf in the kitchen, and some cotton out of the top drawer in the bureau in the bedroom." She turned to Mrs. Rope. "Lay it on the couch there."

The baby, tiny and faintly blue with cold, was still bloody, its black fuzz of hair plastered to its unshaped head.

Brown Woman solved the stove, hung her shawl and a rug on chairs in front of it, and then, after a moment's thought, put plenty of coffee on to boil. That, she thought, would be welcome. She had seen babies born; she wasted no time dithering. Anne was appalled by the infant's appearance, but she managed to do what she was told, and then hovered, willing but not much use. The men came in and stood by the door. The baby gave out a faint, tinny cry and the Navajo quivered. Marty passed him the makings. He rolled a cigarette, then squatted. Holding his hand with the cigarette in it up over his mouth, he wept silently, the tears joining the trickle of water from his disordered, long hair.

Jane and Mrs. Rope worked together with a minimum of needful words. Once Mrs. Rope turned and asked the man, "How long has it been born?"

He said, with difficulty, "As long as it takes to ride from Natahn Kai to here, and a little longer."

Just over an hour, Jane calculated. They oiled and wrapped the child, deciding from the noise it made that it was all right, and not seriously chilled. They set it on the kitchen table, in a wash-basket.

"Don't you give it milk or something?" Anne asked.

"Heavens, no! Just leave it so, it's fine."

"Is it a boy or a girl?"

"A girl."

"What happened? I mean, how————"

"I don't know. We'll find out now."

The man asked, "Is it all right?"

"Yes, it's fine. Tell us what happened."

"We were coming home from Tsayai in the wagon, and we stuck in the mud. It was late when we got to Natahn Kai, and then she—then it began to come. It was dark then, and raining hard. And then the child was born, just now, and she————" He made the downward-diving gesture of sudden death.

Jane interpreted to Anne and Marty.

"I took one horse out of the wagon," the man continued. "I saw there was nothing to do there. I wrapped up the child and came here. That is all."

Brown Woman brought the coffee-pot, sugar, and some cups from the kitchen, setting them in the middle of the floor.

Mrs. Rope said, "Give him some."

Brown Woman served him, not going nearer than she had to, since he was tainted with death. They all helped themselves.

After a minute or two, the man turned to Jane, saying, "*Shamah yazhie*—little mother—will you do something else for me?"

The strong relationship term implied an unusual request. "What is it?"

"She is out there, by the wagon. There is just her shawl over her, and I hate to think how the rain is coming down on her. I hear this rain on your roof, and I can feel it on her. You *Belicana* are not afraid of—of them. I—I cannot go right there, at night, with this storm and lightning. I cannot do that. Will you, will this man here, just go and cover her up? You have your car. I will go with you to show you where, if you will do that. I ask a lot, I think. Perhaps you can imagine her there, too. Perhaps you will feel what I feel."

Mrs. Rope broke the silence which followed. "We are Navajos. We cannot help how we are. It would be a kind thing for you to do."

Jane nodded. "His wife is lyin' dead beside his wagon, down by Natahn Kai Wash. He says she's just got her shawl over her, and it hurts him terrible to think of this rain beatin' on her. I don't blame him, it does me, too. I knew her, she was a nice woman. Well, he wants Marty and me to drive down and cover her up."

"Hell," Marty said. "Why don't he go himself?"

"You know how these Indians are about dead folks; scared to death of them. He nor any Navajo wouldn't dare go near her now, on a black night with rain and lightning and all. He'll show us where she's at. I think we ought to go."

"Lot of foolishness," Marty said. "If the Injun's too yaller to cover up his own dead wife, jest because of some fool idees, I don't see why we should. No reason to buck five miles o' mud on account of a dead squaw."

Anne spoke unexpectedly and sharply. "Superstition is real to the people who believe it. We all know that. Look at that man's face, look at his eyes. We've *got* to do it. I'll come with you, Jane."

Marty shifted his ground immediately. "O. K. I guess I wasn't thinkin'. Sure, I'll go. I'll git the car." He rose and stretched. "Let's go. And tell that girl to make plenty more coffee."

Jane said, "We shall go."

The man raised his face to look at her. "Thank you."

Jane turned to Marty. "You got a slicker? It's goin' to be wet and chilly. I'll just get mine, and then I'll come right out."

When she returned from the bedroom, she told Mrs. Rope: "If my boy wakes, see that his blankets are over him, and leave the door open a crack. Don't pick him up. You'll know what the baby needs, I think. Make some coffee."

The motor was at the kitchen door, the Navajo and Anne standing beside it.

"Goodness," Jane exclaimed, "get in out of the rain."

Anne popped into the car.

"Here, you ain't comin' along are you? There's no need, and it's a mean night."

"Should I be in your way?" Anne asked.

"No, but———"

"Well, then, I'd better come. I might be useful."

"All right." She perceived the girl as she had not formerly. There must be more in an Eastern background than just elegance. She told the Navajo, "Get in beside that woman," and seated herself in front, by Marty.

She could tell at once that he'd taken more whiskey. That was his business, but she didn't like it. She knew Gentiles who could hoist a lot of it without apparent effect, but this did not seem to be just the right time. She forgot about the driver in his driving. Getting a car through adobe mud at night is an art; slow though the pace is, it seems racing fast, and the technique is exciting to watch. She clung to the edge of the door while the machine lurched and pounded, her eyes fixed on the enigmatic pools and stretches of grey mud under the headlights. The rain had lightened to a drizzle, making it possible for the spotlight to bore a slight distance ahead.

The five miles took over half an hour. She had time to think about Pete, camped somewhere on the other side of the wash, in a hogahn probably. He would be sitting by the fire, his slicker on against a slight drift of rain through the smokehole, joking with the Indians and drinking coffee. On a night like this no one would go to bed, they would make a party of it, and Pete would be a welcome guest. Some men might think it pretty tough, but Pete always allowed that such occasions were delightful. Pete and she drank an awful lot of coffee, for good Mormons; how could you blame Marty for smoking and a little liquor? He'd been out in the big world, where things were different. He certainly drove all right. She didn't mind Anne's smoking, but then, she was only a Gentile.

They stopped on a rise, from which the ground sloped steeply down to the wash, which rumbled clearly and steadily not more than a hundred yards away.

"Down there," the man said, "where the little level place is."

Marty swung the spotlight till it found a wagon, with one horse standing in a tangle of harness by the tongue. Just beside the nigh wheel was some sort of bundle in the rabbit brush.

The man took in a slight breath and said, simply, "*Kodi*—there."

"We'll leave the car here," Jane said. "It might not be able to get back up the slope. Anne, wait here; Marty and I'll go down."

She switched on her flashlight and got out. Marty followed slowly. The Navajo winced as a distant streak of lightning came to the horizon just in line with the wagon.

"Rain's lettin' up, praise be," she said.

Marty grunted. "Let's go."

They sloshed and slid through deep mud. The horse had whinnied when the searchlight fell on him, now at their approach he became restless. Jane, stumbling, let the flash turn in his eyes. He plunged. The mess of harness caught him, he stumbled against the wagon tongue, got one foot over it, and began to fight.

"Why didn't the fool turn him loose?" Marty said.

"More important business. We've got to get him out now, or he'll kill himself."

Marty reached cautiously and ineffectually for the bridle, jumping back when the animal lunged forward. Aware of the presence of death, frightened by tangled bindings, lights, and the distinctive smell of white men, the horse was in full panic. Jane gave a snort of disgust and grabbed at the outside trace-chain, yanking it from the whiffle-tree. The horse's hind leg caught her glancingly and knocked her sprawling. She heard breaking wood, Marty swearing and saying "Whoa, boy," and "Easy, now," in a soft, shaking voice. He's no good, went through her mind. He's just no good.

Strong hands took her by the armpits and almost threw her, clear of the horse's range. Then Marty's all right, maybe; she saw the man dive past jerking heels, and could tell dimly, by outlines and motions, that he was cutting the inner trace. How'd he know where an axe was? she wondered, without pausing as she moved to the animal's head. But Marty was still there, holding out a hand and saying, "whoa." Then who———?

Anne, out of nowhere and panting, as if she had come on the run, said, "Here's your flash. You dropped it."

"Thanks."

The horse jumped forward, clear of the wagon, and this time Marty caught the animal's bridle and hung on. The Navajo rose from beside the wagon-tongue, axe in hand. So it was he, then. Jane turned the light on him, and thought she had never seen a man so much afraid. He dropped the axe, and a piece of the breeching to which he had been mechanically holding.

"Better go back to the car, Grandfather," she told him.

"What use, now?" he answered in a dull voice.

"Do as I say."

"All right."

"Marty," she called, "take the harness off that animal, will you? You can just turn him loose."

Marty made no answer, but began undoing straps.

"Come on, Anne. Let's see what we've got to do."

The woman lay under her shawl, in an inch-deep puddle of water. Anne was breathing hard and her teeth chattered, but Jane felt that she would stay with it.

"We can't let her lie there, that's a fact. We've got to get her into the wagon, I think. There ought to be a tarpaulin." She turned the light onto the wagon floor. "Here it is. Now, so. She don't weigh much; a thin woman."

The burden they lifted was amazingly heavy, now that it was lifeless; they got it into the wagon awkwardly, with unpleasant bumping and scraping. Jane drew the tarpaulin over it.

"Poor woman," Anne said, "poor woman."

"She had a hard time with her first baby, too. Don't let anyone tell you Indian women have it easy. They don't. Come on, let's go home."

"Yes."

Marty was standing with the harness in his hands.

"Leave that stuff here. There ain't a Navajo livin' would touch it at any price."

Marty dropped it, and led the way back to the car without speaking. She could tell that he was sullen. He threw the gear in viciously.

After a few minutes, Anne leant forward. "This man is just trembling and trembling," she said. "Is he going to have a fit?"

Jane looked back. "No, he's plumb scared to death. He's just done what he was most afraid to do—gone right in where her ghost was trampin' round in the dark, and used an edged tool, too, which is terrible bad medicine. I didn't know you could get an Indian to do it. And he took his chance with that horse, too."

"That's real courage," Anne said.

"Yes, it is."

Marty suddenly put the car to a dangerous speed.

"Easy, easy," Jane told him. "We don't want to spend the night here."

His answer was unintelligible, but he slowed down.

The stone-walled post looked solid and protective; the light in the kitchen windows was golden, warm, and delightful. They climbed out gladly, hastening to the stove. The Navajo hesitated at the door, Marty was attending to something in the car.

"Come in, elder brother," Jane said. Then she turned to Mrs. Rope and Brown Woman. "He came down by the wagon to help us when we got into trouble with the horse. He did not touch her. And in any case, no *chindi* can follow into this house; *Belicana* medicine is too strong."

The man warmed himself at one corner of the stove, apart from the others. The Navajo women looked dubious.

Mrs. Rope said, "Here is coffee."

Marty came in, looking glum and angry. He had taken yet more whiskey, Jane noted; he must have a good-sized bottle in the car. He was a weak man, angry. He took coffee, and then moved over near Anne, seeming anxious to get her apart. He wants to justify himself, Jane decided, he's lost face, and he wants to get a fresh start. Well, he's not going to do it. She's almost hysterical herself.

"It's late," she announced. "For heaven's sake let's turn in before something else starts. Anne, will you bunk with me? I'd kind of like some company."

"I'd be glad to, if you don't mind."

Marty started to say something, then stopped. He looked very angry. Jane ignored it.

"Marty, you can bed down on the couch in the livin'-room, and this man can make a bed on the floor in there. These ladies had better sleep here, so's to be handy if the baby needs something." She spoke to them in Navajo, telling them where to find rugs and blankets. "Come on, Anne."

They left Marty standing, still unjustified to himself and the world. Jane nodded toward her child in the crib. "Don't mind him. Once he's asleep, cannons wouldn't wake him."

They undressed without many words. As they got into bed, Jane said, "Thank heaven, the rain's stopping. I guess Pete'll get in some time tomorrow mornin'."

The remark started Anne going. Jane saw that she was too wrought up to sleep yet, and let her talk along, half listening, answering her questions pleasantly. Through the excited run of intimate, low-voiced speech she caught at more of the substance of the girl, some vague idea of background and home and present condition. She was surprised to learn that Anne was but a year younger than herself—twenty-four; she had guessed at eighteen. Never saw a new baby before, or a corpse, or a grown man in terror. Never saw much of anything. But she was all right. Genuine intimacy grew in the lamplit room. Jane, as the Eastern girl became real to her, worked out her thoughts and made up her mind.

"How long have you known Marty?" she asked.

"Since I came out West—three months. He's one of the guides at Rancho de la Mesa. You know him well, don't you?"

"Since we were kids together. I came close to marryin' him."

"Oh. He——he's attractive, isn't he?"

"Yes. I guess he's the most fun I ever knew, to fool around with." Anne hesitated, then said, "He didn't act very well tonight, did he?"

"No. He wouldn't."

"How do you mean?"

"Well, he's all right, only he ain't real. Like his lettin' on to be a cowboy. He never was a cowboy." Jane was watchful as she said that. It was her main attack.

"Oh! But—are you sure?"

"Well, I guess he went out and got his daddy's milch cows into the barn, when he was little. And like any kid round home, he learned to ride and throw a rope some. But he never worked on a ranch; no ranch at all, not till he took up dude wranglin'."

Anne said, "Well——" and then stopped.

Jane followed up her point. "First job he ever had was jerkin' soda-water. Listen—you notice what bad English he talks? Sayin' 'you was' and things like that, real Western?"

"Yes."

"He's picked that up in the last three years or so. He used to talk real correct, havin' been bright at school. Now with the movies and tourists, its kind of popular to be a cowboy. Him and lots of other self-elected cowpunchers have gone back to the saddle-blanket, you might say. They've got all the clothes, and the manners, only if he was ridin' night-herd and it come on lightning' and the herd started to shift—well, he wouldn't be there, same as tonight. He's just an attractive imitation. And right now his bluff's been called; that's why he was so glum, and went out and had more drinks. Did you notice?"

"Ye-es, I did."

"I like Marty; always have, since were little shavers. But he ain't real, and he ain't a sport. That's true."

After a pause Anne said bitterly, "Then it's a sham out here, just the way it is at home?"

"About the same, I guess, no more, no less. There's plenty of men out here, earnin' twenty-five or thirty a month workin' cattle and riskin' their necks all the time. Yes, or these sheepherders now, pullin' their flocks through blizzards and workin' day and night at lambin' time. And traders here on the Reservation, and men carryin' mail through the desert and the mountains, and some of the Indian Service people and forest rangers, and all sorts of others." Jane talked quietly, not using too much emphasis, letting her slow words carry conviction. "There's dude wranglers that have been through it all, too. Those people've got everything you ever read about in the books, but you've got to find 'em, just the same as you do back East. And a phoney Westerner is just as phoney as a barber passin' himself off as an Eyetalian count, the way you read in the papers."

She stopped, seeing that Anne was crying. "Why, honey, what's the matter? I guess you're overtired."

"No. It's just—well ———" She braced herself, drew a breath and began again. "I suppose I hardly know you, Jane, but I feel as if we were old friends."

"After the way you acted tonight, you're my friend as long as you want."

"Thank you. I do want. Well—well, you see, we—that is, we planned, after the Snake Dance, we'd go on to Flagstaff and get married. All the men I knew in the East looked so dull and weak to me, after I got to know Marty. I thought, well—you know ———"

"Sure. A real man, from the wide-open spaces."

"Yes. And he isn't." Anne's voice cracked. After a pause she said: "It looks awkward, doesn't it? How am I going to drive back to the ranch with him? The situation isn't covered in Emily Post."

"It is in Tradin' Post. You lead off by gettin' some sleep. I guess you'll miss the Snake Dance, that's all. Don't worry, we'll fix it easy. Anyway, you can't make your plans while you're so excited. Better sleep on it all."

"All right, if I can."

Jane leant over and blew out the light.

As was her habit, she woke early, wondering first why she felt so sleepy, then starting into full thought as she remembered. It was a quarter past five, soon the boy would wake, and he would rouse the whole house. She slid out of bed quietly, dressed with quick, thrifty motions, and left the room.

Marty snored in deep sleep on the couch. A faint smell of whiskey remained about him. The baby in the kitchen, well covered, was quiet. She found the Navajo women out by the woodpile. It was a clear, fresh dawn, with most of the clouds gone from the sky. The damp sand was rose-tinted, the mesas and rocks and cedars stood out in clear, full colour, without harshness. She took a deep breath, looking around her. Pete had said once that such moments were like the Urim and Thummim to reveal God's tablets to ordinary mortals. It was true.

Mrs. Rope told her that the man had gone with the first peep of dawn, to find a medicine man to cleanse him. Meantime, she would take the baby to her hogahn. Jane approved and returned to the house.

Marty was hard to waken. She wondered if he had taken more to drink after they went to bed. He had trouble collecting himself, when he did get his eyes open.

"Get dressed," she whispered, "and come into the kitchen. I'll have some coffee in a jiffy."

She set the coffee-pot right down on the new fire, to bring to a boil quickly. Thank goodness, Mrs. Rope would take charge of the baby; she guessed she was plenty competent. Marty came in, poured water into the basin, and sloshed himself. Combed, and with scarf adjusted, he was presentable and more or less himself. The women came in, bringing ample firewood.

"Here's coffee," Jane announced, pouring off a cup and handing it to Marty.

He drank it willingly, then rolled a smoke. "How's Anne?" he asked. "That was a hard day for that little girl."

"She's still asleep. I aim to let her sleep late." Jane faced him fully, feet apart as though preparing for physical effort. "She don't think she wants to go to the Snake Dance."

"How?"

"Nor to Flagstaff, neither."

Marty changed colour, started to speak, then didn't.

"I think she'll just stay here and rest with Pete and me for a spell. Pete'll be here pretty soon. I guess you'll have to drive back to Rancho de la Mesa alone. It's a long trip, you'd better make an early start and get breakfast at Shiprock."

"What ——— *Damn you* ———"

Jane raised her hand, her voice changed to true anger. "That'll do for you, Marty Gorton. That's more than plenty. Get out."

He was snarling and his eyes were wicked. Jane thought he was going to hit her. As surprising, as unexpected as if the earth had moved to help her, Mrs. Rope handed her the 30–30. She took it, held it as though to test its weight, and laid it on the table.

"I don't need that," she told him, "and you know it. Get goin'."

He turned and left. She returned the gun to its scabbard. The Navajos made no comment, but poured themselves coffee. She heard the car start, go into first gear, then second as it passed the gate. An idea had died, a part of past life been destroyed. It hurts a little. Pete would get across soon, and she could rest some of this on him. She still saw the bad look on Marty's face, and shook herself to get rid of it. She went on cooking. This past night had been a heavy burden, with no one to help her. When she told Pete about it, she'd be rid of the weight.

Brown Woman said, "Show me how you put all these things on the table."

She came out of her concentration on herself. Not altogether without help: Pete was right.

"I'm glad you two stayed the night," she said. "I surely needed you."

Mrs. Rope chuckled. "There's always something doing hereabouts, and that always means work for the women."

ALL THE YOUNG MEN

O ld singer was one of those Indians the trader would point out to strangers whenever he came into the store. "See that old buck there? That's the real thing, a medicine man, too. You'd never think he was eighty, would you?" The trader would nod, and then add the fact which is a special badge of distinction among Navajos: "He was one of Haskinini's men; you know, the band that never was caught when Kit Carson rounded up the tribe and took them into exile."

He dressed well, in the later Navajo style of velveteen, calico, and silver; he carried himself with easy pride, his strong, dark face was stamped with the kindness and control of a religious man. His word carried weight in council.

As a young man, in the long past warlike days, he had been called "Hasty Arrow." Whatever the hastiness was, it disappeared after he became a medicine man, governed by the precepts of the Navajo religion. He was known as "Mountain Singer," and latterly "Old Singer."

When his wife died he began to go to pieces. From being a tall, straight old man he became bent and aged and frail. Not even the trader had realized how completely his wife had managed their business, Old Singer being wrapped up in the mysteries of his chants and dances. Now he made little or no effort to collect his fees, pawned his jewelry thoughtlessly, seemed to have become oblivious of material things.

*Originally published in *All the Young Men* (Boston: Houghton Mifflin, 1935).

95

He talked a great deal about old times, when the Navajos were true to themselves; and occasionally to men he knew well, like the trader, he would tell about the terror of that day when artillery opened on them, when they thought they had the Americans trapped and beaten, and they broke and fled under the shrapnel at Segi Chinlin.

His wife's clan divided her sheep. He let them all go, saying, "Take them. She herded them. I don't want them." With the flocks gone, and his carelessness, and a habit he developed of buying real turquoise and mother-of-pearl for his ceremonial offerings, he became poor quickly. It meant nothing to him that his clothes were ragged, that he had no jewelry, that he lived in a leaky hogahn, sometimes cooking for himself, more often eating with the Indians roundabout.

The trader urged him to change his ways. Old Singer made a cigarette and smoked nearly half of it before he answered.

"As a man full of needs and wants, I am finished," he said. "I know so many songs and prayers, and the stories that stand behind them, that it would take me from the first frost to the first thunderstorm just to think them all over to myself.

"Behind all those stories, in turn, is a greater truth than they have on their faces. I am thinking about that. It is all that really matters. I am thinking about the faces that are behind the masks of the gods. I am reaching behind Nayeinezgani's mask to the one great thing."

The trader sighed. Since he was a young man Old Singer had been especially concerned with Nayeinezgani. The name means "Slayer of Enemy Gods." He is the great war god.

The trader said: "I have better than five hundred dollars' worth of your jewelry in pawn. I won't sell it, but it stands for so much goods which I bought, and I have to pay for them."

The next time Old Singer held a mountain chant he collected his full fee, and paid the trader fifty sheep on account, which released almost all his pawn. He didn't want to embarrass his friend, so when he borrowed on his goods again, he did it at other trading posts, with men he did not know so well.

He looked so poor and unworldly that the Indians stopped listening to his counsel, but as a singer—a medicine man—his reputation remained great. When he was not holding ceremonies, he meditated, or discussed with other old men like himself, who had worked on the philosophy of their religion so long, and penetrated so deep into its mysteries, that no ordinary Indian would have understood what they were saying.

His granddaughter heard how poor and ragged he was, and finally she sent for him to live with her and her husband, Homer Wesley. They were a smart pair of educated Indians who dressed well and spoke good English, and affected to despise Navajo ways. Sometimes they professed Christianity, but really they had no religion save, in the secret part of their hearts, a little longing for and a real fear of the old gods.

Wesley might have made a warrior once—he had strength and brains—but, like so many school Indians, he wanted chiefly to be slicker than white men in their manner, and he was pretty slick. It was trying to be up to the minute, and wanting a new car, that got him started running liquor into the reservation. That was dangerous work, but he did it well, drank little himself, and made big money.

They lived south of the reservation, in one of those sections where Indian allotments and white homesteads and public domain are all mixed together, the breeding grounds of continual trouble. Old Singer did not care. It was right that his granddaughter should house him. He wouldn't have to go visiting for his meals any more; he would have more time for his religion. That was enough.

But he was seriously disturbed when he found out what Wesley was doing. He'd tried liquor when he was young, knew it was fun, and a bad thing when it got going the way it had among the Navajos in recent years. He had seen the spread of drinking, and was worried about it. He hated to see bootlegging right in his family, and tried to persuade them to stop.

Even down in that section there was reputation to be gained from a famous medicine man, and Wesley was careful to collect the fees, so they bore with his talk. When Old Singer would hammer at them about being Navajos, and being true to themselves, and how completeness inside a man or a woman was all that mattered, the young man would grow sullen.

He minded being lectured by an old back number, and minded doubly because fragments of belief, and his voiceless blood, responded to what was said. In anger he conceived the idea of getting Old Singer to drink, and he finally managed it. He had known a Kiowa once, who belonged to the peyote cult, and, borrowing the idea from that man's talk, claimed that his liquor would bring peaceful, mystic experiences and religious communions, and thus persuaded the medicine man to try it.

Old Singer did have an extraordinary experience. For an hour or two he recaptured the full flavour of the old days, and later thought he was talking almost directly with Nayeinezgani. Wesley kept at it, building up the habit, aided by a nasty, raw, wet autumn. By mid-winter Old Singer was drinking regularly.

His granddaughter objected at first, but Wesley convinced her. He said he was afraid of the old man's telling on them, but his taking to drink would keep his mouth shut. Besides, they could chalk off the value of the liquor against his fees if he ever tried to claim what they had collected. So she let things slide until it was too late, and her grandfather was a drunkard.

Early the next winter he got drunk in the course of conducting a hail chant, and messed things up so that another singer had to be called in to do it all over again. After that no one sent for him. Leading the prayers and chants was the breath of his nostrils. He felt more and more empty and lonely as the months went by without a call. He attended many ceremonies, watching how the younger medicine men were careless and cut things short.

He was utterly apart from his granddaughter and Wesley, who began to let him see that he was a nuisance to them. The liquor did not bring him such happy experiences now. He would catch the glorious feeling, but it was confused, and then he would fall to thinking of the old days, and the decay of his nation, and at last would have a kind of horrors, talking disconnectedly about the boom of the fieldpieces at Segi Chinlin and the white man's lightning, which destroyed the lightning of Slayer of Enemy Gods.

They built him a small hogahn at some distance from the house, and fed him what was convenient when he came round. Wesley let him have liquor, hoping he would drink himself to death. As he grew decrepit, he lived further and further into the past until he was surrounded by the shades of his youth, against which the miserable present was thrown in sharp relief.

That winter and summer went by. The first frosts of autumn came, bringing again the longing for the ceremonies, his mind full of the sacred names which could not be spoken in the thunder months. He fingered his medicine bundle sadly. It contained sacred jewels, real turquoise, mother-of-pearl, red shell, and black stone. It contained the strongest kinds of medicine, and was wrapped in a perfect buckskin, which is the hide of the animal killed without wounding, absolutely unblemished.

Wesley, feeling cheerful over a big profit he had made, brought the old man two bottles of whiskey. He hadn't had a drink for nearly a week, and he needed it badly. Now he took a big pull, and sat back, looking at his bundle. It was the time for ceremonies. He took another drink and began softly singing a song for Nayeinezgani.

Now, Slayer of Enemy Gods, I come
   Striding the mountain tops . . .

This was a bad country. These people here might be Navajos, but they were lost. Living with them, he, too, had lost his way. In Zhil Tlizhini, on the slopes of Chiz Lan-Hozhoni, were still Navajos who were men, he knew. There he could find himself; he could give them the message, to keep the gods, the power of the gods, the strength of Nayeinezgani. He started reciting the names in a half chant:

Slayer of Enemy Gods, Child of the Waters, White Shell Woman, House God, Dawn Boy, Thunders All Around—their names fall down; the great power of their names falls down. Here the people turn them back, here the air turns them back, here the earth turns them back, here the water turns them back, their great names, the great power of their names.

He took a long drink. Quite steady and not apparently drunk, he went to the house. Standing to his full height, so that he filled the door, he said to Wesley:

"I am going away for good. Give me a horse."

Wesley stared at him. He said, "Take the pinto mare in the corral."

By the time he had his rickety saddle on the mare he was stooped again; his hands were uncertain. On the saddle he tied his blanket, with the untouched bottle in it, and his medicine bundle. That was all he owned. He took another drink and mounted.

He was dressed in cast-off overall trousers and a grotesquely ragged coat. Of his ancient style remained only the long hair, knotted behind and wrapped in a dirty, red turban, and his moccasins. The toes of one foot came through, and, having long ago sold his silver buttons, the footgear was tied on with bits of rag around the ankle.

The mare followed a cart track leading from Wesley's house to the road, then turned south. Old Singer took no heed of her direction. Whenever the liquor began to die in him he took a drink, so that by mid-afternoon he had emptied the first bottle. Everything he saw made him feel worse—badly dressed Indians, automobiles, men on horseback in the clothes of white labourers, usually pretty ragged.

Always he saw short hair and the stupid-smart expression of the young men. They wore clothes over clothes. No one stood up clean and straight in breechclout and moccasins; no one let the sun strike on strong chest and shoulders; no one wore the dignity of the old, strong blankets.

These shapes moved in and out through his dream of the past, so that he rode in a nightmare. The Navajos were dead; these were the children of dead people. He and a few others had been condemned to go on moving around after the big guns on wheels had killed them all. The lucky ones were the ones who stopped right there.

With that he remembered Hurries-to-War, who had been his friend. He remembered with longing how they had hunted and gone on the warpath together, and the warrior's figure as he stood ready for battle. He remembered this, and looked at a boy going by in an old flivver. He groaned, and started on the second bottle.

About sunset he reached a town. At first the houses had no reality to him, then he realized he was entering a white settlement, and drew rein by the roadside. The houses were strange to him. Raising his eyes, he saw cliffs to the eastward, very bold in the level sunlight with their banding of dull, greenish-white and orange strata. He recognized the cliffs. This was Tseinachigi. They passed this way when they raided Zuñi, two hundred men, when he and Hurries-to-War were just beginning to be warriors.

This was country over which the Navajos swept at will, their raiding ground and their plaything. Now here was a big town, and the railroad. He began to be dismayed, realizing how far he had ridden in the wrong direction, regaining at this sight his urgent intention to head north for country that was still Navajo.

100

He dismounted and sat down wearily, cradling his medicine bundle. He needed to think. He took a little more whiskey, having reached the stage of weary intoxication where each drink braced and confused him, then quickly died away. He decided he must not sleep yet, drunk as he was, and knowing in what condition he would wake.

White men spoke just behind him; he turned to see two coming toward him. They had badges on their shirts, and one carried a gun. They spoke to him in English, then in Spanish, out of which he understood something about liquor and being drunk. He told them in Spanish that he was a good Indian, the Americans' friend.

They laughed, and took away his bottle. He let it go. Then they reached for his bundle, but he clutched it to him. They laughed again. Each took one of his elbows and hustled him along to a house, into which they took him. There was a desk, at which sat a big Mexican, also wearing a badge. He and the Americans talked together, and he wrote something in a book. Old Singer stood all hunched up, hugging his bundle. Now they went seriously about taking it away from him.

After they got it, one of them had to hold him. He went on struggling and protesting in mixed Navajo and Spanish. When they opened the bundle and saw its contents, they seemed to find it funny. They poked around with their fingers among the sacred objects and made jokes. Old Singer was frantic. One of them said something. The Mexican nodded, wrapped the bundle carelessly, and gave it back. Old Singer held it tight and mumbled over it. They took him along a corridor, opened a door, shoved him into a room, slammed and locked the door.

He sat down with his bundle in his lap. For several minutes his mind was blank. Then he looked around. The room was narrow and quite bare. The door was of metal. There was one small, high, barred window. This was jail, then; they were going to keep him in jail. With the Navajos' horror of being enclosed, he went into a panic. At last, wearily, he set his bundle on the dirt floor.

This was his end; he might at least pray. This was his great need. He might at least meet his end talking with the gods, if they would hear him, if he had not cut himself off from them forever. He had everything here—prayer sticks, breath plumes, sacred jewels.

As his hands performed the familiar acts of arrangement, he gained a little courage. Life pollen, sacred cigarettes, Nayeinezgani's cigarette, clear stones, blue feathers, yellow feathers and a perfect buckskin.

That was the keystone of his power, to pray sitting before the unwounded skin. Having taken everything out of it, he began smoothing it out, his hands moving slowly. Then his hands stopped; his heart jumped downward, and his eyes ceased seeing. It was torn, ripped wide across near the head.

After sunset the cell grew dark and chilly in a short time. In the complete blackness, with the fumes of liquor and great fatigue, his fear reached fantastic depths and grew into a kind of exaltation. His right hand began to move forward with a slight downstroke, and back, as though he were shaking a rattle. His lips formed a prayer to Slayer of Enemy Gods. By the second verse his voice had risen to a soft whisper. His eyes were closed and his ears were stopped.

The cold slid in along his skin; he might as well have had no clothes on. As though in opposition to the reality, he began the prayer, "Dawn Boy, little chief." It was very chilly.

He would have done well to have brought a blanket, but then one would not want to seem soft. It had been long and slow, lying out on the mesa, watching just that one line of pass against the night sky for a movement, a quiver of the horizon, that would mean the Americans were coming. Now when he rose and stretched he was stiff. He reached his arms out to the white line in the east, intoning his prayer softly.

Day seeped into the sky overhead, but had not yet touched the cañon below him. The east was brilliant. He looked to the south again, and his blood leaped. A column of smoke rose from Tletsosenili—broke, rose, broke, rose. He read the code, twanged his bowstring, and ran down the gully to where his pony was tethered.

In the cañon he met Hurries-to-War on his blue roan.

"Come along," his friend said; "it is time."

They rode together. Hasty Arrow was surprised to see how handsome this man was. Everything was familiar, but he seemed to have new eyes, a new perception. He felt a sharp pleasure at the sight of a warrior stripped for battle, at the long hair on his brown shoulders, his muscles, his lance. The rich, strong colours of his blanket almost sang.

All the Young Men

He saw Segi Cañon, too, as though it had just been made, the wide valley and high, red cliffs with spruce trees on the upper ledges; the brilliant, gold sunlight touching the highest places. They loped, feeling the morning air tingle against their chests.

More and more men joined them until they led an army. Hasty Arrow looked back at the tossing, feathered spears, the bright headbands, the brown torsos and strong blankets and lively horses. He felt the vigour of his people. We cannot be beaten, he thought.

Hurries-to-War said, "Over here."

They turned into a narrow side cañon and mounted a precipitous trail where their ponies climbed like goats, now at a fast walk, now at a scrambling trot. They came out on a high, small mesa where a clump of spruce trees stood by a clear spring. Halting, the two friends looked about them.

From here one could see all around to the blue, distant boundary mountains at the extreme ends of the four directions. Mesa and cañon and plain, the immensity of the Navajo country was under their hands. From Tletsosenili the smoke of the signal fire still rose.

"Make a prayer for us," said Hurries-to-War. "You have everything."

Hasty Arrow put his hand behind his saddle and felt the bundle. Dismounting, he spread the objects around his buckskin, just as though he were an initiated singer. The young men gathered behind and on each side of him, save Hurries-to-War, who sat his horse just in front. Hasty Arrow looked around, half smiling, at the familiar, brave faces, thinking about their true names, concentrating himself.

He offered the cigarettes and threw the life pollen, then he began to sing. He did not follow a prescribed ceremony. Songs came to his lips in an order which seemed to be dictated to them.

Now Slayer of Enemy Gods, alone I see him coming;
Down from the skies, alone I see him coming.
His voice sounds all about,
His voice sounds divine!

He went on through the four verses, calling the warrior gods. Looking up at his friend, he was disturbed by his beauty. It was almost intolerable.

Now with a god I walk,
Striding over mountains . . .

103

It was not just his friend, not just a man. The blue pony stood on the ground, but it was high above them. Hasty Arrow swung into another song.

Now, Nayeinezgani, on my turquoise horse I ride . . .

He sat above them on his horse, standing on the end of a bent rainbow; not the masked impersonation of the dances, but the great, young war god himself in majesty. The turquoise horse struck lightning with his hoofs. His mane and tail were rain; lightning rustled as it played around the arrows in the god's quiver; sunbeams were gathered above his head. He looked down, smiling.

Hasty Arrow was rent with joy and exalted fear. His heart was high above him.

Lightnings flash out from me; they zigzag
Four times.
Striking and returning, they zigzag
Four times.

He began the final song.

I am thinking about the enemy gods . . .

An alien voice sounded somewhere, and heavy footsteps. A cold fear without meaning rose in him. Behind what he saw was something trying to be seen. He sang louder. The heavy voice spoke again, and there was pounding. The big guns began to boom, the white men's lightning flashed in the air, and Nayeinezgani's arrows stayed in his quiver.

He was two things at once; he was fighting down a knowledge in his mind. All the young men were dead long ago; they faded before his eyes, and the war god was high upon his rainbow. He clung desperately to his song, singing with all his voice and all his being. The young men, the beauty of the Navajos, were riding off into the sky. He was alone, making a prayer with a torn buckskin.

The enemy gods, the enemy gods, I wander among their weapons.

104

All the Young Men

He sang, trying to keep that vision, to keep away the cell walls. He was an old man praying in agony. White men were opening the door to do something to him. Over Nayeinezgani came a mask of a ragged, drunken Indian with a bottle in his hand. Old Singer's voice rose frantically:

Now on the old-age trail, now on the path of beauty walking,
The enemy gods, the enemy gods . . .

Slayer of Enemy Gods leaned down, smiling, and picked him up as one might pick up a child. He placed Old Singer behind the saddle on his turquoise horse, wheeled on the rainbow, and galloped up after the warriors, beyond the reach of white men.

COUNTRY BOY

That spring, when it came on time to plow the north meadow, Buck Langdon felt even worse than he had through the winter. So he told Tom Whittaker, the boss of the T Slash, that he guessed he needed a change, and Tom let him go without questions. So he went drifting south and west into Arizona, and reached Pistol Flat at the time of the Stampede.

Just mentioning the north meadow brought things up too clear. He remembered how he'd been cultivating there the year before, thinking to himself that cowpunching had got altogether too much mixed up with farming, and wishing he'd been born into the old times, when he saw the couple riding over the sky line. From about as far off as he could see them, he could tell they were a dude wrangler and a lady. For a minute or two he might have taken her for a boy, but then he was sure. It was still too far to pick out the colors of their clothes, but the wrangler was easy to spot by his extra big hat and the line of his silk scarf around his neck. Pretty soon Buck recognized Slim Sterling from the Rafter 8. He went on driving his horses, with the dust rising up around him, wondering what it would be like to work on a dude ranch and wear clothes like that all the time, and take ladies out riding. If Slim could do it, why, a cowboy ought to be able to, and they paid as high as ninety dollars a month.

They rode up to the gate in the line fence, and when Buck saw

*Originally published in the *Saturday Evening Post,* March 5, 1938.

Slim dismounting, he got down and walked over to them. Slim saw him coming and swung his leg back over his horse.

"Hello," he said.

Buck said, "Hello," and went to untie the gate.

"Don't trouble yourself," Slim told him. "We just want a little information."

Buck didn't answer, but stood there, looking hard at him.

After a moment, Slim said, "Mr. Langdon, meet Miss Ross."

Buck took off his hat and bowed slightly. "I'm pleased to meet you, ma'am. You'll excuse me not comin' over to shake hands."

"How do you do," she said. "Of course."

She was a good-looking girl. She was more than that, she had a kind of style that Buck wasn't used to, and a look of spirit and gentleness you see in some top horses. It was partly in her eyes and partly in her nostrils. What make-up she had on was put on so well Buck didn't spot it, and he thought her coloring was sure pretty.

He didn't keep looking at her, of course, not wanting to be rude.

Slim said, "We was lookin' for the trail up to that high point over Horse Lake. Can you tell us how to pick it up?"

Buck explained about the trail. Slim told him thanks, and so did the young lady. She said it pleasantly, and her voice was nice, but yet there was something in the way she spoke and looked at him—as if she didn't quite see him, and also as if she was being nice to him—that made Buck feel hot under the collar.

Then Slim said, "Well, so long, cowboy."

Buck said, "So long. You can't miss it if you spot that rock."

The lady had turned her horse away already, and Slim was turning his as he said with a grin, "How's farmin'?"

Buck just stood there for a while, feeling mad and looking after them, then he went back to the cultivator. He knew what he looked like. He was all over dust. He was wearing a small hat with a four-inch brim that had a couple of holes in it and had lost its shape, an old work shirt, and ordinary, broad-toed, flat-heeled boots. He guessed he did look like a farmer, and he guessed that lady dude could only see cowboys, and there was Slim with her, a tall, well-got-up rider, dressed right out of the moving pictures. Yeah, he thought, slapping the reins, there might be something in dude wrangling after all.

Country Boy

It was the very next day that Tom Whittaker told him to wrangle up four horses from Long Canyon and take them over to the Rafter 8. He had a long morning's work getting them to the home corral, but he sure enjoyed it as a change from farming. After lunch he got ready to take them to the dude ranch.

Tom took a look at his new hat and yellow-and-black shirt, and said, "You ain't got nothin' but horses goin' along, have you?"

Buck said, "No, but I figure it'll be relievin' to them visitors to know that cowboys wear clothes like this too."

He didn't let on that he had a blue silk scarf in his pocket.

The horses made a little trouble on the way, wanting to graze and getting mixed with another bunch, and it was after four when he came down off the mesa to the Rafter 8 corrals. Chuck Linderman was in the corral, and he started taking bars down as soon as he saw them coming.

"Hello Buck," he said. "How's things?"

"Hello, Chuck. Can't kick. How you gettin' on?"

They had punched cattle together in Wyoming and out east in Colorado, and they always made a joke of their names sounding so alike.

"Here's your gentle horses," Buck said. "Where's the boss at?"

"He's around somewheres. Get down. Take your saddle off."

He was just explaining to Chuck about the bay being truly gentle, but a little head-shy, when Slim and Miss Ross rode up. Slim sort of waved his hand and said, "Hi," and Buck answered, "Hyah." He admired the quick way she fell to untying her own cinch, and then swung her saddle off.

Half apologizing, Chuck said, "They like to do it for themselves, and it spoils their fun if you offer to help. She's been here a week, and she's sure learned fast."

After she'd turned her horse loose, Chuck called to her, "Miss Ross."

She turned toward them, and Chuck said, "Meet Buck Langdon. He's top hand on the T Slash, and one of the best cow hands in the Southwest or anywhere else."

Her eyes widened, and she colored up a little as they shook hands. Buck saw she didn't recognize him at all, and he was partly glad, partly angry. She acted as if he was someone important, and Buck

109

began to figure she was younger than he'd thought. He'd put her down as his age, close to thirty, but now she seemed about twenty.

When Slim saw the three of them hob-nobbing together, he came on over and began asking professional questions about the new horses. Buck said he'd have to find the boss and get his receipt, and Chuck offered to go with him.

It was after five by the time Big Jim MacAllister had looked the horses over and accepted them, so he told Buck to stay and eat. Buck was plenty willing.

The hands ate in the main house along with the guests. As far as Buck was concerned, Miss Ross was the only person there that mattered, although he did give some attention to a young feller who wore his spurs to table. The guests all got a lot of pleasure out of calling the hands by their short names and talking Western subjects. Buck could see how good Slim was at feeding it back to them, so that they felt they knew more than they did. He kept on watching Miss Ross. Sometimes he thought she was young, sometimes not. It was her knowing manner—living in the city, he supposed—and then all of a sudden she'd turn enthusiastic about something and go all young again. Either way, he liked watching her.

Big Jim questioned him about the T Slash, and when they got the idea that he was from a sure-enough cattle ranch, they all paid him a lot of attention. It embarrassed him some at first, but he found that all he had to do was give honest answers, and he rather enjoyed it. No one brought up the farming to raise winter feed, which was what made the T Slash a good proposition, and Buck didn't mention it.

Pretty soon after supper he said he'd better start for home. He was sitting near to Miss Ross, and Slim was on the other side.

"You're riding back tonight?" she said.

"Yes, ma'am. I got some cows to move tomorrow."

"How far is it?"

"Seven miles, I guess."

"That's a long way to ride so late, isn't it?"

He'd never thought of that, and he felt strong as he answered, "No, ma'am. It won't take but a little over an hour, with the good horse I got."

Big Jim told him, "We're goin' to have doin's here Saturday week. Barbecue starts at noon, and we aim to rope some cows and ride some horses. Tell Tom and the boys to come on over, and if you all have a horse you think is fast, bring it along."

Buck said, "I'll sure tell them."

He and Chuck went down to the corral together. He could hear his spurs jingling, and the ground under his feet seemed springy, and at the same time he felt sad.

Big Jim's party got going fine. The T Slash boys brought a fast sorrel, and put on their best shirts and scarves and chaps, and the H Bar S outfit came with their best horse—a gray, also a black that could really buck. They had surcingle riding and races of different kinds, and steer riding and roping, and so on. Chuck was the clown, wearing a straw hat and horsehair whiskers.

Some of the men guests went into different events and did badly and laughed at themselves. Miss Ross and another young lady went into the women's race along with John Avery's daughter from the H Bar S and the Rafter 8 waitress. Buck watched that race keenly, and he saw that Miss Ross could ride all right, and never held her horse in or tried to take the edge off its running on the bend, and knew how to get the best out of it. It wasn't her fault she came in second, and he guessed she'd ridden a lot in the East, and could make a good rider, with practice. She was certainly pretty in the saddle, leaning forward and all excited, and when she came past the line with her hair all blowing out and her face flushed and her mouth half open, he made up his mind she was as young as he'd suspected.

About four in the afternoon, Chuck got bucked off a burro he was clowning on. No blame to him in that—everyone knows that burros can be snaky—and he was busy clowning when the little beast came apart. It looked as if the donkey jumped on him once before it lit out. Anyway, Chuck stayed lying down.

Buck got to him first, then Miss Emerson, the hostess, who was a trained nurse, followed by Big Jim and Dick Connell and Miss Ross, and then the crowd.

Buck knelt down and said, "Are you hurt?"

Chuck said, "No, I'm just lyin' here, admirin' the sky." His lips were pale.

Buck held his head while Miss Emerson felt him over and began strapping him up. He saw that Chuck was having trouble keeping a grin on.

111

"Well, you stayed ten seconds," he said. "That might be some kind of record."

Miss Emerson and Miss Ross looked at Buck reproachfully.

Chuck answered, "I thought you was the pick-up man. Why didn't you come and take me off when I'd stuck out my time?"

Buck said, "I thought you'd put your legs down and let him go right out from under you."

Miss Emerson shushed him. Miss Ross looked at the hurt man and then at Buck, and she got the idea. Buck didn't notice her; he was watching his friend.

"Well," he said, "you make a funnier clown than I thought you would. Do you do this regular?"

"I'm goin' on the rodeo circuit with it if I got enough ribs," Chuck told him.

Miss Emerson spoke to Big Jim, and he said, "Here's the car now."

Buck and Dick Connell loaded him in, as gently as they could. The nurse got in with him. There was another Rafter 8 wrangler driving.

Buck said, "Well, you're goin' to have a nice rest. Give my love to your nurse at the hospital."

Chuck grinned again. "She won't need it."

The guests had kind of lost their taste for the show, so they called it off. Buck was just as lief: he felt upset about how bad Chuck had been feeling, and he hated to think of him going over that bumpy road to town. Pretty soon they were passing round more barbecue meat and other fixings, and Slim got out his mandolin and he and Dick were singing cowboy songs.

Big Jim came over to where Buck was standing, figuring out a reason for working his way into the group where Miss Ross was.

"I been talkin' to Tom," he said. "My busy season's startin', and I need a good man in Chuck's place. There ain't but two other cowboys in this outfit."

Buck didn't say anything.

"Tom says he can spare you till roundup time. I'll give you ninety a month. How about it?"

"Sounds all right," Buck said. "If you don't mind, I'll just talk it over with Tom a little."

Tom told him there wasn't anything the boys couldn't handle during the summer, and he reckoned the extra thirty a month would help. Buck nodded. He had a good section of land homesteaded next to Tom's range, and as soon as he had five hundred dollars saved they were going into partnership.

They had lit a big bonfire to gather round, and he walked toward it, feeling plenty good. He wished it could have come some other way than on account of Chuck, but however you looked at it the Rafter 8 was where he wanted to be that summer. He found a place not far from the one he would have liked, and sat down. They were singing Little Joe the Wrangler.

When the song ended Dick said, "I hear you're goin' to be with us this summer, Buck."

"It looks that way."

Miss Ross said. "Oh. That's nice."

Slim looked at her quickly and said, "Well, it'll be a change from farmin'."

Buck answered, smiling, "I guess I'll catch on pretty quick. At least, I used to be a cowboy."

He kept on smiling and staring at Slim. Slim got red and pretty soon he turned away, asking, "What'll we have now?" After that, Buck's evening passed very pleasantly, although he didn't get much of any chance to talk direct with the girl.

He brought his string of horses to the Rafter 8 the next morning. He wondered about things as he rode down off the mesa, seeing the ranch and corrals below him, and people moving about. He guessed he could do his job all right, but it was a funny world he was moving into, and he was just a country boy. He wondered if he'd have trouble with Slim, and what a feller said to a girl like Miss Ross if he rode with her, and if you could interest her if you weren't smooth and couldn't sing. He wished Chuck was there to teach him the signs and blazes. *I dunno,* he thought, *but there ain't nothing the matter with me, and I reckon I can have a good try.* He came down at a good pace, feeling hopeful and excited and determined.

II

The first part of that summer went by fast. Buck found the work easy enough, and that the chief requirements were to be patient and polite, and never get tired of answering questions. Big Jim called him down only once, at the beginning, when he told a dude, who asked him who painted the painted buttes, that it was done by the early Mormons, so they could tell this part of the country from another section which looked exactly the same, and that copying those stripes was how Navajo blankets originated.

He and Slim had always been cool to each other, and pretty soon Slim was feeling hostile, for, without doing anything special, Buck cut him out with Miss Ross, at least to the extent that she stopped admiring him or looking to him as the main authority on Western matters. Slim didn't try to do anything about it, but he didn't waste any time doing little favors for the new hand either. Buck figured that his advantage was mainly in being known as top hand from a cattle outfit, on loan for the summer.

Two middle-aged women came out that Slim had taken care of for two seasons past, and who always gave him a handsome tip. He was put to wrangling them as his main job, so Buck got to ride with Miss Ross. She was a fast learner and easy to talk to, and a lot of fun to listen to. She was smart, and had a lot of city expressions and funny cracks that amused him as much as his Western way of talking interested her. He was calling her "Eleanor" in no time, and he knew he was in love, the way he'd never imagined it could be.

She didn't take any sugar in her coffee, and neither did he, and every time he drank a cup of coffee he remembered that, and just that simple act seemed to have some deep connection with her. When he was explaining something to another dude, he'd think that she knew this, or she might like to hear it, or remember telling it to her. She became the flavor and color of every minute of his time. He couldn't touch anything without its having some kind of relation to her; hardly even make a cigarette. He taught her how to do that too.

Chuck stayed in the hospital. It came on July and then August, and little by little Buck's happiness evaporated. At first he didn't think past the little signs that she liked him, and the fact that she seemed to love this half-desert country, and wasn't planning to go home at all. She said she might winter right here, and he thought he might have something to do with that and it made him feel fine. But as he learned how rich she was, his feelings changed. He knew that anyone paying ten dollars a day to stay at a dude ranch wasn't exactly poor, but as she talked about her home, he came to see how her folks might even be millionaires, and some of the things she said about her life made him feel sort of blinded, and like he was standing outside a camp circle, looking in, with a cold wind blowing on him.

Any way he figured it, he couldn't get away from the idea that the gap between himself and Eleanor was too wide to be closed, and that the whole thing was wrong and hopeless. He'd seen how Slim played up to her, and he knew that Slim was thinking of what he could get out of it. Dudes come out dazzled by the West, and they get the man mixed up with the country. She had too much money and her world was too far from his. All she knew about the West was the dude ranch's false front. He had it out with himself different ways, pretty well spoiling his days and nights. Finally he made up his mind, because he could see that Eleanor was liking him better and better.

He pulled in his horns, and she noticed it. First she tried to brighten him up, then she got annoyed and became very cool to him. This went on for four days, neither of them quite liking to ask Big Jim to change his assignments, and Buck not seeing any excuse to make for letting Jim down in the middle of the season by quitting. Buck kept feeling worse and worse, seeing her puzzled and then angry at him, and not knowing how to explain, nor just what there was to explain.

Then came the time of the moonlight picnic, which had been planned way ahead, with everyone going who liked to ride. Buck couldn't get out of it. It was pleasant, too, with the moonrise over the desert and the mountains beyond, and the campfire, and good grub, and plenty of singing. All the time he just ached all through himself. Eleanor made up a lot to Dick, and some to Slim, and that didn't help any. He watched her face across the fire, its softness in the light, and all the good things in it. She caught him at it and started a smile, but he ducked his head. When he looked again, she was studying him in a puzzled sort of way, and right off she turned her eyes away, and then got up and moved. He was plenty miserable.

Some of the boys had a pretty good idea that he and Eleanor had been right close, and that now there was some sort of trouble. Figuring to do him a favor, they divided up so that he'd have to be her escort home, and Dick Connell quietly herded her horse off into the brush, leaving it up to Buck to find the animal when it came time to go.

So there they were the way Buck had dreamed it when the picnic was first planned—the two of them alone in the moonlight, with their horses stepping slow, and the others out of hearing ahead. After a good deal of trouble he managed to say that it was a pretty night, and she said yes. Then he told her that moonlight was confusing to horses; they're likely to take flat shadows for things with thickness in them, and she said, oh. Finally he allowed that an Indian he'd talked to was right when he said it was going to be a late fall, and she asked him, in a polite way, how that was. So he told her the Indian's reasons, and his reasons, and she asked some more questions. They were both working hard, and finally they gave up and went on in silence. At least, it didn't seem so plain indecent as if they hadn't spoken at all. In this way they got near to the mesa rim above the ranch, when she spoke up all of a sudden.

"What was that crack Slim made when you were hired?"

Buck was surprised. "He said it would be a change from farming."

"And then you said that at least you used to be a cowboy?"

"Yeah."

"What was that all about?"

Buck thought this might be a chance to explain himself. "It was on account of the first time I met you."

"You mean, when you brought the horses?"

"No. When I was cultivatin' that time."

"Cultivating? Oh, was that you?"

"Yeah, that was me."

She didn't say any more, so, after a pause, he went on. "You see, that's what the cattle business is nowadays. Cowpunchers are country boys in flat shoes, like the way you saw me that time. Of course, we ride plenty, too, but if they wasn't a good crop of feed to raise on that ranch, Tom would have to go out of business. Yeah, we're just country boys, only here on the Rafter 8 we're paid to dress up and do nothin' but amusin' things. I aim to stay in the cattle business, and that means I'm a farmer, like Slim said. There ain't much o' romance in it, and fellers like me ain't got no business gettin' out of our class."

He thought over his own words for a moment, "Of course, we do all the things I told you about, too, and I ain't told you no lies, no time. Only they ain't but the half of it."

They went on in silence again. He felt better, but he couldn't see her well enough to guess at what she was thinking. The big night was all round him and the night air on his face, and he heard the horses' feet moving. He felt eternally waiting, and then they came to the rim of the mesa, where they could see the lights of the ranch down below, and his heart went down again. He couldn't think of anything worse than riding in and speaking to people.

She reined in her horse. "How pretty the lights look. Let's get off for a minute."

He didn't know what was coming next, but his heart was pounding as he dismounted.

They both lit cigarettes. He wondered if she'd understood what he'd tried to tell her. He guessed he'd made it plain enough.

She said, "And then, you told Slim—you meant he never was a cowboy?"

Buck hesitated. "Not that I know of."

"But he seems—he looks so ———"

"Yeah. That's easy; you can learn that by readin' the magazines." He took a breath. "That's one o' the things made me think maybe you hadn't got it figured out right."

After a wait, she said, in a low voice, but not hesitating, "You mean, you don't think I'd make a farmer's wife?"

It was so direct it took his breath. He puffed at his cigarette before he answered, "I mean, I guess you ain't been figurin' on what it means to be a farmer's wife."

"You think," she said, not angry at all but soft and slow, "I might—well, just fall for a pair of spurs and a big hat?"

"I dunno," he said, feeling a little confused. "When I talk too much I get snarled in my own rope. I ain't never took you for a silly girl."

She turned toward him, so he could see all her face under the shadow of her hat in the moonlight, shadows under shadows, her eyes and mouth, and yet he could make her eyes out clearly.

"How about you, Buck? Have you ever figured out whether you could be an Eastern girl's husband?"

What he'd thought about that, and what he wanted, all his contrary thoughts and feelings jammed in him while he tried to say something. He said "Eleanor ———" and then he stopped again, and he put out his hand as if to help himself talk, and he touched her and

117

then his arms just went around and he was kissing her; it was the sweetness and coolness and warmth of her mouth, and her arms holding tight onto him.

There was no happiness in the world that even came close to this, and it was like being in church.

By and by they came halfway down to earth, and backed off enough so they could see each other. She was smiling at him.

"Oh, Eleanor," he said. "It ain't right."

"Hush, darling," she told him: "we can talk about that later."

That word "darling" went right through him. He just held her tight making up his mind he'd never let her go, no matter what happened. After a long time, they decided they'd better go down to the ranch.

That first moment of high happiness spread out and became a condition like sunlight. He could hardly believe it but it was true. Eleanor knew her own mind so well that she cleared the last of his doubts away easily. At first she was all for buying into the T Slash right away and setting Buck up. She wanted to put a lot of money into it, and hire a foreman, so that Buck could winter in the East. He wouldn't have any of that. He aimed to support himself, he said, and you can't run a ranch that way. With the extra money he was laying by that summer, he'd have the price of his half share soon enough, and if she wanted to come in as an equal partner on a regular business basis, all right. But a little outfit like that couldn't go hiring foremen, so one of the bosses could loaf, and besides, it would be letting Tom down. Then they planned how the outfit could grow little by little, and Eleanor began figuring on buying the Gallegos place which had irrigated land.

All this talk about business made the impossible seem real and solid. She wanted to see a roundup, so they agreed that she'd stay at the Rafter 8 until the T Slash roundup was over, then she'd go East and prepare her folks a little, and in about a week he could come along. Chuck was due back at the ranch in mid-September, in time to let Buck go back to the T Slash.

She told him not to worry about meeting her folks, but the prospect panicked him some. It had to be done, he knew, and even if his English wasn't so good, he saw no reason to be ashamed of himself.

One night late in August, the boys got into a big talk session in the bunkhouse. Without any of them meaning anything, the talk swung round from the general subject of dudes to the particular subject of

Country Boy

marrying them. They told about a couple of cases where some smart wrangler had got him a rich girl, and come out of it in a couple of years with a nice little ranch of his own. They bore down pretty hard on the men who'd do it. Buck sat quietly. They didn't know he and Eleanor were engaged. Of course, he wasn't doing anything like that, but the talk made him uneasy.

Timberline Smith said there'd been some honest tries at sure-enough marriages, too, but he didn't know of any that hadn't come unstuck. He allowed that Eastern girls couldn't stand for ranch life. Dick said he knew of one case where the couple got hitched all of ten years ago, and was still going strong on a ranch near Cimarron. Someone said she must be a remarkable woman, and Timberline said she was, and the man was a good one too. It was Utah Crane, he said, who used to live around Medicine Hat. Several of the boys knew Utah, and they said, yes, he was sure a good man.

Then Slim spoke up and said, "Well, it calls for a good man." He didn't look at Buck, but Buck felt he was talking at him, and he sounded kind of pleased with what he was saying.

"They come out here," Slim said, "lookin' for romance in a big hat. They ain't never heard people talk the way we do, but they've been readin' about it. And they're far from home. They ain't got the faintest idea of how ordinary we are when you live with us day in and day out. As for us, when a feller's new to the dude game, the Eastern women hit him pretty hard too. And for much the same reasons."

His tone of voice changed, and Buck decided he was talking about something he knew right well.

"So we're both in a fog, you see. And if you tie onto one, you don't know what you're up against. If she goes home and the pull o' the country wears off, she comes to, and it's all over." Buck saw the twist on Slim's mouth, and he remembered something Chuck had told him about Slim being kidded by an expert his first year at the ranch. "And if you marry 'em," Slim went on, "they come to, only slower and in another way. Well, I don't see no point in holdin' the bag for 'em. They're lookin' for a kick. All right, jingle your spurs and slant your hat and give it to 'em, and play it for what it's worth, or some o' them will play you." He looked quickly at Buck. "We're wearin' scenery. We are scenery, that's how I figure it."

Just then Timberline noticed Buck's face, and he said, "Well, it can be done, like Utah Crane."

119

Dick said, "Sure it can," and right away he said, "That reminds me," and got off, in a rambling way, onto an Apache and his wife who came by the ranch two days ago, and they all fell to talking Indians.

Pretty soon Buck went out and had a smoke by himself. Slim had aimed all that at him, he knew, and more than halfway enjoyed doing it. And then the way all the boys caught on, and turned the talk aside, that was upsetting too. He thought hard, and made up his mind. The scenery had to come down.

He was due to go into Santa Fé in a couple of days for supplies, and Eleanor was going with him. They planned to stay into the evening, dancing. So the next morning he told her that he wanted to celebrate, and go to the Conquistar, which is the big resort hotel. Mostly they went to cowboy places. She said that was all right with her. So then he told her he had to go over to the T Slash to get his really good clothes, and would she mind driving the truck that far and getting him there? It was a pick-up easy to handle, and she was a good driver, so she didn't mind that at all. She liked coming by the ranch, and wanted to get to know Tom and Mrs. Tom better.

He got there shortly after noon, giving himself time to borrow what he needed to complete his outfit. It meant the boys there guessing how he felt about Eleanor, but he figured they were onto that already. He took a lot of pains with himself, and was proud of the result, although he felt a little awkward and self-conscious too.

She came by at 3:30, and when he walked out to the car she gave a little start of surprise. He was wearing his pin-striped blue suit with the snug-fitting coat, and a light blue shirt and a bow tie. His silk handkerchief matched his shirt and socks, and he had shined his yellow shoes until they gleamed, and his hair was well slicked down with something that smelled good. The only thing he lacked was a small hat.

She moved over for him to take the wheel, saying, "My, but you are dressed up."

"Yeah," he said. "I figured if we was goin' to the Conquistar, I'd ought to put on my good clothes."

It felt more like scenery to him than if he'd been wearing his brightest riding outfit, but he guessed to her it was just clothes, and that was what he wanted. He had a knife-edge crease on his pants, and he was careful, sitting down, to pull them so he wouldn't spoil it.

Just as they started he said, "I aim to practice up for meetin' your folks back East."

"That's a good idea."

It was only a little more than an hour's drive to Santa Fé, and they didn't talk much. She asked him some questions about cattle they were passing, especially some Polled Angus, which were new to her, and they passed a few remarks about happenings at the ranch. Then, in town, they each did their shopping, and met at the Conquistar for supper. There's a café there, Spanish style, with a dance orchestra.

It was when they had ordered supper, and their cocktails were in front of them, that he realized she was working a little to keep up her end of the talk. It wasn't anything he could put his finger on; she looked just like always, and she laughed the same way, but he knew her too well not to catch her shades of feeling. He kept getting the idea that she was being game.

This made him self-conscious. He commenced to notice the other men in the place; those that weren't wearing Western clothes. He'd never paid them much mind before, barring to wonder why they didn't dress up when they went out with a lady. They ran to coats and pants that didn't match, and the coats hung loose on them, not seeming to fit; their shoes were dull, and their hair dry. It didn't look snappy to him, but he began to wonder if he was all wrong.

He'd never thought so much about clothes, but now they were getting important. First, his farming outfit against Slim's get-up, and now this; maybe what he was wearing was still scenery, but the wrong kind. With him thinking like this, their talk got thinner and more awkward, and both of them were fooling with their food. He asked her to dance and she accepted gladly. It relieved them to be occupied that way.

Buck liked to go straight at things, and he knew he could count on Eleanor for a straight answer. So he asked her, "The way these men are dressed, is that the right way?"

She looked around. "Some of them." She picked out two or three, and they weren't the ones Buck would have picked. "That's the style. It's English, the way women copy the French."

Buck took that in, then he said, "Would you sooner I'd worn cowboy clothes?"

121

She didn't hesitate. "Yes. I think I would. I like you to be what you are."

"Maybe that's what I'm bein'."

She smiled at him. "I don't care if you dress like a Chinaman, so long as you're Buck inside."

Warmness came all over him, and they began talking and enjoying their food. They danced some more, and talked while they were dancing. Buck clean forgot what sort of clothes he was wearing. It was about an hour later when a couple came into the café and recognized Eleanor. They were Easterners, they had heard she was near by, and had been hoping to see her.

The two girls fussed over each other, and the man was glad to see Eleanor. When she introduced Buck, they looked at him like a poker player picking up the wrong card when he wanted to fill a flush— guarded, but not pleased, and a little surprised. Eleanor said Buck was top hand at the T Slash, and had been lent to the Rafter 8 for the summer. They said "Oh," and looked at him a little differently, and when they'd all sat down they asked him questions about his ranch. It was all slightly stiff, and it came over Buck that a cowboy was a kind of exhibit, and he felt angry.

They talked about New Mexico for a while, and then the three Easterners shared some news from home. Buck was out of it, but Eleanor gave him an explaining smile, and he felt better. Then it came out that these two, the new couple, were all steamed up over a big musician—Buck couldn't get his name; it was a tough one—who had just arrived at the hotel. That excited Eleanor, too, and the three of them got going for quite a spell on this man's music, and other music, and performances they'd heard, and Buck, who couldn't carry a tune in a bucket and didn't know much beyond liking the Old Chisholm Trail and Cielito Lindo, just sat helpless.

By and by Eleanor brought them round to horses. Buck could see her do it, and he wondered if he knew anything to talk about besides animals, and he felt as if his conversation was all thumbs. Everything he said sounded dull to himself, and he couldn't stop being serious and heavy and short. He wanted to get up and tell them "to hell with you"; he wanted to take them out to where he could get on a horse and show them something; he craved action.

By and by they broke up to dance again, and when she spoke to him the only answers he could make were short ones. He didn't want to be like that, and hearing himself made him feel worse.

Eleanor said, "Are you angry, Buck?"

He said "No," and then "Yes, I guess I am. At myself, that is. I guess I'm pretty dumb."

"You don't need to know about symphonies."

"No."

"Supposing we call it an evening and go home."

"You'd like to see some more of your friends, wouldn't you?"

"I see plenty of them back East."

"Well, look——— I got to get used to your kind of folks and not just quit on them."

She smiled at him. "You can't do it the way you're feeling now, Buck. Take it easy and it'll come."

That made him smile too. "All right, let's go."

He felt a lot better as soon as they were outside. It was always all right when they were alone. They got into the car and headed back for the ranch. Their lights on the road ahead of them held their eyes; they sank into one of those dry silences that won't break. He was studying hard, and he could tell her mind was busy as she sat beside him. By and by she reached out her hand, and he let go of the wheel with one hand and took it.

When he knew what he wanted to say, they'd been silent so long it was hard to make his voice come out; and when he did finally start, he sounded rusty and had to stop and start over again.

At that, all he managed was "Eleanor."

"Yes."

"Well, Eleanor ———" He took a firm hold on himself. "Darlin', I think it would be a good plan if, say, you went home like you planned, but you kind of looked things over before you said anything to your folks."

"I don't."

He looked at her and saw her fighting chin set.

"You been thinkin' about this out here, with the ranch and all that takin' up your mind. Well, we want to be real sure. We want to know we ain't overlooked any bets, and then we can go ahead feelin' just right."

"How about you, Buck?"

"I'm sure of everything, barrin' whether I can make the grade."

"It's me, not you, should worry about that. There's nothing the matter with you," she told him. "I don't ever hope to meet a better man."

They turned in at the ranch gate, and came to a stop by the shed where cars were kept. There was no one around; it was dark shadow under the shed, and silent and empty outside, with one wall of the barn and part of the corral in sight. With the noise of the car stopped, the hush shut in on them.

"Oh, Buck, it's hard to know," she said; and then, "You don't want to get out of this, do you?"

He pulled her to him, hard, and they kissed. They hung onto each other, kissing long and desperately, and by and by whispered a little, telling about love. They had a hard time separating, and, even at the door of the main house, clung together again before she went in.

They went on like that for two or three days, talking things over and getting nowhere, and then making love as if someway they could wipe their minds out with it, as if, by going deep enough under, they could make the world fade out of being.

Then one morning she said to him, "Buck, this is no good. We'll have no rest till we're sure. I'm packed and I'm going home this afternoon."

When it came as near as that, Buck was stunned, but she said the only thing to do was to go now and get it over with. They went up on top of the mesa together, and as they talked Buck saw that all she wanted to do was to end the doubts, and that this was the best way to get to where they wanted. They fell to planning again, how he could come East, when things got slack on the T Slash, and by then they'd both be sure; and she told him a lot about her family, and what he'd see in the East, and what would be difficult there. It was a good morning, and they came down confident.

When she was gone, Buck certainly lost interest in dude wrangling. He was glad when Chuck came, and he could get back to the T Slash, where his work took him out by himself a lot of the time.

She had wired him from the train and then written, and wired again from New York. After that she wrote short letters, and sometimes long ones, almost daily.

Buck carried them around and reread them when he was alone,

and it seemed wonderful that she could put those words on paper. He did the best he could in return, though the pen came hard to him, and he had an awful time putting his feelings on paper.

The letters slackened in October, and they changed. They were almost the same, but there was more news in them, and something different. Then the change was more marked, with a lot of variation back and forth, sometimes like at the beginning, sometimes as if she was fishing for what to say, and there were long waits and letters beginning with a lot of reasons for not having been able to write.

At Christmas she sent him six fine silk scarves and a plaid flannel shirt. He sent her a pair of beaded gauntlets he'd had an Apache make for her. He got a lot of pleasure out of sending his present, but not so much out of getting hers. The things were right, and carefully chosen according to his tastes, and having his shirt size right, and he felt as if they were relics of something finished. He spent a bad Christmas.

He wasn't surprised when the letter came thanking him for his wisdom, and telling how they'd both made a mistake and it wouldn't work. It was a nice letter, and she took all the blame for failure on herself. She said she hoped they'd be good friends, and that she'd see him sometime. He had thought he was all ready for it; and now that it had come, it hit him like being slugged. He didn't hardly speak to anyone for several days.

That was a bad winter, and he was kept plenty busy. He went into town sometimes with the boys, or to other ranches, but it wasn't like it had been. Now the girls he saw, those he'd known and those he met now, seemed flat and tasteless. He knew some of them were as fine as any man could ask for, but he felt sort of sorry for them, and he didn't even want to dance with them. Eleanor had a perfume she used just a little of, and it mixed with herself and her hair when they danced together. These girls used a different perfume, and too much of it, and he'd feel uncomfortable. Then, Western girls put on their make-up so that it shows, and now it looked coarse to him.

In the early spring he got a plain friendly letter from her. He decided not to answer it; there was no use trying to electrify a dead horse. After spring roundup he asked Tom to let him go for a while, and Tom did, without any questions. He drifted till he got to Pistol Flat in time for the Stampede.

He was a good rider, who did just a little better than average well at local rodeos, that was all, until that Decoration Day. He drew the Cyclone. If the Cyclone threw him and stamped on him, that was all right with him, the way he was feeling. He didn't care much what happened to him. The result was, he stayed on and broke a record, and came out with a nice lot of money.

They came after him to go on the rodeo circuit, and he thought it over. He didn't see that traveling got him any farther from what he carried inside himself. Any way he took it, it looked like a long gray road, and he wasn't much interested in where he was going to end up. But long ago he'd said he was a cowboy, and he aimed to be a cattleman. About all he had left, he figured, was not being licked. So he took his winnings, which made what he needed for the partnership, and headed back for the T Slash. He didn't care, but he figured it was the best way to keep going.

POLICEMAN FOLLOW ORDER

From the top of the ridge they could look back, down onto the town of Peña Roja, clearly visible in the cool silence of dawn. From it their eyes rose to the changing colors of the sky beyond. Anne sighed faintly. For a moment they faced each other, at once grave and half smiling. Then they turned their horses westward and spurred them into a fast trot, the pack mule following at the end of his lead.

To Linton, their very hurrying emphasized the fact of flight, even while the fast motion exhilarated him. The escapade excitement of saddling up and sneaking the animals out of the corrals with daybreak pressing hard upon them, of the sense of freedom when they got far enough away to dare to trot, died away. Danger for himself, grief for Anne: it was up to him to be alert, to miss no bets. Yet what could Campbell do, he thought. Nothing really. He saw Campbell in his mind, clever, powerful, ruthless, holding Atascosa County in the hollow of his hand. There was a man who always knew what to do. Not far ahead of them now lay the boundary of the Apache Indian Reservation, Federal soil, where Campbell's sheriff's had no power. It was a good plan. Then he looked at the girl riding beside him, thinking of her courage. He knew he must not fail.

At the top of a long rise, they paused to breathe their horses.

"I think you can turn the mule loose now," Anne said. "We're far enough from home."

*Originally published in the *Saturday Evening Post,* August 20, 1938.

Jack took off the lead. "We'll be over the reservation line in another hour. I'll feel safer then. But I won't really feel all right until ———" He broke off and smiled at her, his face alight. "I wonder if we're fools, doing this?"

"Perhaps we are. I'm glad."

"So am I. Well, let's go. We can make tracks while it's still cool."

They pushed on westward trotting most of the time, occasionally loping, enjoying the still crisp air and their lively horses. From a slight distance they looked like any other young couple taking a pack trip, heading into the mountains to fish perhaps. A tall, pleasant-faced young man and a pretty, blond girl, both wearing checked shirts, big hats and Levis, both comfortable in the saddle on handsome cow ponies, with a chestnut pack mule following like a big dog. The pack was small, well tied on, competent. The man didn't sit his horse or hold his reins quite like a Westerner, and they traveled unusually fast.

It was about eleven when Burns, the chief clerk at the Jicarilla Apache Agency, who was acting superintendent in Mr. Littlefield's absence, came to the door of his office. He told Jack Grover to go find Spotty and Ted, and bring them here, then he returned to his desk.

Jamison, the sheriff of Atascosa County, sat in a chair facing him.

Burns said. "Old Spotty's the feller for you, and Ted can do the English talking. Spotty's a real scout."

Jamison nodded. "Yeh. I know Spotty. But ain't you got a white man you can send along? I don't know as Mr. Campbell'd be pleased ———"

"Oh, they'll act nice. I'm pretty sure that Mr. Campbell knows Spotty. And who can we send? They've called Littlefield to Washington right at lambing season, and our stock supervisor's sick. All the men we can spare are down on the lambing grounds now. We're lucky to catch Spotty. He has sheep of his own, you know."

"Yeah. I guess that's right. I wish I could go along."

"Why don't you?"

"With this strike on at the mines? Hell, I hated to take the time even to drive over here, if it wasn't to oblige Mr. Campbell."

Burns nodded. That was in both their minds. He, too, was not averse to doing a favor for the boss of the county.

128

Spotty and Ted appeared in the doorway. Burns told them to come in. Spotty was a heavy-set Indian with a stony, wide, pock-marked face. He looked stupid and rather brutal. His hair hung in two heavy braids, wrapped with green and yellow tape, from under a regulation Army hat which perched on top of his head. He had a feather stitched to one side of the hat. His uniform jacket was partly unbuttoned over a checked shirt. Besides his police badge, he was adorned by a shell necklace and beaded arm-bands. He wore khaki slacks, and had replaced the soles of his Army boots with softer ones of rawhide.

Ted was a young Indian, with a leaner, liver face. He wore his hair short, and needed a haircut. His uniform was neat and properly buttoned, with an added touch of gayety from an orange silk scarf tied closely about his neck and allowed to hang down his back. He wore high-heeled Western riding boots with big spurs.

The two of them stood side by side, facing the desk.

Burns said, "Well, looks as if we had a job for you boys." As neither Indian responded, he added impressively, "This is Mr. Jamison, the sheriff from Peña Roja."

Ted glanced at the sheriff, Spotty seemed not to have heard.

Burns felt irritated. He didn't like being ignored.

"Now see if you can get this straight," he said. Spotty fixed his eyes on him. He went on, speaking very slowly. "There is a man came onto the reservation this morning. A sheepherder saw him coming this way, by Wide Valley. He is a horse thief. There is a lady with him. He may head on west, to cross the Arizona line. He may head some other way. The horses are stolen. You are to bring them in. Savvy? . . . Ted, you better interpret that."

The young Indian spoke in Apache, Spotty nodded and turned back to the chief clerk.

"What kind of horses?"

Jamison said, "An iron-gray with black stockings and a Rafter Eight brand on the right arm, a sorrel with a white blaze and a Lazy C bar on the flank, a chestnut mule with the same brand. Savvy?"

Spotty nodded heavily. "Savvy. Mebbe-so catchum."

"Don't hurt anyone," Jamison said. "Be nice to the lady."

Burns added, "Yes, that's right. Treat the lady nice, you hear? . . . Translate that, Ted."

Ted interpreted. Spotty said, "All hraight. *Entiendo.*"

129

"O.K., boys. Get going."

As they left the building, Burns told Jamison, "Spotty's kinda dumb, like most o' these Indians, but he's steady. The kid's name is Theodore Roosevelt," Jamison laughed.

Ted, whose Indian name was Iron Feather, heard him through the open window, and told the other man what they had said, adding, "I don't like Fat Writer."

Spotty said, "There are so many white men I don't like." He smiled briefly. "He's one of them. I think superintendent would not have sent us on this errand, if he were here."

"Why do you think that?"

"I don't know. Fat Writer was keeping from telling us something."

They got their guns and saddled up. They rolled their coats with their blankets, for it was hot now at midday, tied on some grub, and got going. In a little over an hour they reached Wide Valley. They had not talked on the road.

Spotty was annoyed at being sent out when he ought to have been let go to tend to his sheep. His brother was all right, but no one takes care of another's sheep the way he cares for his own. Horse thief. Two saddle ponies and a mule for two people. Campbell's brand on two of the animals. Rafter 8 on the other.

They reined in when they came to the long, faint slope of Wide Valley.

Spotty said, "That iron-gray with the track over two loops, it belongs to that man who was at the Gathering last fall. Do you remember it?"

"It has a barbed-wire cut in one ear?"

"That's the one. The man held the reins crossed through his hand, with an end coming out each side, instead of holding them through his fingers."

"Yes."

Now they traveled at a walk, while Spotted Shield studied the ground. His expression was alert and live. By and by he pointed. The tracks of three shod animals were clear enough, and one was obviously a mule. He sat leaning over in his saddle, studying them.

"They went by here before the morning bell rang to go to work."

Iron Feather grunted.

"Look, my son. Learn to tell."

They dismounted. Spotty showed how a little sand had drifted

130

into the tracks from the north. There had been a northerly breeze which died about nine o'clock.

The two horses were about of a size. The one on the right had rather narrower hoofs, and its print showed that it was carrying less weight. Pretty soon the tracker saw a cigarette butt stained with lipstick on that side. The woman Fat Writer had mentioned was along, all right. The other horse was being ridden by a fairly sizable man.

Sometimes the people they were following had trotted, occasionally loped, occasionally slowed to a walk. Where the tracks were clear, they followed at a lope, other times they slowed down. Ted didn't speak to his leader, knowing that if he called the tracker's attention for a moment, he might lose the trail by letting his thoughts slip, and have to find it again. Any Apache knows that it's your mind, as much as your eyes, which keeps you following those faint signs without hesitation. They could see that as the morning went on, the riders had slackened their pace. The part they were following now showed a good deal of walking and no loping. They were pretty sure that they were gaining.

Spotty stopped, pointed and grunted. He looked amused. Here the horses had been going at a slow walk, side by side, and you could see where they must have been pressing together, and the one the woman was riding—the one which made a shallower print—had been thrown off its stride. Ted grinned, and Spotty half laughed.

"That's why white men like to have their women ride beside them," Spotty said. "So they can put their mouths together." He looked at the tracks and laughed again. It was like having the action repeated for you, or hearing a story retold, and it still tickled him. "That mule is running loose; it must be an old friend of one of the horses."

"Campbell's mule and Campbell's horse." Ted said.

"And what else of Campbell's?"

They pushed on. In the mid-afternoon, they reached where the two had made their noon halt.

"No more hurry," Spotty said as he dismounted. Ted grunted agreement.

They had eaten crackers, canned tomatoes and canned tongue. They had sat close together, reclining against the base of a pine tree, and taken time to smoke before they got going. Spotty laughed again, studying the marks in the sand.

"Very much love," he said. "They sat very near together, they

131

leaned together. Then here, he rose, and then pulled her to her feet." He pointed to where the man's heels dug in. "Then kissing again, see?"

Ted nodded. He was faintly annoyed by the old man. He had learned something of white-courtship ways while he was at boarding school, and he felt a sympathy for these people he was trailing. Spotted Shield's show of amusement was partly embarrassment. The exhibition was so public. They should have smoothed out the signs.

He studied the base of the tree carefully. He pulled a couple of long bright hairs from the bark and held them out. He squatted, looked carefully at the footprints, a handprint, at the length of leg shown where the man had sat.

"Campbell's girl," he said. "Campbell's girl has run off with Crossed-Reins. She took one of his horses and one mule, so Campbell makes Crossed-Reins a horse thief. That is just like Campbell, I think. It is his way. He wants to stop them: he wants us to stop them for him."

Ted said, "Let us let them go. Why should we take care of Campbell?"

Spotty took up his reins, "We are not policemen for fun. Come on."

The Indians did not like Campbell, but they were all keenly aware of him, as was shown by the fact that he was known to the tribe by his English name. He had made various attempts to crowd them off parts of their reservation. Through his political power he had prevented them from getting a water hole on the east side of their line, which they badly needed.

Out of a long silence Spotty said, "One white man or another, who cares?"

Ted didn't answer. He wanted this couple to escape. There was something appealing about the way the two of them rode side by side.

The old man was hard to move, though. Spotted Shield: riding behind him, he resented his firmness, and at the same time felt the young Indian's deep respect for older men of proved distinction.

Immediately after leaving the halting place, the trail had turned sharply south. Spotty kept on meditating as he followed it. In his long career as a policeman, he had learned a lot about the white man's law. A horse thief would head due west, strike into the Navajo country, and cross over into Arizona deep within that reservation. It would be a safe move. These people were heading toward the settlement of San Gregorio; they should reach it tomorrow. You wouldn't do that, riding stolen horses with a famous brand on them. According to white man's law, there is safety in crossing a state line when you've done something wrong, but if you take an unmarried woman across, then it becomes wrong. He had thought of that whole strange superstition about lines a great deal. None of it made sense, and yet, the way white men handled it, there was a lot of power in it. Including protection for Indians. So these people were pushing on to San Gregorio, and making fast time for whites, even though they weren't hurrying the way they had this morning.

Late in the afternoon he told his companion. "They are not married yet, but they intend to get married, I think."

"Yes. They will do it at Town-on-the-Flat."

"Yes."

Just at sundown they saw the campfire. They dismounted in the cover of a patch of scrub oak, then Spotty went forward to scout. He returned in a few minutes, saying, "Let us, too, eat. They have turned their animals out to graze."

They supped on bread and cooked meat. When it was dark, Spotty said, "Let us go look."

It was easy for the two Apaches to creep close in without being heard. Spotted Shield watched with interest: he always liked studying the white men's ways, and it wasn't often that he got a chance to do work as much like the old warpath as this. The man helped the woman washing dishes, as white men do. They talked gaily while they were at it, then they made themselves comfortable against the packs, with their arms around each other. The man dragged out two bedrolls and arranged them at a distance from each other. Then the two of them, standing by the fire, held onto each other tightly and kissed for a long time. Then they said good night and went to the separate bedrolls. After they had turned in, Spotted Shield touched Ted's shoulder. They crawled to a safe distance and walked back to their camp.

"What did they do that for?" Spotty asked.

"Do what?"

"What they didn't do. When one steals a woman ———— If it was a warpath, they would not touch each other. Why is that? Is it another law?"

"No. It is a custom. It is a rule of honor, they say. Those who are going to be married, they stop at that point with each other. So they told us in school. In that way the man shows highness towards the woman. Thus he honors their marriage."

Spotted Shield nodded. It seemed an odd custom, but he could understand a point of high behavior. White men had all too few. That these two lived up to a hard thing raised them in his estimation.

"All people have their ways. It is well to live up to one's own."

He made and smoked a cigarette. While he smoked he thought hard, partly about the couple and Campbell and Burns, partly about himself and his companion, young Iron Feather. Iron Feather spoke too much English, he decided. He figured out how to get around that. If those two did get off the reservation, they'd be spotted at San Gregorio. The brands on their horses would do for them. They were properly caught.

"We must arise very early," he said. "Let us sleep now."

It was still dark when they rounded up the fugitives' animals and took them behind the scrub oaks. The whiteness was only beginning in the east.

"Now, my son," Spotty said, "ride to the agency. Tell them that I have them, and will bring them in. Say just that, and don't change it."

"Why do you want me to do that? Why don't we just let these people go? They are all right, and I don't like Campbell."

"We are police. For many years I have been policeman here. I do not wish to lose my job. I do not wish to be ashamed. If we say we lost them, anyone can follow up our tracks and see the truth. Do as I say."

"Why do you want to send a message? Why not wait, and we can go back together?"

"Because you speak too much English. You understand it too well."

Iron Feather shrugged with annoyance.

"You mean that I will try to help those people, I think."

"My son, do as I say. I know what I am doing. Eat now, then go."

"Very well."

When he was alone, Spotted Shield settled down to wait, in a place where he could watch the camp. He was figuring how to get another breakfast out of this.

Jack woke to see dawn already bright in the east. As soon as he was awake, intense happiness ran through him. Looking across the

134

camp circle, he saw that Anne still slept under the white tarpaulin of her bedroll. He couldn't hear the bell on his horse, so he supposed they'd drifted. That was all right. They wouldn't go far in this country of good grass, and he liked showing that he was able to wrangle like a Westerner.

He started the fire and set the coffee-pot on it. This had been a crazy way to elope, but it had turned out all right. By noon they'd be in San Gregorio, then they'd be married. The thought still appalled him with wonder. And they'd never forget this ride; it was something to have back of you, a beginning that couldn't be improved on. His thoughts ran on as he watched the fire, and he smiled at their sentimentality. You just didn't know how a person felt until it happened to you, he thought. He considered again the strangeness of coming out here on vacation last fall, idly choosing the West, to have this happen. His senior year at Harvard had been her first at Wellesley, just up the river from him, but they met in Atascosa County. The long winter at home with certainty growing upon him, then returning here, Campbell's blind opposition, and now this.

He'd hoped she'd like it. Of course, they'd come West often, but not until he had made a home for Anne. In a couple of years, the way things were going ———— The coffee came to a boil. Deliberately he made a noise with the cooking outfit.

Anne sat up. He thought that she looked pretty when she was tousled. He took a cup of coffee over to her.

"I can't hear the bell, so I think the horses have strayed," he said. "I'm going after them."

"Is there enough firewood?" she asked. When he nodded, she went on, "I'll have breakfast started."

He drank his coffee standing, took his bridle and a nosebag with oats in it, and walked off, whistling. Anne watched him out of sight before she reached for her comb. Her father thought that only a Westerner could be a man. She was completely filled with a sense of great contentment. A man worth living in the East for. She knew the East well enough not to fear it, nor to doubt that there would be difficulties. Marriage was more important than difficulties, and she knew her mind.

Jack picked up the tracks shortly, heading pretty definitely in one direction, as though something had startled the horses. He followed along, his eyes on the ground most of the time, so that he was startled to see the animals suddenly quite near them, being driven by a big ugly-looking Apache on a scrawny roan. He stopped still. This was peculiar. The Indian came on toward him, wrangling the animals. He wore a police uniform and badge, and was armed.

When he reached the white man, the Indian said, "You horss?"

"Yes."

"All hraight. I bring."

Jack unhobbled the gray, bridled him and mounted. The sorrel and the mule kept trying to get at the nosebag. With the policeman following, he rode into camp. Anne had finished dressing and was busy at the fire.

"We've got a guest," Jack said.

"So I see."

"I found him wrangling up the stock for us. He'd taken the bell off Dusty."

"Oh. That's funny."

The Apache dismounted. Then Anne recognized him.

"Why it's Spotty. . . . Hello, Spotty, *como estamos?*"

He shook hands with her, saying, "*Como 'stá.*"

"Sit down. Have breakfast with us."

He made himself comfortable without speaking further. Anne thought hard while she cooked. That was a very odd thing for an Indian to do, but you couldn't suspect Spotty of having been caught in the act of stealing the animals. Everyone knew him to be a real cop, with a love of making arrests. He was on duty, too; his revolver was on his belt and his gun on his saddle. She had thought that by crossing the reservation, she'd put herself out of daddy's reach, but now she wondered.

Jack finished graining the horses and came over to the fire.

"Gloomy-looking old duck," he murmured.

"Careful. He understands more English than you'd think."

She dished up canned beans, bacon and flapjacks. Spotty ate steadily, in large mouthfuls. He had not responded to the few remarks she made to him in Spanish, although she knew that when he wanted to, he could speak that language reasonably well, nor had he asked her any of the usual questions about where she was going, how long she had been on the trail, which are the standard Indian social gambits. The more she thought, the less she liked it. The singing bliss of her awakening this morning had gone, and in its place was a slow fear.

She would have been willing to bet that Superintendent Littlefield wouldn't let her father use his police the way he did the sheriff's office. This was particularly so, because, after all, there was no legal offense of which he could accuse them. But Spotty was behaving in an odd way. That expression of total stupidity on his face meant many concealed thoughts.

She decided to break through somehow. The Apache accepted a cigarette with a grunt.

"You look as if you were out on business," she said.

Spotty didn't answer. In the back of his eyes she thought she saw amusement. Apaches have a funny sense of humor.

"You look like you going to arrest somebody," she said slowly.

After a pause he answered. "Yess. T'ief horss."

"Horse thief?"

"Horss, t'ey been t'iefed"

"Stolen horses?" She felt relieved.

Jack, sitting beside her, tried to copy her unconcerned manner. More from her than otherwise, he caught the feeling that something was wrong.

"Yess."

"Navajos stole them, mebbe-so?"

"Catchum."

"Catchum? Where?"

"Catchum." He said it as if it were funny, then made a gesture with his left hand toward their animals. His right hand dropped idly onto his revolver butt.

Jack turned all taut beside her. He glanced quickly toward his pack, in which his pistol lay, but that was hopeless.

"How do you mean?" she said.

"Sheriff say horss been stole. Two horss one mule. Now my catchum. Takum back to agency."

"But those are our horses."

"That gray is mine. I bought it six months ago from the Rafter Eight," Jack said.

"Mebbe-so. You come back agency, come back Peña Roja, tell sheriff?"

Jack said. "My God."

137

Anne's face paled while she thought. No matter how ridiculous the horse theft charge might be, her father would jail Jack for it, and then—the phrase "work him over" came horribly to mind. Remarks she had heard pass between her father and various deputies. There before her was the Indian's face, utterly unreachable, blank and closed and grim, and the latent spark of amusement or enjoyment behind his black eyes.

Jack said slowly, "You mean you want to take us back to Peña Roja?"

Anne laid a hand on his arm. She could see that he was keyed up for action, and Spotty's hand still rested limply on his gun.

The Indian answered, "Take horss back."

"Take the horses?"

"Yess."

"But they're ours."

"You wantum, you come back claimum."

A light began to gleam in Anne's mind, and some of the constriction left her heart.

"You mean, we let you take the horses, and then we can come and claim them?"

Out of inaccessible stupidity, the Apache said, "My order, catchum horss. My catchum. My bringum in. Policeman follow order."

Jack said. "But you'll leave us afoot. And all our tack? Our saddles?"

"Bringum agency. You come getum."

Anne whispered in a low voice. "Don't you see? It gives us at least a chance to get away."

Jack fell silent.

"How far is it to white men's houses?" she asked.

"T'at way," he pointed due west. "Little bit." Making a circle of finger and thumb, he showed the sun moving over about an hour's space, "'Mericano ranch sit down. Catchum car. You money"—he crossed his hands in the trading sign—"road go round Taneville."

"Can't we go to San Gregorio from there?"

"Road heap bad. Damn bump-bump." He rose. "Heap bad t'at way."

Jack said. "Well. I guess there's nothing for it but to walk. Gosh, I hate for this to happen with you, Anne."

"That's all right. And I think I know the ranch he means; Catlum's. He'll hire us his car all right."

The policeman said, "Mebbe-so you saddle up. My watch."

Jack smiled sourly. "You know your stuff."

They made small packs of personal belongings for themselves, then saddled up and put their camp goods on the mule. Spotty tied the animals in a string and mounted, lead rope in hand. Turning in the saddle, he reached out his right hand, rubbing his thumb over his forefinger.

"*Cigarro, si gusta.*"

Jack looked angry. Anne said. "Oh, give him one." Jack handed him a cigarette.

Spotty said, "All hraight. *Adios.*" He hit his pony with the end of the lead rope and started off.

Jack and Anne stood looking after him a moment, then they picked up their bundles.

"Now we're hoboes," Jack said. He put his arm around her. "But we're lucky at that."

They trudged along, feeling the sun slowly growing hotter. After they had gone about half a mile, Jack whistled.

"Say! San Gregorio's still in your father's county. Tanneville is in San Juan, and besides, he'd never figure on our getting that far on horseback. If he's got a horse-stealing charge against me ———— I never would have thought of it if it hadn't been for that bad road, 'damn bump-bump.'" He laughed. "It's lucky for us that Indian was so dumb."

"I'm not just sure how dumb he was," Anne said thoughtfully.

Spotted Shield, pushing on toward the agency, sighed within himself. He remembered just what Burns had said. "The horses are stolen. You are to bring them in, savvy?"

He sighed again. Now he was going to have to stand and listen to Fat Writer make a lot of noise about dumb Indians.

He put his animals to a faster trot. Lifting up his voice, he sang a gambling song with a fast tempo. Into it he wove new words, "The policeman follows orders." Suddenly he began to laugh, and for some minutes rode on, laughing.

THE HAPPY
INDIAN LAUGHTER

Three men sat, each on one of three wooden steps. The one on the top step was young. His hair was cut short. He wore a fairly large, neat, light gray Stetson, a blue Air Force officer's shirt, a blue silk scarf at his throat, neatly pressed Levis, and cowboy boots. He was waiting for something. He sat as quietly as the others, but you could tell that he was waiting.

The two others were past middle age. Their large black felt hats were battered. One had a beadwork hatband, the other a hatband made of dimes. From under the hatbrims, just behind their ears, their braided hair hung down, wrapped in two colors of tape, crisscrossing. These two were not waiting for anything, they were just relaxing.

When a big blue convertible with the top up came around the corner at the end of the dusty street, all three looked up. The car seemed to hesitate, then came toward them slowly.

The man on the middle step said, "Tourists." He looked at the one below him, who was thin, and older than he. "Show your moccasins, brother; perhaps they'll pay to take your picture."

"Run tell your wife to weave a basket."

They both laughed. The young man's face had become blank.

*Originally published in the *New Yorker,* August 6, 1955

141

The old man said, "Just one tourist—a woman, young. Perhaps we can be Apaches and frighten her."

The two laughed again—the pleasant, light laughter of Indians. The young man said, using the title of respect, "Grandfather, I know this woman. She was a friend when I was in the Air Force."

The old man said, "Good. Let her walk in peace."

The girl had put up the top of her convertible when she encountered the penetrating dust of the road that led from the sad little town of Arenosa to the Indian Agency. The road appalled her. The dirt was hard, cut by ruts, and washboarded, and, for all its hardness, produced fine, clayey dust in quantity. She came to a cattle guard, a strong barbed-wire fence, and a sign reading, "Department of the Interior—U.S. Indian Service—Gohlquain Apache Indian Reservation—No Trespassing." She stopped the car and studied the sign, half minded to turn back. Then, with a jerk, she started forward again. She had overcome too much opposition, in herself and from others, to turn back now.

The Agency was five miles inside the boundary, Ralph had written, and the high country of grass and trees not far beyond. She could see the high country ahead of her, blue and inscrutable. She'd find out soon enough what it was really like. She'd find out a lot, and above all the difference between a handsome—you could almost say beautiful—Air Force pilot with a bronze skin and an Apache cattleman. As she had pointed out to friends and relatives, he was a college man as well as a pilot, and he would be the same in any setting, with the same nice manners and the same humor. She wished now that she were sure of that.

The Agency was a village, strung out along a wide, straight section of road. There were white wooden houses, some adobe ones, and a couple of dreary brick buildings. Ralph had written that he would be waiting for her in front of the Agency proper, which she could recognize by the sign over its door and the clock in the little tower on top. She came almost to a stop, looked about, then proceeded slowly.

She passed two women walking in the opposite direction, on her side of the road. Their hair hung, rich and black, over their shoulders. They wore calico blouses and full calico skirts. As she passed them, they did not glance but looked at her for a measurable time, their faces impenetrable, their eyes dismissing. So those were Apache women; even their manner of walking was alien.

She identified the Agency, which was one of the smaller structures—she had expected it to be large—and saw the three men sitting. That was surely Ralph on the top step, and by now he must have seen her Ohio license plates and recognized the car, but he did not get up. She felt a sudden anger.

The Agency building stood on the left-hand side of the street. She came to a stop opposite it, on the right. As she did so, the young man rose, came down the steps, and walked to the car, not hurrying. The two older men sat gazing at her. All three faces showed nothing but blankness it was difficult not to read hostility into.

Ralph stopped with his hand on the door. "You got here." The remark was neutral.

She said, "Did I?"

A trace of smile showed about his mouth. "Hard to tell in all this dust. You'd better let me drive; I know these roads, and I can take your car over them with less of a beating than you can."

She was within a hairbreadth of saying "Thanks, I'm going back now," but she didn't, for the same reason that she hadn't turned back at the boundary, and because she remembered how guarded and withdrawn he had been, for all his wings and ribbons, the first time she took him to the country club. She said, "All right," and moved over.

He drove without speaking for nearly five minutes, handling the car carefully and well. Shortly beyond the Agency grounds, the road began to climb. Instead of the hard, dust-yielding baked mud, its surface was of a coarser, reddish earth, less dusty and less dramatically rutted. Scattered cactus and sagebrush on either hand were replaced by occasional piñons and junipers. The land seemed greener; she could not decide whether there was actually more vegetation or whether it was merely that the grass and small plants were not dust-coated and showed up more strongly against the warmer-colored earth.

The cowboy outfit was becoming to him. He was tanned, darker than when she had known him at the base. His nose was high and straight, his lips sculptured, his chin strong. There was the intriguing extra height of his cheek-bones, and above them the dark eyes,

143

slightly Oriental. They were not slanted, but at the outer corners of the upper lids there was a fascinating curve. All this was familiar, but the expressionless face remained strange.

They passed a single tall white pine by the side of the road. As if reaching that point released him, he looked at her and said, "You know, I didn't really believe you'd come until I saw the car." His face had come alive. This *was* Ralph, after all.

She was astonished to feel so much relief. "I wouldn't have missed it for anything. It isn't everyone who gets formally invited to spend a weekend with Indians."

"My dad was tickled with the whole idea. Mother said I was nuts; she said it would be too strange for you. Still, she's kind of looking forward to it. I think you'll find it interesting."

Of course he had not mentioned the real purpose of her visit, any more than they were able to speak of it between themselves; it mattered so much and seemed so beyond reason. She wondered what that dark Apache mother was thinking, and the sisters—especially the one who had served in the Waves.

He slowed to a stop alongside a pickup truck parked by the road. The driver of the truck wore his hair in braids, heavy ones, the hair black and shiny where it was not wrapped. Ralph had told her once that long-haired Indians were mostly over forty. This one looked middle-aged. He had a blobby nose in a broad, heavy face. As the two men talked, she thought he seemed a cheerful type.

The language sounded slurred, soft, with a good many "sh" and "l" sounds, punctuated by harsh, throaty consonants. There was a rise and fall of tone. The speech was milder than she had expected, faintly musical, and yet virile. She did not think she could ever hope to understand it.

Presently the man in the truck laughed. Ralph turned to her. "This is my uncle, Juan Grijalva. He and Dad and I run our cattle together."

She smiled at the Indian, who studied her gravely. "You got a gun with you?" he asked.

She saw that his intent was humorous. "No. Do I need one?"

He shook his head. "These Inyans are mighty rough people. And these Inyan veterans, you gotta watch them all the time. You need help, you let out a whoop and I'll come. I gotta keep my nephew in line."

He and Ralph laughed. She didn't think it particularly funny, but she liked the friendliness. She said, "Thanks, I'll remember that."

Ralph said to his uncle, in English, "All right. You'll bring up the salt then?"

"Yeh. Your friend ride?"

Ralph looked at her. She said, "Pretty well—that is, I've been on dude ranches."

Uncle Juan told Ralph, "You pick her out an easy horse, and we can take her along while we set out the salt, and let her view the configuration of the landscape."

As he said the last words, he was watching her closely and his eyes were dancing. Her mouth twitched.

Abruptly, he said, "well, so long. *Ta'njoh.*"

Ralph said, "*Ta'njoh.*"

Both men started their cars and moved along.

"He took two years at Colorado A. & M.," Ralph told her. "He's really a fine cattleman; I'm learning from him right along. He's my dad's brother, so we kid each other all the time."

"Do uncles and nephews usually kid each other?"

"Only on your father's side. On your mother's side, you use respect. It's the custom."

"Oh." It sounded surprisingly complicated and artificial.

Pines were appearing among the smaller evergreens, and the grass was definitely richer. Presently Ralph said, "Anthropologists call it "the joking relationship'—I mean relations who kid, like Juan and me. When I marry, he'll kid my wife the same way. It's fun if you're used to it."

For a moment she stiffened, feeling the remark probe toward the central, unmentioned thing, the thing that had seemed possible at the officers' club, at the country club, in the city, and so totally impossible when the young man came down from the steps. She let it pass before speaking the thought that came to her, lest the connection be apparent. "You aren't going back into the Air Force?"

"Not unless they call me back. I belong here. These people are coming up, in the cattle business and a lot of other ways. There are only four of us in the tribe who've been all the way through college, besides maybe half a dozen like Juan, who went part way and then came back. Besides, it's good here. Look at it."

They had never ceased climbing. The air was fresher, the country greener and more rugged. At some distance to their right, a handsome bank of red cliffs paralleled the road, contrasting nicely with the pine and spruce at its base. They came into a long, wide, open meadow on which a score or more of beef cattle were grazing. It was good country.

He asked, "Did you bring a tent, and all?"

"Yes, one of those little green tents, and a cot."

"Good. It's not so long since we lived in tepees, and we're used to being kind of crowded together. There's five of us in the two rooms in Dad's house. You'll be more comfortable in a tent of your own."

When they had driven a little farther, he said, "I'll show you where I'm laying out my house. After the cattle sales this fall, I'll have enough cash to go ahead and build it. I'm going to put in butane gas for the kitchen, and there's a spring above it, so I can bring water in on straight gravity. I figure on three rooms and a bath to start with, and then build on later. Maybe you can give me some advice. There's good stone handy, as well as lots of timber; I don't know which to build in."

He could not possibly have sounded more casual, nor could she as she answered, "I'd like to see it."

Even so, she was relieved when he started reading brands on the cattle near the road and explaining to her which were good Herefords, which off-color or poorly made. As she already knew, he had delicacy; his capacity for perception and tact had surprised her friends.

Ralph's father's name was Pedro Tanitsin; she must find out, she thought, why Juan had a different surname. Tanitsin had put his house in a fairly narrow, craggy-sided valley with an outlook to the south. It was a simple, small frame house, slightly overdue to be repainted. There were no grounds—that is, no fenced area, smooth grass, or planting of any kind. At the east end of the house was a large, flat-topped shelter, its roof thickly covered with evergreen branches. Beyond that was the bare pole skeleton of a tepee. A heavy truck with a tarpaulin over the hood stood by the house. A hundred feet or so behind it, she made out the horizontal bars of a corral crossing the lines of the ruddy stems of the pines around it and she saw a horse move. Ralph parked the car beside the truck.

146

Two dogs came skulking, but no human being came to meet them.

At the east end of the shelter was a wide opening. When they came to it, Ralph stopped, so she did, too, beside him and a step behind him. Inside were the people—Ralph's father, sitting on a bench, and his mother and his two sisters, standing. There was an interval of silence; she felt awkward, and saw before her the same blank, guarded faces that had repulsed her at the Agency. She was aware of a camp stove, a fire pit in the middle of the floor, some cooking utensils, and a large barrel, in addition to the bench.

Pedro Tanitsin's hair was braided, and he wore a brilliant beadwork vest over a bright flannel shirt, and Levis and moccasins. Ralph's mother wore the native dress; so did the older of his sisters, but instead of wearing her hair loose over her shoulders, she had it clubbed at the back of her neck. That must be Juanita, who had been in the Waves. The other, then, was Mary Ellen. Her hair was bobbed and curled, and she wore one of those gaudy silk blouses servicemen bring back from Japan, and slacks that had never been intended for outdoor life.

The mother spoke a single word, in Apache, and followed it with "Come een." Ralph moved forward, and the girl followed. She felt that she was moving against a wall of rejection. Ralph said something in his own tongue; then, gesturing, "This is my father."

She turned toward him. He nodded once, slowly.

Ralph said, "And this is my mother."

The older woman put out her hand, so the girl took it. The clasp was limp, there was no response to her motion of shaking, and the hand was quickly withdrawn. Then the mother spoke, ending with a laugh.

Ralph said, "She says—Well, you see, a while back one of the government women, some kind of social worker, came here, and she came in talking her head off before anybody had time to get used to her. You came in quietly, like an Indian. So she says, 'This one has good manners.'"

The woman laughed again. "Yess, not walk in talkin'."

The girl felt pleased and relieved. Then she saw that all of them were smiling except Mary Ellen.

Juanita gave her a somewhat firmer handclasp and said, "We were wondering whether you would really come here, to an Indian camp. I hope you like it." Mary Ellen's touch was limp and even more fleeting than her mother's; she kept her eyes down and did not speak.

It seemed that in summer they lived in the shelter, using the house only for sleeping and storage. Their housekeeping was easy and relaxed, rather like a well-organized picnic. She thought it better not to offer to help with getting supper; instead, she watched and took it easy. Hold back and go slow, she had decided, were essential elements of Apache etiquette. Cooking was well advanced when Pedro addressed some commonplace questions to her in heavily accented English. It was a little as if one of the pines had decided to speak, and the product, she thought, should have been less banal.

They all settled on the ground to eat, in a half circle. Ralph's mother insisted on giving her an angora skin, dyed deep blue, to sit on. The food was good, the utensils clean. In the middle of eating, to which the Indians devoted themselves with very little talk, Mary Ellen said something that made the others laugh. Juanita interpreted. "She says Ralph said that you were the kind who would wear Levis and sit on the earth, and you are."

She began to see that what she had taken for hostility in Mary Ellen was defensiveness, just as the inappropriate, pseudo-elegant costume was. The younger girl had not been out in the world, like her older brother and sister; nor had she the self-assurance, the satisfaction with plainly being Apache, of her parents. Her English was limited and unsteady. The presence of a strange white woman made her uneasy, and in an Indian, the visitor was beginning to see, uneasiness takes on the face of guarded enmity.

She herself was beginning to feel at home here. She looked around her. The incoming night air from beyond the shelter was chill. A generous fire burned in the central pit. About her were dark, friendly faces. In the air she breathed were the smells of smoke, food, coffee, pine needles, and the near-perfume of juniper boughs that had been brought up from lower county to make the walls of the shelter thicker and more fragrant. It was incredible that she should be here at this moment, stirring the sugar in a fresh cup of coffee, listening to the musical rise and fall of a woman's voice saying something in that mysterious tongue. She looked sidelong at Ralph. In the shifting, reddened firelight, he was darker, at once familiar, loved, and alien, primitive. Could it be possible, after all? Was it anything more than a remnant of a madness that had seized her when she went visiting a friend who had married a fly-boy major?

By the end of the third day she had to remind herself that all this was as strange as it was. Ralph planned to build a modern house, but the family's half-camping mode of life was agreeable; come winter, though, the inside of that little house would be on the grim side. The family were friendly, easy to be with, especially once Mary Ellen, feeling secure, had returned to native costume.

They had a radio, which they listened to chiefly for news, weather, and cattle price reports, Ralph or Juanita translating for their parents. Mary Ellen read movie magazines. Juanita dipped into textbooks that would help her in college (the University of New Mexico had accepted her for next fall) and, for the same purpose, was struggling through *Vanity Fair*. The white woman was able to help her there, realizing as she did so what a staggeringly broad context an educated white person moved and thought in, learned without effort, all of which an Indian had to grasp item by item. To speak English, read, and write was only the beginning.

Ralph and Uncle Juan, who visited daily, went in for bulletins from the extension service and agricultural colleges, reading them and then expounding their contents to Pedro. She was amused by the automatic gesture with which Uncle Juan would brush a braid back when it fell on the page. She had thought she had learned a little of the cattle business on a dude ranch near Tucson, where they made a big thing of running beef stock; not until now had she imagined it could be a bookish vocation with a highly technical vocabulary. Ralph and Juan turned to her to verify the meaning of "it is a far cry from," and in the same sentence were two words they had to explain to her. This amused Pedro greatly; he didn't know much English, but he had learned those.

Reading was occasional and in the daytime. After dinner, in the firelit dark, they told stories. Pedro, it turned out, was a noted storyteller in his own language. He talked and Ralph translated and explained. The stories had quality, and through them she saw that the Apaches, too, had a considerable context to be learned.

In her cot that night, with the sweet, cold air on her cheek, hearing the shushing rise and fall of a soft breeze in the high pines, she thought that it was possible, it could happen. It was just possible.

Ralph in the saddle was magnificent. Uncle Juan sat his horse like a rock that had become one with the animal, but Ralph was fine-waisted live whalebone. They were fun to ride with—considerate, instructive, humorous.

As they went about the range, there was nothing that moved, nothing out of place, that they did not see, at the farthest distance to which good eyes could reach. They made no apparent effort, she was not conscious that they were scouting, but they saw everything and were not content until it was explained. A pinto horse, an over-age steer with long horns—whose? A truck, two mounted men—to her, when she finally made them out, no more than dots on a distant road—who were they? Where were they going?

It made her think of bygone days and Apaches on the warpath. Some of those warriors had still been alive when Ralph was a boy. The warpath training had not been dropped. It made her think, as well, of Ralph high in the air alongside the Yalu, and his record of kills. There was a closer link between a deadly grandfather with a painted face and the skilled pilot than one would have thought.

Nothing was quite what she had expected, and least expected of all was the constant thread of laughter—the happy Indian laughter running through everything, so light and so easily provoked. And it was possible, just barely possible—that is, if *they* accepted *her*. Before she came here, she had not thought of that. What was definite was that she was in love with Ralph. When she had fully faced that, tired as she was, she was long in falling asleep.

The following afternoon, Ralph told her, "There's a neighbor of ours had a curing ceremony a while back. What he had was a virus and a touch of pneumonia, and they cured that at the hospital, but he had a sing, too. They do that a lot. There's something to it; the doctor takes care of the physical end, and the medicine man takes care of the psychosomatic. Anyway, now he has to 'pick up' the ceremony, as they say. It's a kind of thanksgiving. He puts up a tepee, and they make *tulapai*—that's a kind of beer made from corn. The neighbors come in, and there's a little singing and a feast, and we drink *tulapai* and talk, then at the end everybody gets blessed."

She said, "It sounds interesting. Do they get drunk?"

"You'd have to work hard to get drunk on *tulapai*. It just makes everybody happy. While you're seeing the Apaches, you ought to see this, only—Well, it's kind of unsanitary. They fill a lard pail and pass it around. Of course, you're not an Indian, so it will be all right if you want to use a cup."

"I don't think that's necessary."

Ralph was pleased. "All right. Anyway, it will be just us and Uncle Juan's family, and this man's—his name is Pablo Horses. They're all healthy, and they're clean."

Near sundown, they drove the mile to Pablo's place in her car and the truck. That was her first sight of a real-life tepee; she was struck by its symmetry, the way in which the curved canvas caught the light, the effect of the long, sloping white line against a green background. Inside, the tepee seemed even roomier than it had looked from the outside.

The door faced east. In the middle, there was a small, fragrant fire, and a kerosene lantern hung near the host's place at the back. The men sat on the south, the women on the north. All of them were wearing elements of Indian costume—items of buckskin, beadwork, Navajo silver, and Pueblo turquoise and shell. Pedro had his beaded vest on again; she knew now that his donning it that first day had been in honor of her. Ralph had put a wide band of beaded work around his hat, and at his throat, instead of his cowboy's scarf, he wore a broad choker of elk bone and beads. It was becoming.

All of them had blankets. Juanita had insisted that she take one, and had given her a handsome, soft, expensive Pendleton. The idea of wearing it had embarrassed her, but now she felt that it helped her to blend in. She'd turn into an Apache yet, she thought.

Their host, a craggy man with definitely gray hair, was older than Pedro Tanitsin. Because this was a ceremony, he had an eagle feather tied to the top of his head.

All of them, and especially the women, were amused that a white woman should come to drink *tulapai.* There were comments and laughter. Juanita, sitting next to her, said, "You mustn't mind. It's good. You are giving people a good feeling, so that helps what we are doing."

Pablo Horses took up a rattle and began a chant, in which the older men joined. The time was slow and monotonous, the music

151

narrow in range, and heavy. It was dull, and yet, as the girl listened, the monotonous rhythm and droning voices took hold of her. There was a curious power there.

After four songs, Pablo's daughter brought in a pail of *tulapai,* which was passed around solemnly, clockwise. Unsanitary, certainly; the girl wished she had asked for a cup, but they did seem a healthy lot. The drink itself was good, like beer but with a fresh quality that suggested hard cider. There were four more sets of four songs each, with a circuit of the pail after each set, and then the business of sprinkling a yellow powder and brushing the air with feathers. Everyone had sat still during the chant; the refreshment period was a break, when people changed positions. Pablo's women brought in food. The girl felt no noticeable lift from the small amount of the beer she had taken, but it did seem to have sharpened her appetite.

When they had eaten, Pablo said, "Young lady, where you come from?"

She said, "Ohio—Cleveland."

A young man, Uncle Juan's son, said, "I was there one time when I was in the Army. They got a good U.S.O." That took care of Cleveland.

An elderly man—Pablo's brother, she believed—asked, "How you like it here?"

"I like it. This is beautiful country."

Ralph took the trouble to translate that. Pablo said, "Yess. This is our country, Apache country." Then he went on at some length in Apache.

Juanita explained, "He's taken what you said as a kind of text, and he's telling how this is our country, and we must keep it, and we must live up to our Apache traditions."

More *tulapai* was brought in. The women were speaking up more than usual. There was an atmosphere of geniality and relaxation, but no ugliness, nothing one could call drunkenness.

The man she believed to be Pablo's brother, after a good draught of beer, launched upon a long story. Soon someone laughed. A little later, they all laughed. There were interruptions of laughter all through the latter part of the narration.

When he had finished, Ralph translated. "This is Tomás Horses speaking. He lives about five miles from here, and in between Pablo's place and his there is a place called Yellow Spring, where people camp. That's important.

"He says there is a Pueblo Indian called Malaquias he knows pretty well, a smart trader. Three or four times, when Tomás had visited that Pueblo, Malaquias has given him wine, then traded with him when he was high, and outsmarted him. So he's been waiting for a chance to get even."

They were all listening eagerly. Hearing the story a second time, knowing the point, made it all the more delightful.

"Well, about a week ago Malaquias came trading jewelry, and he camped at Yellow Spring. Tomás had some whiskey, so he made his plan. He came and borrowed Pablo's buckskin; that's a fast, strong horse and hard to hold once he gets going."

There were giggles.

"Then he drove to Yellow Spring in his wagon and told this man, 'My friend, put your goods in my wagon and come to my house. I'll give you a drink, and you can have supper with me, and perhaps we can do a little business.'"

This, it seemed, was hilarious.

"So he went along, and Tomás poured whiskey for him." More laughter. "Tomás went light. All the same, they traded, and the Pueblo traded him out of that buckskin for that string of turquoise he's wearing. The poor Apache had been gypped again." Ralph's own voice shook as he said this.

"So he gave the man some more whiskey, and kept him there for supper. Meantime, his two boys—this one here and another one, who's away now—went down the road about a mile and strung wire across between two trees."

The punctuations of laughter were almost continuous.

"So Tomás gave Malaquias a hackamore for the buckskin, and Malaquias started for his camp after dark, and good and tight. The buckskin was headed toward home, you understand, and Malaquias could not stop him when he started running. So they came to that wire, and it took him just right, under the chin, and threw him right off the horse. The horse came on back to Pablo's."

The telling had to stop for seconds of laughter.

"Then Tomás and the boys went and got the wire, and he sent this boy to the ranger station to tell how there was this foreign Indian lying in the road with his neck all torn and they'd better pick him up. By and by, they picked him up and took him to the hospital. He's still there."

Ralph looked about him, chuckling over the humor of it, feeling the successful narrator's glow. His audience was given over to laughter—all but the girl he loved, who seemed somehow alien, remote, so that he was unusually conscious of her paleness. He caught Juanita's eye, and she threw back her head to laugh again. Then he looked at the girl once more. She was so still, her eyes fixed on the ground. Wanting her to share in this as she had in so much else these last days, he forgot his satisfaction with his performance and studied her with concern, trying to reach what was in her mind, what was the matter. At that moment, she raised her eyes and looked directly at him. The last traces of pleasure left his face, because, as he read her now, her thoughts all laid open, he knew that this had ended it, and that she would start home the first thing tomorrow.

THE BRIDE AT
DEAD SOLDIER SPRING

If, as some Indians believe, there is a *gann,* or god, for every tribe of people on this earth, then the *gann* that looks after white men must surely have heard Molly Houghton's cry of anger and despair in the house at Dead Soldier Spring. Betty Natahnn, who came to clean for her on Mondays, heard it, halfway between the spring and her father's camp. She thought of going over to see what was the matter, but she decided not to. Although Mrs. Houghton had recently tried to be friendly, in an awkward way, Betty thought that she disliked Indians. So Betty continued on her way, with the water-basket heavy against her back.

Dead Soldier Spring is a wide, harsh, many-colored, arid valley in the western end of the Gohlquain Apache Indian Reservation, many miles from the Agency. The one little red sandstone house, neat and astonishing to come upon in that wilderness, had been built by the Soil Conservation Service, which had since withdrawn. It was not more than an easy day's ride on an average horse from Noon Mountain to the south, where the Gohlquain say that the *ganns* live. If there is one *gann* who has special charge of white people, he had probably already taken notice of the young woman who had started her married life, one might say, almost under his hand.

*Originally published in *American Magazine,* August 1955.

But Molly Houghton was certainly not feeling any divine influence at that moment. She sat down hard in the kitchen chair and uttered an unladylike word. Everything was wrong, everything, in this dreadful little house in this desolate, hideous waste. Why, why, did Bob have to ask that awful Jackson to dinner? Had he no consideration at all?

She was being unfair to Bob, but she did not care. She was getting dangerously good at being unfair and not caring, because in that way she avoided feeling ashamed of herself. Harry Jackson was a member of the Gohlquain Tribal Council and delegated by it to see that the oil company lived up to the conditions under which the council agreed to let them run a pipe line across the reservation. He could make Bob's job virtually impossible, or ease it greatly.

Molly knew all that, but when Bob told her at lunch what he had done, she nearly blew up. Lunch had got off to a bad start, as too many meals did recently. She had been lost in a book when she suddenly discovered that it was almost twelve. Bob drove an extra twenty-four miles every day to have lunch with her instead of at the work camp. She had hastily put a pot of beans to warm, and then found she was out of catsup. She had served him the beans and a nice canned aspic, and apologized about the catsup.

Bob tasted the beans, and said, "You could have got them a little hotter." That was the kind of thing he was saying these days, as though an evil spell had been cast over him. Then he nodded, "I don't blame you for living by the can opener out here, but you can do a lot with canned goods if you work over them."

She almost cried. Then, a little later, he told her he was bringing that Apache—he called him "Harry" and spoke of him with liking—not only to dinner, but to spend the night. He would sleep on the couch.

She said, "Oh, no!"

"We have to have him, honey." He went on to explain the situation that had arisen, which required getting the Tribal Council to amend an ordinance. He and Jackson had to work it out during the evening. It was important, she had to admit.

Then, as he was starting back to work, he said mildly, "Harry's a big eater. Let's have a good, solid dinner for him."

The Bride at Dead Soldier Spring

She almost threw a plate at him. Men—stomachs! That was marriage, a contract to fill stomachs. Men made an altar of their stomachs and sacrificed their wives on it, daily.

As for Harry Jackson, the one time she had seen him was more than enough. Bob had brought him to lunch once, unannounced, and the sight of that heavy, dark man, not as tall as her husband but just as broad at the shoulders, had startled her. She had picked up a towel to avoid shaking hands with him. She had been surprised when he handled his knife and fork correctly, although she could not have said what she expected.

He had looked at her just once, when he first came in; then somehow seemed to erase her presence. He did not speak, ignored a couple of attempts at small talk; he was just there at the table, his face dull and hostile. She knew very well that he talked freely with Bob; Bob even said that he had a fine sense of humor. With her, he was plain hateful.

That was what Indians were like, she decided firmly, having spoken with just two in all her life. Perhaps somewhere there were noble red men, such as you read about, but not on the Gohlquain Reservation. She was marooned in a wasteland inhabited by savages who did not even dress picturesquely, and her husband, her wonderful, gentle Bob, had turned into a despot complaining about the food.

When they had come here, in the early spring, life had seemed a wonderful prolongation of their honeymoon. Housekeeping was a grown-up game, in which her successes were a series of little triumphs. The hours of Bob's absence went rapidly, between work, reading, the radio, and just sitting and watching the brilliant, eternally changing landscape. It seemed to her that she had everything; with the new washing machine and the electric stove Bob had put in to supersede the original, kerosene one, she gaily wrote her mother, she had no chance to be a frontier wife at all.

Honeymoons will not last forever. The lightest of housekeeping grows dull, and loneliness seeps in before you realize it. Even the most loving bride needs someone besides her husband to talk to, and who else was there? Occasionally Bob brought one of the con-

157

struction men home for a meal, but since, in the hot weather, Molly had let her cooking slide, he had stopped. Talk with the Apaches? With Harry Jackson, the voiceless wonder, or Betty Natahnn, her sullen neighbor? They were just alike, hateful and hostile.

When the wind blew, fine sand sifted in around the window frames, so that the place was gritty, no matter how often she swept and dusted. In July, the afternoon sun burned on the kitchen window, until the room was like one huge oven. Planning a whole week's menus for the Saturday shopping trip to town was an exasperation. Even the electric stove was unpleasant to stand over, in the summer heat. A washing machine was a wonderful thing, but men's work clothes are backbreakingly heavy. There was a window that always stuck, and a door that rattled. It was years since anything had been painted.

Molly stopped admiring the play of the shadows on the sandstone walls, she would not look at the cactus coming into bloom, and she hated the house. Then, when Bob began criticizing the meals, she felt betrayed and sorry for herself.

Bob had changed. Associating with the Indians had corrupted him, she thought; he was even losing his cheerful look. Twice, recently, they had actually quarreled. This place was cursed, she told herself. If there were Apache gods, most probably they had hexed it. Dead Soldier Spring—Dead Marriage Spring, it should be called.

The sun was beginning to touch the west kitchen window when Molly reluctantly began to study the matter of dinner. The outside thermometer, she noted, showed ninety-one degrees in the shade, which meant that something in the neighborhood of a hundred and twenty degrees of heat was boring into the west windows. As she moved slowly to the storage closet, she faced one of the reasons why having Jackson or any other guest for dinner just then made her angry: It was Thursday, her last week's shopping had been slapdash, and the stock was low.

The stock, from the point of view of feeding healthy men at the end of a hard day, was downright pathetic. Presented with the equivalent of such a situation, her mother would lift the phone, talk to the butcher personally, and have a nice steak sent around. Send a runner to town—forty miles each way—and have a steak sent around?

Molly thought firmly: Boneless chicken—four-ounce can; Vienna sausage, tuna, sardines. . . . Hadn't she heard that Apaches had a religious objection to eating fish? You entertain to advance your husband's career. *The Senator sat back, smiling, after one of young Mrs. Houghton's delicious meals.* Harry Jackson, no doubt, that eminent statesman of the Gohlquain Apaches. . . . Sardines, black-bean soup—that would help. She took out the can. At the back of the shelf she saw a box of pie-crust mix and a can of cherries. Early in the spring, when it was cool and she had been ambitious, and a thousand years younger, she had made Bob a pie. She had never got around to making another.

Suddenly she felt better as she saw a presentable meal becoming possible: black-bean soup, and a slice of lemon; Vienna sausages on mashed potatoes—a trifle odd, but it would do; peas with a touch of onion; chilled, canned tomatoes with a little vinegar and mint; and cherry pie. She checked the mint; there was plenty in the refrigerator, which ran by kerosene like the original stove. Maybe she was a bit of a frontier wife, she thought, as she switched on the oven and went to work at the pie. She made a nice job of it, with a latticework of pastry on top; then opened the oven. It was cold, distinctly cooler than her kitchen.

She turned the switch off and on again, tried the hot plates on top. She decided to check the connection, then looked in the fusebox on the wall. The fuses were intact. She tried the lights; they did not work, either. Then she knew: Somewhere in the miles of drooping wire that led to the main line, her line was down.

It was then that she gave the cry that Betty Natahnn heard, and threw herself into the chair.

She looked forlornly at the pie, resisting an impulse to throw it out the window. That was why the government people had hung on to the kerosene stove and refrigerator after electricity was brought in—break one insignificant wire, and all the machines go dead.

Well, she decided, that was that. No dinner, no breakfast, nothing till the line was fixed. Bob would just have to take them into town, and they might as well stay overnight there. She would forget for a few hours, at least, that the house at Dead Soldier Spring existed.

With her mind made up, she felt calmer, although a little afraid of what Bob might think. For a real frontier wife there probably were ways—she would not imagine any ways. She lit a cigarette and got

159

up to fetch an ash tray. Then, of course, her eye fell upon the kerosene stove, still in place, which for so long had been nothing to her but a table space beside the sink that she had ceased to see it. Her supply of oil for the refrigerator was low, but there might be enough. Her heart sank at the thought of trying to fill and light the thing, of setting up the oven which fitted on top, and which was in the back of the closet. She went to the gallon bottle in which she kept the oil, and with profound relief found it all but empty.

The sense of relief faded, and she stood irresolute in the middle of the room. She had to know that she had really tried, and the Natahnn family had oil lamps of some kind. The idea of going to them was thoroughly unpleasant. Betty Natahnn was worse than Jackson, because she subjected Molly to the same blank silence, the same dismissal, every Monday all day long. Molly had hoped to get to know the girl when she first came to work, although she was at a loss how to act toward an Indian servant and wondered if they stole. She had tried to be friendly and watch Betty unobtrusively, but had finally given up on both.

To face a whole family of those stony, hostile faces was almost impossible. But she had to try, to be able to say that she had tried everything. She took money; after all, she would be asking no favors. She made herself go out in the sunlight and walk along the sandy, faint path, past the spring to the camp.

The place was primitive. Molly believed that the family used it only part of the year, and had a house somewhere else. It consisted of two large A-tents and a square shelter of leafy branches, open to the east. Inside the shelter she saw Betty and an old woman. When Betty came to work she wore an ordinary faded cotton dress; now, like the older woman, she wore a full skirt of bright calico with a blouse in contrasting color, and her hair was in two braids.

Molly stopped a few steps outside the shelter. She did not know what to do next. There was nowhere to knock, and she couldn't just breeze in and say hello, so, in indecision, she did exactly the correct thing: She waited. Betty glanced at her, then spoke to the older woman in Apache. The old one answered, and the girl said, "Come in." As Molly entered, the old woman spoke again. Betty rose, pulled a wooden box out from a corner, and said, "Sit down."

Molly sat down, feeling confused. The reception had not been effusive but it was far better than she had expected. Betty, as she made herself comfortable on the ground again, said, "That's my grandmother. She does not speak English." Molly looked at her. She was the lean, spry type of old woman. Her face was thoroughly Indian, but it was also universal; it had the lines and character of those who have lived much, know their own minds, and are accustomed to running things. Molly wished she knew how to say how-do-you-do in Apache.

The grandmother spoke. Betty said, "She says she's glad you came over, she's been wanting to look at you. She says now you can see how we live, and then maybe she can go and see all the things you have." She added, "I've been telling her about your electric stove and the washing machine and all."

Molly hadn't known the girl was capable of that much speech. She said politely, "I'd be glad to have her come."

There was an extended silence. Finally Molly said, "I wonder if you could spare me some kerosene for the stove. You see, the electric line has gone out, and my husband is bringing your Mr. Jackson for dinner, and I—" Her voice trailed off.

"Harry Jackson?"

"Yes."

There was another exchange in Apache; then "It's too bad. My dad and mother went to the Agency yesterday, and took the can with them to get it filled. They'll be back maybe Monday."

That was conclusive, and Molly should have been greatly relieved, but she was not. She said, "Oh," and then, "I don't know what to do."

The grandmother spoke. Betty interpreted: "She says, did you take Home Economics?"

"Yes."

The old woman said something else, and laughed. Betty said, "So did I, at Indian School in Santa Fe, and when I came back I didn't know what to do, either. I had to learn again." She pointed to the circle of ashes and arrangement of smoked stones in the center of the shelter.

"The only thing I ever cooked over a fire was a steak," Molly said, "If I had one, I'd do it." She did not know why she was telling these people all this. "I made a nice pie—" She started to choke and fell silent.

There was more talk in Apache. Betty seemed to make an objection and to be overruled. Finally she said, "Grandma says if you have a dollar, you can have steak. The people at Twin Hills butchered a yearling yesterday. She says she'll go along with you and get you started, and I can ride over for the steak. I know how to see that it's cut right." She smiled slightly. "I learned that in Home Ec., too. She says your husband is a good man, they say, and men don't like it when they come home hungry and there's no meat."

Molly was bewildered. It seemed that she was being taken in charge, and somehow it was reasonable and relaxing to let this strangely familiar old lady give the orders. And all the while she was coping with these feelings, she was also wondering what had happened to the sullenness, the stolidity of these people. The old lady's face was full of life, and Betty's had lost its masklike rigidity.

"Thank you very much," she said in a small voice. "I think that would be fine."

It was all strange, and she seemed to have no will. Here she was, lugging a big Dutch oven and following an elderly Apache woman who carried a long-handled fork in her hand as if it were a scepter. Here she was in the house, and the old lady was looking at the pie and laughing but not mockingly. And then, under directions, she was taking the racks out of the stove, and shortly she was gathering firewood.

You make a roaring fire of little sticks piled loosely, she learned, to burn into coals and hot ashes quickly. A small fire of logs at the back of these makes more coals for future reference. You take your nice clean racks and set them on stones for a grill. Around your fire is a small sphere of heat, which you move in and out of as you cook, but beyond that sphere the shade under the cottonwoods is cool and sweet. Water is slow to boil, all cooking is slow, and you wait, sitting on the ground, in company, even though you have no words in common.

Betty rode up with a bundle wrapped in burlap. "They gave us some corn," she said. "It's not really eating corn, but it's tender, and

162

it'll be nice roasted. You'd better take this steak and wash it off. Then put it in your icebox until the men come."

It was a magnificent piece of meat. In the kitchen, Molly set another can of tomatoes to chill in the refrigerator. Nothing had been said, but Betty and her grandmother would eat here, of course. Roasting corn and potatoes in ashes requires little more than patience but baking a pie in a Dutch oven takes skill. The old lady took charge of that.

Betty came out with a big, graniteware coffeepot which Bob had bought and Molly never dreamed of using, and set it on the grill.

"It's a picnic," Molly said, "Let's eat out here; it's so much nicer."

They went in to get things. Molly said, "What's your grandmother's name?"

Betty considered, "I guess you'd say, Spotted Bead Woman—only, you don't use it in front of her; that isn't polite with us. That's all the name she has; she never went to school."

"Then you have an Indian name, too?"

"Yes." She did not volunteer it, and Molly, beginning to realize that these people had an etiquette of their own, decided not to ask.

"What do I call your grandmother, then?"

"Just 'Grandmother.' That's all right."

"How do you say it?"

"*Schichoh.*"

Molly repeated it, and, outside again, she used it. The old lady laughed delightedly.

Molly said, "Could you people help me build a shelter like the one you have?"

"A *topaste?* Sure." Betty looked her directly in the eyes. "Say, you're halfway turning Indian, aren't you? I thought you didn't like us."

"I didn't know you. I thought you didn't like me."

"I didn't. You were watching to see if I was going to steal anything."

Molly blushed. "I—I didn't know." She sifted sand through her fingers. "I wonder you didn't quit coming."

"I have to work, anything I can get. I've had two years of college, and I won't stop until I graduate. The Tribal Council can't help me, because it's paying three scholarships now, and Dad can't cover it all, the way cattle prices have dropped. That four dollars a week I get from you goes in the bank, all of it."

"So you just kept at it and didn't like it, and that's why you wouldn't look at me or talk to me."

"Yeah, sort of. You see, the way white people stare at people—the Indians think that's rude. And then, you never know how a new white person will behave, so you make yourself real quiet and wait. You kind of shut yourself in."

"Is that why Mr. Jackson wouldn't speak to me?"

"Harry? Likely. And then, likely he never sat at table with a white woman before. He was probably shy."

Molly laughed. "And so was I, and it was awful. Listen; would you be willing to work for me right along? Could I hire you by the week?"

Betty's face lit up, then it darkened. "You don't have that much work."

Molly looked at her with new respect. She'd wait a day or two, she thought. They could paint and calcimine all over, and build a *top*—whatever they called it. "Anyway," she said, "you'll come and visit, won't you?"

"Sure."

The old lady wanted to know what was going on. Betty was still interpreting when Molly saw the dust cloud that meant the car was coming. She went into the house, seasoned the steak, brought it out, and put it on the grill. Over the slow coals the thick slab would be perfect by the time the men were ready. She went to the front of the house and stood by the road.

Bob stopped the car in the shadows of the trees. Beside him sat Jackson, bulky, Indian, withdrawn.

"I guess you know your line's down," Bob said. "I'll send a crew to fix it in the morning. For now, we can drive to town for dinner."

"And spoil my picnic? Go in and clean up, both of you. You'll be just in time."

Bob stared at her. Then he looked past her, past the corner of the house, saw the fire and the other women, and at the same moment Jackson said, "I smell steak." The Apache opened the door on his side. "Come on, boy." He was smiling.

Bob swung out of the car. "I thought—when I heard your line was out—"

164

"You thought I'd quit, and I don't blame you. But I didn't; I'm through with that."

A great relief filled his face like an inner light. He lifted her clear off her feet to kiss her.

"Now, hurry," Molly said, "or the steak will be overdone."

She stood by the grill with the Natahnns' long fork in her hand. She sniffed the steak; she was hungry, and imagined how much hungrier the men must be. The leaf shadows on the wall of the little house were charming, and beyond the wall was the stranger, haunting beauty of that vast, fierce land.

Dead Soldier Spring, she thought; there must be a story back of the name. Perhaps Betty could tell her. She heard the front door open and close; the men were coming, and the meal was ready. She was happy; for several hours now she had been entirely happy, in good company, working like a frontier wife by the house at Dead Soldier Spring.

A PAUSE IN THE DESERT

Along this stretch the highway turned almost north, letting the afternoon sun roast the driver's side of the blue sedan. The black road kept extending itself ahead, undulating over minor rises, its farthest point evaporating as a black mist in the vibrations of heat haze. This part of New Mexico, speaking by the book, was not desert. There was vegetation, there were areas of greenish overtints, but they failed to provide contrast with the yellowish or reddish earth. The rock outcrops were brown; under the force of the sunlight they seemed black. Whatever its correct classification, the country had the quality of howling. It had the sentient, hostile personality of a desert.

The man, Huggins, drove intently, wanting to get through and come as soon as possible to where the road had punctuations, divisions, and places. He had driven between Los Angeles and Albuquerque twice before, and rated this the most repulsive stretch of all. His wife, beside him, younger, agreeably pretty, alert, was affected differently. She kept studying the landscape as if she were trying to master it. Mostly she kept her eyes on the far distance, where streaks of red, brown, and yellow with occasional pale greens and washed-out blues, hot yet subdued, led to the semblance of mountains.

The man was acutely conscious of the woman. He watched her with occasional quick side glances, estimating her thoughts. He was disturbed that she was not repelled by this sorry wilderness, as he

*Originally published in *A Pause in the Desert* (Boston: Houghton Mifflin, 1957).

167

was. Had she been, he could have developed a little more his role of the experienced traveler, the guide, alleging himself to be unaffected by it, using a faint touch of masculine mockery. It would have been another little addition to the structure of himself he had been erecting, for her and his own sake, in these last four days. Instead, she seemed attracted by it, and that renewed the uneasy feeling of losing hold of her that he had been putting behind him.

He shook his head slightly, remembering the beginning of their marriage, before he was out of uniform. A little thing like this would never have troubled him then. He told himself he was a fool, and to stop worrying, and he glanced at her again. He could not for long forget the hope that by bringing her on this trip he could restore what had been at the beginning; the obverse of his hope was anxiety.

She said, without properly looking at him, "It's frightening, really, but it makes you want to go way out into it and see what's there. I mean, you can't imagine, you feel you have to look."

"You'd find plenty of nothing."

"Not even Indians?"

He visualized where his road map showed the Navajo Reservation border. "Not for a hundred miles or so." As he had done since they crossed the San Gabriel Mountains, he spoke with assurance, the man who knew the country. Then he told her the story about putting green glasses on the burros so they could eat the desert. It struck the right frontier note, and it pleased her. I'm doing all right, he thought.

His own principal thought demanded expression. "We ought to make Albuquerque in two hours more. Then I'll have fun introducing you to the Southwest Area gang."

She detached her eyes from the distances to answer. "Past time you brought me along, too. You can do with an eye on you. You and your sales conventions."

The trite, affectionate suggestion that he was a dangerous male when on the loose warmed him with a reassurance he constantly craved. He was clearly older than his wife, in another stage of life. His bare head showed a thinness of his fine, brown hair at the crown, and his forehead ran back beyond its original line. He was dressed in a brightly figured shirt with short sleeves and an open throat, and blue slacks of light material. He was not fat, but he had a soft little extra layer under his skin; looking at his face and throat, one would assume a slight roll on his belly. His forearms were round, smooth, and white. Judging by his wrists, he was a small-boned man who used to be lithe. In these last days of driving and getting out to see the sights he had acquired a pink flush on the top of his head, his face, and the backs of his arms and hands. The back of his left arm, after a couple of hours of direct sun since the road had swung northward, had more than a flush; it would be painful later, but he did not know that.

He said, "This *junta*" (he was proud of the Spanish word, the use of which he had picked up the year before) "may mean a lot to us. This is the third time now I've been picked to represent the California area; I'm pretty sure that there's something good in line for me, and of course the big shots will be here. That's where you come in, Dot. I've really got a better half, and I want them to know her."

He spoke sincerely, warmly. She really looked at him, and gave him a smile. Then she lost herself again in the tumbled distances, showing him less than a profile when he looked toward her, her neat ear and the live, gold-brown curl of her hair under the bright bandanna, mostly blue, with which she protected her head from the wind and dust.

He grunted suddenly. "The car's overheating. Look at the gauge."

She turned to see the needle at the red line. "That looks bad."

He slowed down. He read the speedometer, frowned thoughtfully, then he said, "I think there's a sort of a service station just ahead." On the face of it, the statement was improbable. No land could look emptier, less promising of help. Her doubt was plainly visible. "I think it's about a mile further on." The tenths of miles turned slowly on the speedometer. He kept looking from the figures to the road and back again. "There it is. See—where that clump of trees is."

"Nice work."

He concealed his triumph. The bad luck of whatever had happened to the car was his good luck, giving him the opening for the most impressive demonstration of himself as the man, the guide, the ready and experienced traveler, that he could possibly have asked for.

After a thoughtful pause she asked, "Why is there a station here, of all places?"

169

"People get into trouble, like us, or the kids get to yelling for pop. Bet you it changes hands every couple of years."

"Well, I'm glad it's here. You're sure they filled the radiator at Gallup?"

"Yep. I checked."

He was now driving under twenty, and the heat of the outside air, of the roasted metal of the body, and of the engine assailed them with a blanketing fury. As they drew near they could see that the place consisted of a large, one-story building with a metal roof which blazed a painful silver. Its walls, broken on the side toward them by the one high, square ink spot of a window, were made of local stone which camoflauged itself into the desert. There were some small shacks at the back. On the near side stood two big cottonwoods, wonderfully green; on the far side, at a little distance, a cattle-loading pen thrust its platform at the highway. There was no apparent reason for either building or pen, unless the miraculous existence of those trees somehow required that something be placed by them.

Now they could see that two horses were tied to a hitching rack under the trees, and a big, black truck with slat sides, shiny and new, was parked partly in their shade. From the front of the building a long roof carried well out beyond the gas pumps. Along its edge a sign said that this was a garage, a trading post, and the post office of Huesos, New Mexico. Signs on the ground advertised cold pop, ice water, curios, and cabins. From the opposite edge of the highway two roads ran off in a wide, regular V, the kind of roads made by the frequent passage of wheels in the same track. Their existence was the most unreasonable thing of all. It was impossible to conceive that there was anywhere for them to lead to in the jumbled, color-streaked barrenness toward which they separately meandered, and yet their presence, plus the signs on the store, stated that some-where, somehow, in unimaginable spots beyond sight, in God only knew what desolate canyons, beside what water holes guarded by the skeletons of cattle, there lived people, from whom this enter-prise drew a sustenance of trade.

There were several figures, seated in the deepest shade, by the wall of the establishment. Huggins turned the car in to park just outside the pumps. As he shut off the engine, he said, "Listen to her boil."

A Pause in the Desert

Dot studied the people reposing along the front of the store, while a tall boy not quite turned man hoisted himself slowly from a seat on a wooden box and moved toward the driver's side of the car. The man followed her eyes. "Local yokels," he said. After a moment he added, "There's a real Sioux Indian for you. Look at the braids." He pronounced all the letters in "Sioux," *Sigh-ooks.*

He got out as the boy came to the door. They looked under the hood together. The boy said he needed a new fan belt. He said, "Damn. Okay." He told his wife, "Might as well get out and stretch. How about a coke?"

"You bet." She was still studying the loungers.

The three men by the store front looked at them with mild, friendly curiosity. The Indian was sitting on the ground. His face and hands were mahogany-dark. He and his face were broad. He wore his hair in two braids wrapped with yellow and blue tape, reaching, as he sat, almost to his thighs. There was a beaded band around his very large, floppy black felt hat, which he wore square on his head. Otherwise his costume was disappointing, cowboy boots and denim, all of good quality. They had been seeing Indians since Needles, but this was the first with the braids one had always heard about.

The other two men sat on a bench. One was tall, spare, with very wide, flat shoulders, a seamed face, a lantern jaw, and a humorous mouth. Under his smallish felt hat his hair showed gray. He, too, wore cowboy boots. The other man was slight, worn fine as old silver is worn. His dark face was slender, thoughtful, strong. He had noticeably handsome brown eyes and one of those thin mustaches with the ends drooping well below the corners of his mouth that one sees in Remington's pictures, but his was snow-white. He wore a neat, moderately wide black hat at a good angle. It went well with his white, collarless shirt and black alpaca suit. His black, elastic-sided shoes, small and narrow, were wonderfully old-fashioned. On his shirt, visible under the open coat, was pinned a badge. A sheriff or something, Huggins thought. It was a congregation of old gaffers. At first he had not thought the Indian old, but on second look he saw he was not young, but ageless.

The broad-shouldered man said, "Afternoon, folks. Make yourselves at home."

Huggins, feeling Western, answered, "Howdy."

Yet another man came out of a side door marked GENT'S. He was taller than the broad man, and lean. He wore a work shirt, Levi pants like the Indian's but older, a large hat, boots, and spurs. At the moment he was bowed over. In his hands he was holding objects of some sort.

"Look," he said between chuckles. "By heaven, first time I ever knew you could smoke while you was brushin' your teeth." He extended his hands. "Look." In his left hand he held a toothbrush and a set of uppers, between he fingers of his right hand was a cigarette. He put the cigarette in his mouth, took the brush in his right hand, and demonstrated, shaking with laughter. The white men on the bench smiled, the Indian laughed aloud. The lean man straightened with his back to the strangers. By the motion of his hand, he had put the plate back in place. Seen from behind, he gave no indication of age. He simply looked like a horseman, tall, narrow-hipped, and erect now that he was through clowning.

Huggins looked at Dot, registering disgust, and saw that she was delighted. The lean man turned around. He raised his hat, saying, "I beg pardon ma'am. I come out so tickled I couldn't stop. Hope I didn't upset you."

"Oh no. It was so funny."

She pulled off her bandana and shook her curls. Huggins was astonished, the gesture was so profoundly one of being at home.

The lean man smiled. His smile was good. His eyes were intensely blue, his face was aquiline. She smiled back at him, then at the others. Their eyes received her with appreciation. Huggins said, "I'll get us some cokes." He went into the store.

The broad-shouldered man followed and sold him cokes and cigarettes in a leisurely, friendly, desultory way. He told the storekeeper that they came from Los Angeles and were going to Albuquerque for the Central Supply Company's area sales convention. The storekeeper told him that he'd never been to California but always wanted to go there, and that it was sure hot around here daytimes but it always cooled off at night.

Huggins glanced over the place with its old-fashioned, general-store quality, noting as an oddity the saddles hanging from the wooden ceiling. He took the cokes outside. His wife was sitting on the wooden box, at an angle to the bench. With the Indian sitting facing inward, and the lean man standing at the far end, she and the other three formed a group. As he came to her she was saying, "Do you mind my asking—are you a Sioux Indian?" Like her husband, she pronounced the word as it is spelled.

The Indian said, "Huh?"

The storekeeper, behind Huggins, interjected, "Soo. No, Steve ain't Sioux."

The Indian said, "No Sioux round here. They live up in Dakota. I'm 'Pache."

The lean man looked down at him affectionately. "A murderin', scalpin' Apache."

Huggins glanced at his wife, then at the man they called Steve. Apache was a word full of connotations and wonder. He felt the same discomfort he had known at Grand Canyon when he had been caught out identifying some Hopis as Navajos. It was important for him to be master of this wild country, and that was not easy when before he had always driven straight through, stopping only to eat and sleep.

Steve said, "Just like in the movies."

Dot and the three old men laughed. The storekeeper had sat down on the bench again. Huggins felt ignored. Because they intrigued his wife, these old yokels had become important. He handed her a coke, then, having thought of and discarded the word "gentlemen," he said, "Any of you boys care to join us?"

The storekeeper said, "Thanks, don't use 'em." The others refused vaguely. The rebuff was plain. He had struck a wrong note, as if he had spoken too loudly.

The slender man with the badge spoke in the manner of one who has finally decided to voice something that has been bothering him. "Pappy, if a horse bucks on you, will those teeth stay in place?"

He had a Spanish accent. The pronunciation was not so marked as was a certain gentleness with which he spoke, as if the alien words had to be handled delicately. The Apache, in contrast, had been heavy in his speech, bearing down on the English.

The lean man pushed back his hat, revealing a forehead that extended to his crown. "I'd been wonderin' about that myself. This mornin' I went out with the boys to pick out these off-color bulls I aim to pass off on Steve here. I was ridin' my *grullo* horse and he busted in two first off. They stayed in fine."

The storekeeper said, "You're too old to be buckin' out horses."

"He wasn't buckin'. It was just early in the mornin' and he felt good. Didn't have a mite of harm in him." The lean man chuckled. "When my oldest boy was seventeen I was watchin' him buck out a bareback at Winslow. He was throwed on the fourth jump and nearly got stomped on. I realized then and there that now I had a boy to be a damn fool for me, I didn't need to be one myself any more. Slim, I need somethin' to wrap this new toothbrush in, to take it home."

The storekeeper jerked his head. "Small sacks behind the counter by the till. Help yourself." The lean man went in.

Dot said thoughtfully, "You call him 'Pappy'? How old is he?"

Slim said, "He ain't so old—seventy-two. You see him ride, you'll know he ain't old. It's just that when that kid he was talkin' of was born—Steve and him and me was punchin' cattle for the Rockin' Three, up in Steve's country—he bragged so on him that we took to callin' him Pappy."

Not so old—seventy-two. The question fluttered in Huggins' mind, he saw it in his wife's face, but neither of them liked to ask it. Steve said, as if he were giving an order, "You guess how old we are." He gestured with his whole hand toward the woman, then toward the others.

She hesitated. The sheriff said in his soft voice, "Go ahead, miss. It's a game always with the Indians, guessing ages."

Steve took off his hat. His hair was iron-gray. The uncovered braids behind his ears were much too thin to justify the thickness or length of the wrapped portion which fell so handsomely to his waist. They were stuffed, then. Huggins saw his wife's mouth twitch as she grasped this incongruous femininity. You had heard that Indians' hair did not turn gray until they were very old. Dot said, slowly, "Well, if your friend—oh—I'll guess seventy."

"Now him, Anastacio." The Indian indicated the sheriff by turning his head and pointing with his lips. The slender man took off his hat. His plentiful white hair, carefully brushed, curled about his ears. He challenged her with smiling eyes.

Pappy came back. "We're guessin' ages," Slim said, "only you're out. We told on you."

Pappy said, "I'll help you out, ma'am. The shameful thing about these poor old crocks is not how old they are, but how young they are, considerin' their condition." At that Huggins thought, he looked the youngest of the lot, excepting possibly the Indian.

The sheriff was live and alert. He was fine, but he looked as if he had always been fine, and he was not at all withered. For him she guessed seventy-two, and for the store-keeper, sixty-eight.

The Indian pointed to himself. "Sixty-nine," Anastacio said, "I'm seventy-three." Slim said, "You called the turn on me. I'm the baby, sixty-eight."

She laughed. "Not a one of you looks it."

Huggins felt a shock of jealousy. There was a flirtation between her and these four men. She was sparkling, giving her charm for them, and they were responding. He did not understand it, he felt uneasy, and his glibness, his usual, easy approach to any group, seemed to have dried up in him.

"Now we guess you," Steve announced.

Slim licked and lit the cigarette he had just rolled. "That's easy. Sixteen." It *was* a flirtation.

"No, go on, really guess."

Pappy said, "Twenty-four."

Slim said, "Twenty-five, to be different."

The Californian considered his wife. She did not look that young. They were being gallant.

"I'll string along with Pappy," the sheriff said thoughtfully.

Steve studied her. "Twenty-eight." No gallantry there.

"That's right," she said, "twenty-eight."

Next, he thought they would guess his age, and with that he could cease to be excluded. It would be all right them. His wife was looking out over the desert, then she turned to the lean man. "You are going to sell him bulls, Pa—Mr.—?"

"Pappy to you, ma'am, Pappy Evans."

"Thank you. I'm Dorothy—Dot—Huggins. Where do you raise cattle around here?" The moment for inclusion, if it had existed, was gone. That was not like Dot.

"I got a little piece over yonder." Like the Indian, he pointed by thrusting his lips toward one of the dim, improbable roads.

"In that—desert?"

"It does look hard around here, don't it? You see where that dark red streak is about ten miles from here? Well it dips there, and there's a strip of good country, grass all year round."

She stared out along the road. "Aren't you lonely there?"

Slim answered for him. "Him nor me. He's got his folks, and we got lots of neighbors; Steve's cousins."

Steve said contemptuously, "Navajoses."

Slim laughed. "It's all Navajo country from here on. They're my main customers. The Apaches don't think too much of them, even if they are related."

Huggins seized a chance to join in. "You say this is Navajo country right here? I thought the reservation was way over west."

"It is, but that don't stop 'em. Matter of fact, they've always been here."

"You mean, they're allowed off the reservation?"

The Apache said heavily, with emphasis, "Inyans are citizens, just like you. We don't have to stay inside no reservation."

His mind was confused with the thought of apology. The sheriff intervened. "You are new to this country?"

Dot answered, a trifle hastily, "I've lived in California all my life." Humiliatingly, he was glad to let that stand for himself, too.

Pappy looked down at her. "Then you never was West before?"

"West?" She digested his meaning. "Oh. No, I never was."

"This is it, or part of it. It ain't all this harsh. If you and Mr. Huggins"—he gave her husband a polite look—"have time to come by the ranch, we'd be glad to have you. It's pretty around there, and the mountains are close."

She looked at Huggins, questioning, wishing. He said, "We'd like to, thanks. Maybe we can make it on our way back." There were all sorts of reasons why they would be unable to stop.

"You're welcome any time. The road's good in dry weather."

Slim surveyed the group. "You got the assorted Wild West right here. One cattle man, one wild Indian, one wicked Indian trader, and one Spanish sheriff. He's sheriff on account of he's a Republican and a García; that's four aces in this county."

"It's the fast hand," Pappy said. "'Stacio's really quick."

She was puzzled. "How do you mean?"

Pappy said, "*Amigo, enseñela.* Go ahead."

The sheriff looked at her mildly. "When I was a boy, my papa worked at Tombstone. Mr. Earp was marshal then, he showed it to me. You must practice all the time. Like this." His delicate hand barely flicked in toward his waistband under the coat and outward again, armed. The gun was big and ugly, blue-black, with the bluing worn off along both sides of the barrel. It lay steady in his light grasp. Then it disappeared as it had appeared. "It is practice, that is all."

Pappy said to the Indian, "We better get started. I got eighteen two-year-olds in the four-mile corral. Pick yours out today. We can take the rest back to pasture with us, and load yours tomorrow." He looked at the black truck. "You can take six easy in that. You got ropes?"

"If I ain't got enough, Slim has."

"That's what I'm here for," Slim said. "You ought to wait a couple of years, Steve. Pappy's just got two new bulls out of Champion Red Royal from Wyomin'. He'll get some real calves out of them."

"I'll come back. We'll be ready for them."

"You and your folks ain't got but about a hundred and fifty head," Pappy said. "How many bulls do you figure on puttin' with 'em?"

"Hundred and eighty now, and we aim for maybe two hundred. We use these bulls two-three years, then sell 'em to other Inyans. Make better stock all over. My father is buyin' registered heifers after the fall sales. Pretty soon, say ten years from now, we'll be raisin' registered breedin' stock altogether. Then you come to 'Paches to buy bulls." There was deep satisfaction in the last statement.

"I aim to keep on improvin' my bunch, too. There's a shortage of good breedin' stock hereabouts, and on over into Arizona. Ten years from now your outfit and mine can trade, maybe?"

"That's right." The Apache rose slowly. "Let's go." Erect, he was a heavy, short man, but his hips were narrow, like the others'.

Ten years from now—Steve's father—the horse was just feeling good. Were these men immortal? Huggins felt almost giddy. Dot's face was full of speculations.

Pappy told Steve, "Get your saddle out of the truck."

Suddenly the young woman woke up. "Wait! You haven't guessed Bob's—my husband's—age. Let's see what you can do with him."

The four old men looked at him. He did not at all want what he had so wanted before; he wished that Dot had stayed forgetful. He did not want their scrutiny, or her seeing him through their eyes.

Slim said, "He's kind of hard to figure. Plump, like Steve here. It fools you."

He was plump, but not plump like Steve, not hard, not ready for the saddle. Under their eyes—yes, and under hers—he knew that he was soft, pale, commonplace. He had thought his full, lightweight California slacks were smart; now they seemed effeminate. He knew that his hips were heavy.

Slim said, "I'll take forty-three."

Anastacio's eyes caught Pappy's, then flickered for an instant toward the young woman. Pappy caught the message. The sheriff said, "I think thirty-seven."

Pappy appeared to consider. "Yeah, close to there. I'll make it thirty-eight."

That was his actual age, but he knew with certainty that both men were underguessing, as they had with Dot, and for her sake, not in gallantry but in a delicacy of consideration. Dot had caught it, too. She was looking away, and what he could see of her cheek was flushed.

The delicacy had passed Steve by. He studied, then said, "Forty-five."

Dot laughed uneasily. "Pappy got it—thirty-eight." He stood foolishly smiling, wordless.

Pappy and Steve went to saddle up. The boy extricated himself from under the hood and said that she was all set. It took Slim time to figure the bill and make change. As they got into the car the two riders came by.

The lean man said, smiling down from the saddle, "Remember, we'll be lookin' for you."

She said, "We'll remember." Again he had nothing to say, nothing to offer but a smile fixed over sheer hatred.

He started the car and let it run for a minute, listening to the engine. "All okay." He let in the gear.

As they gained speed, they came parallel with the two figures on horseback, who followed a trail even dimmer and less reasonable than the two roads. Seventy-two and sixty-nine. Dot's eyes looked past him, fixed on them, until they fell behind. The significant thing was that she said nothing at all.

In a form of pleading, he said, "We'll make Albuquerque a little after five. We can have a drink and a bath, and then we can have a couple of the best of them up to the room for cocktails." He knew she had heard it before, but he had to run on. "Goldbright is a lot of fun, and Tim Loomis from the big office is going to be there. I want you to know him; he's a great guy."

"That will be nice," she said without interest.

THE LITTLE STONE MAN

F ive San Leandro Indians sat in a row on the grass behind the Bonds' house. Charlie Bond, a pleasant-faced youth of twenty, sat facing them. One of the Indians, Agapito Rael (about a third of the San Leandros have Rael as their Christian last name), was elderly. His gray hair was tied in a queue wrapped with red material, his head was bound by a blue headband, and he wore heavy necklaces of shell, coral, and turquoise. The others were young, although all somewhat older than Charlie—the oldest, Juan Rael, being over thirty. Three of them had crew haircuts, and all four were dressed as any Westerner might dress on a warm day.

The pueblo of San Leandro was only five miles from Castellano, New Mexico, where the Bonds lived, and the Indians came to town for much of their shopping. It was not unusual for them to stop and visit. Some of them were Dr. Bond's patients, and, as so readily happens between Pueblo Indians and white people of a sympathetic disposition, he and his wife had developed friendly relations with yet others. Charlie's relationship with the San Leandro people had begun when he was twelve years old, when the Bonds first settled in Castellano, and it was far more intimate and less self-conscious than his parents'.

He had quickly learned never to inquire into Pueblo secrets, but in years of association he had picked up enough to know that Agapito was the Turquoise Cacique—that is, one of the two highest-ranking

*Originally published in the *New Yorker,* June 25, 1960.

priests in the hierarchy—that Juan Rael was important in a society the function of which he did not know, and that Eddie Sota, recently returned from a hitch in the Navy, was Agapito's nephew and had started training to follow in his uncle's path. So far as Charlie knew, the other two were just young men who played good baseball and did their part in the dances.

They had refused an invitation to come into the house and have coffee, made themselves comfortable on the grass, and talked commonplaces for a time—about the green summer they were having after last winter's good snows, about last Sunday's ball game, in which San Leandro had trimmed a team from Santa Fe, and the state of the trout fishing in Chompi Creek. There was a pause, the moment of gathering themselves in, of letting everyone become prepared, without which it would be offensive to broach serious business, then the visitors began talking to each other in Piro. Charlie understood a little Piro, including the greetings, everyday expressions, and a number of things he said to girls; when they talked as they were doing now, he could only catch words here and there.

Agapito said something decisive. Eddie looked at Charlie and said, "We think maybe you can catch another wild ball for us."

Charlie nodded. He felt a little prickle of excitement. Something important was up. At the same time, Eddie's reference called to mind his first encounter with the Piros.

Eight years before, his father, being new to New Mexico, not knowing the difference between a Pueblo Indian and a Navajo, had taken Charlie with him to San Leandro when he went to visit a patient. Charlie had wandered about the village of golden-brown adobe houses arranged in solid blocks—a lonely boy, a boy who had not yet had time to make any friends in his new home, intrigued and rebuffed by the very picturesqueness of this place, trying not to stare at a man with his hair in a queue, at a woman in native costume. Hearing the crack of a bat against a ball, he drifted to the edge of the pueblo, where a young man was batting out flies to a number of boys. They were on a level strip between the last houses and a shallow cliff, below which the cornfields started. The white boy moved slowly to the edge of the cliff, behind the fielders, and stood watching. What they were doing he knew all about. They were mostly

182

a few years older than he; still, they were boys, and he wanted like anything to join them. But they were talking in a strange language, he was of another color, and none of them even glanced at him. He stood watching and wishing, and thinking that the batter ought to have a bigger bat than the one he was using. A boy near the batter fielded a grounder, made a game of winding up, then pitched the ball underhand. Someone had said something funny, and the batter was laughing. Then he swung, really batting, and knocked out a line drive that went past all the Indians and would have landed in the cornfields had not Charlie caught it. It stung his hand like fury, and it was the beginning of everything.

Agapito was now holding forth. While Charlie waited, he thought of Professor McKee, one of the anthropology profs at college, and rather self-consciously wished the Professor could see him at this moment. Then Agapito said something final to Eddie, and Eddie turned to Charlie and spoke in English, while the others listened intently. "We got some trouble, and we been thinking maybe you could help us out. The old men talk it over at home, and they decided we could probably trust you. We know you've learned a few things about our—our old ways, our Inyan religion, you know, and we think you don't talk about it. I heard Telesforo when he was talking to Agapito here, and he was saying that you don't ever ask no wrong questions, you not trying to stick your nose into things, even if you have seen something or heard something that white people don't know about. I'm saying this part for myself, to kinda explain it to you."

He interpreted his words to his uncle in Piro.

The Telesforo of whom Eddie spoke was Telesforo Pérez, who was Agapito's opposite number, the Calabash Cacique. It was typical of Charlie's relationship with the San Leandros that they took it for granted that he knew who these men were, and they did not mind, because he never asked and never told.

Eddie went on. "Now, they say, we want you to do us a big favor, but first you promise you won't tell no one about it. Sounds funny to ask for a favor and then say that, but that's the way we got to do."

"Of course. I promise."

"Not your daddy or your mother."

"Not my daddy or my mother. Or anybody."

Eddie interpreted again. Several of the others nodded, and Charlie understood Agapito saying "Good. Go ahead."

Eddie said, "You know, we got a sacred place—a shrine, I guess you'd say, in the mountains north of here, on the edge of the grant?"

Charlie guarded his expression. He certainly did know about it, because a couple of years ago he had gone that way with a Piro girl, on whom he had a crush, and her brother to pick wild strawberries. He got separated from the others and stumbled upon the shrine, with fresh prayer sticks around it. As soon as he saw what it was, he circled well away, and he had mentioned it to no one. Later, when his friends translated part of a rain-dance song for him and there was a passage, "Holy to the north, Holy in a mountain valley, Someone brings thunder," he guessed it referred to the shrine.

He nodded now, and said, "I heard something."

"We—we keep something there." Eddie seemed to run out of words. He turned and spoke to his uncle, who made an affirmative gesture with his hand—a bit of the old sign language that some older men used unconsciously—and said something.

Eddie faced Charlie again. "Well, it's like one of the images in church, only more like a *bulto*." He meant the primitive wooden statuettes carved a hundred years or more ago by the Spanish-Americans. "I mean, it's little, and the carving ain't so good; only it's stone, not wood." He went on to describe it—a human figure, definitely male, and decorated in a distinctive manner.

Then Juan spoke. "You understand, Charlie, this thing maybe don't look like much, but it's important. Ain't everybody in the pueblo, even, knows what it looks like. All of us here, we belong to the right club, you might say. And if anything happened to this thing—well, it's holy to us, and it's holy to a lot of other pueblos, too." As Eddie had done, he turned to Agapito and interpreted himself.

Eddie then said, "Well, this thing, it's gone. It's been gone now for eight days, and we think either Carlisle has it or else someone from La Aurora picked it up. They run pack trips up that way."

Carlisle was a dealer in curios, a talented fraud, who did in fact possess a fine collection of Indian goods. La Aurora was a guest ranch not far from Castellano. Its original name was Los Jiménez, since it had been the center for the old Jiménez family, but its present owners had given it the resounding, Mexican-sounding title of Hacienda la Aurora.

Juan Rael said, "We *say* Carlisle, because anyone like a sheepherder that mighta taken it would most likely sell it to him. I dunno about La Aurora. Long ago, when they first run pack trips through the grant, they went poking around too much. The War Captains and some of their staff went over and straightened 'em out. They sure don't want us to stop 'em from coming on the grant or visiting the pueblo, and their wranglers have instructions to keep their dudes in line. On the straight and narrow path, you might say."

Charlie nodded. He had heard something of that visitation, from the ranch end; it must have been impressive. And every year, when permission to ride on the grant was renewed, the governor of San Leandro reminded the ranch owners to keep their outfits on the proper trails. "Then it sounds like Mr. Carlisle," he said.

"Yeah. Him or someone. We been to his store, and a couple of our people been to La Aurora, selling curios, but we didn't see nothing. Trouble is, if anyone has this thing, as soon as he sees an Inyan coming he'll hide it and clam up. So that's where you come in. We want you to be our detective."

"All right. I'll try. I don't know that I can do any good."

When Agapito had been brought up to date, he nodded solemnly and said, "Very good; thank you," in Piro. Then he said in Spanish, which Charlie spoke well, "If you find it, better you leave it alone and tell us right away. There is less trouble for you if you do not handle this thing."

Charlie said, "*Muy bien.*" He supposed the old man was referring to ritual contamination.

Jake Pérez, who up to now had simply listened, produced a pack of cigarettes, which was passed around. There was little said while they smoked. Charlie thought they ought to have produced the cornhusk cigarettes that are used on some ceremonial occasions. When the Cacique put out his smoke, the others followed suit and rose. They all shook hands with Charlie, some saying goodbye in Piro, others in English; then they filed off.

Charlie walked slowly about the yard. At first he was carried away by elation. The Indians had turned to, had called upon, *him.* Voluntarily they had opened the door to their inner life a crack more. If he could find that image, perhaps they might even initiate him, take him in. They had come to no one else but him; he was sure of that. At the height of his pleasure, he suddenly saw how ridiculous it was—the only white man the Indians trust. How childish can you get!

Because of his relations with Indians, he had taken courses in anthropology during his first two years at Talvert University, and was seriously thinking of changing his major to that science. His parents and some of their friends were well read on the Southwest, and he had heard them discuss the ethnology, among other things, of the local Indians. The outstanding white man to be received into a Pueblo tribe had been Cushing, at Zuñi, in the eighteen-seventies, and after he had learned all the secrets he could, he went home and published them. The Zuñis had never forgotten or forgiven. Charlie knew he would never betray anything told him in trust, but the thought of Cushing was like a sudden shadow. If I ever become an anthropologist, he thought, I won't do any field work here.

All this dreaming along was well enough, but how should he start trying to find that figurine? To bring his mind down to brass tacks, he told himself, "I want to find a little stone man, an anthropomorphic figurine about ten inches long, that someone not an Indian is hiding." He walked in a circle, thinking about Mr. Carlisle.

The curio dealer would be a tough nut to crack. He really did know a lot about Indian crafts, was something of a connoisseur, and to the discriminating he offered things of quality and value. Some of the best of these he kept in a cabinet in his living room, and along with them articles that were virtually worthless, such as Hopi kachina dolls that he had aged artificially and that he would offer to the gullible at outrageous prices, alleging them to be sacred objects of enormous value, the mere possession of which, here next door to Indians, put him in mortal danger. The Indians knew about his frauds, which made them suspect him. Still, he was no fool, and he wouldn't let you search his place if he didn't want you to. He knew how close Charlie was to San Leandro, and his own dealings with the Indians had always been open and aboveboard. If he really was hiding that thing, it would be a complete switch from his usual practices.

Still thinking about the problem, and not getting much of anywhere with it, Charlie left the yard and started slowly up the street. It was in his mind to go look at Mr. Carlisle's shop. As it was past five o'clock, the place would probably be closed, but looking at it might somehow give him an idea. A block from Carlisle's place, he met his father.

"House call?" Charlie asked.

"No. Through, for once. Finished at the hospital, and no calls at the office. Cross your fingers. Where are you going?"

"Nowhere. Just bored."

They walked along together until they came to the Silver Dollar Restaurant, which was also a bar and a dispensary. It had a carefully frontier facade of logs that had nothing to do with New Mexico's tradition, and it was the only respectable drinking place in Castellano. Dr. Bond said, "Your mother wants me to pick up a bottle of sherry."

They went into the dispensary together. Curley Bostwick was behind the counter.

He said, "Hello, Doc; hello, Charlie. Say, you're just the people I was hoping to see."

The Doctor said, "What's on your mind, Curley?" His son knew he was braced for the usual try at getting a free diagnosis.

"Well, I understand you both know a good deal about these Injuns, and Charlie goes out to the pueblo"—he pronounced it "pew-eeblo"—"a lot, so maybe you can tell me." He paused.

Dr. Bond said, "Shoot."

"Well, a Spanish feller who's one of Sullivan's cowhands come in the other day, and he brought something he wanted to trade on. He said there was a break in the San Leandro line fence, and a couple of his cows had wandered in, so he went after them. While he was in there, he run into sort of a little stone house, and he found this thing in it. Wait a minute."

He went into the back room and returned with a package wrapped in newspaper. He looked out the door, then opened the package on the counter.

There it was. It was as simple as that.

"I give him a pint for it," Curley said, wrapping the little figure again. "Then I got to thinkin'. I hear sometimes the Injuns set a lot of store by things like this. I got customers from several pueblos; I don't want no trouble with them. And then, maybe it's worth a lot of money. What do you think?"

Dr. Bond said thoughtfully, "There isn't much money in a thing like that."

Charlie said to himself, "There's a man you can count on to say the right thing."

His father turned to him. "This mean anything to you?"

"Well, ye-es, it does. That is, I know that the Indians are all upset about something that's been stolen from them. They're pretty mad, too."

"Then it's dangerous to have this?" Dr. Bond asked. Lord, his father couldn't be doing better if they'd rehearsed.

"Yes," Charlie said. "You know they can get tough when someone fools around with what they think is sacred."

Curley looked good and unhappy. "What'd I ought to do?" Charlie said, "Get it back to them, as quick as you can."

"Here," Curley said, thrusting the bundle into Charlie's hands. "You know 'em; you get it to 'em."

Charlie did not see how he could refuse. As a matter of fact, he was glad to be put in a position to bring this object back to San Leandro himself, despite what Agapito had said about not handling it.

Dr. Bond said, "You mustn't be out of pocket on this. How much was that pint?"

"Three-sixty," Curley said.

The Doctor took out his wallet before his son, encumbered, could reach his.

"Let me pay it, Dad," Charlie said. "I've got it."

"I'll take care of it," his father said. "I have it more times over than you."

Curley accepted the money with thanks. Dr. Bond bought his sherry and they left.

Charlie said, "Thanks for saying all the right things. I guess I'd better take this right out."

"It's interesting. I'd like to get a photo of it."

"I'm sorry, Dad. You mustn't."

"The first winter you were in school here, your mother worried that you'd wind up speaking with a Spanish accent. Now, sometimes, I wonder if you haven't turned into an Indian. Will you be able to tell me anything about this?"

"I guess not. The truth is, I don't know much about it myself, except that it was stolen."

It occurred to him that it was odd that the Indians had not mentioned the break in the fence, which they surely would have discovered. Perhaps they did not speak of it because it was the War Captain's business, not theirs.

They took him into a house in which there was no furniture, they prayed and sang over him, making him safe from any harm that could have come from the power of the thing that he had carried. Without asking him to leave, they did what was necessary for the figurine itself, which took half an hour. Then they thanked him ceremoniously, and Juan Rael invited him to supper.

Shortly before he went back to college, there was a Turtle Dance at the pueblo. He went to watch it and, as usual ate at half a dozen houses, taking enough at each to show appreciation. In the middle of the afternoon, when women in full costume took presents to the dancers, two of them brought him round loaves of wheat bread and another a fat, flat cake of blue corn bread, which he knew to be delicious. Shortly afterward, a small boy came to him with a big paper bag in which to put the gifts. He felt singularly happy, and sorry he had to go East so soon, yet in another way eager, for now he knew he would major in anthropology.

Dr. Robert McKee, an assistant professor, gave an advanced course in Southwestern ethnology. Even though Charlie was now an anthropology major, he had to do a little talking to get admitted to it. Once he was in, Dr. McKee became interested in him, helped him adapt himself to requirements stiffer than those an undergraduate ordinarily must meet, and from time to time talked with him about Pueblo Indians, comparing observations as colleague to colleague rather than as professor to student. Charlie began to experience the unity, the closeness, that existed among the faculty and those students who were working toward a career in anthropology.

In November, Dr. McKee invited him to come to his rooms after supper to meet Dr. Sorenson of the University of Northern California, the author of the monumental study *Pueblo Indian Culture.* They would have, McKee said, a Pueblo evening. Charlie arrived at eight. He was the only student present and, not counting Dr. Sorenson, there were only two other guests—Dr. Stronsky, whose specialty was linguistics, and Dr. Elvira Stafford, the only woman on the anthropological faculty. The Southwest was at the extreme northern periphery of her field of interest. Charlie supposed that she was included to lend feminine charm—he himself found her surprisingly attractive for a woman who could not be less than thirty-five. Dr. Stronsky was dark, rather handsome, European-born, and distinctly cosmopolitan. The guest of honor was in his sixties—a tall, lean man with a mop of white hair, who disguised his erudition under an easy, casual manner.

All of these people were good talkers. Their respective educations went well beyond what suffices to earn a Ph.D. in a science, and in their talk they ranged widely. Charlie listened, not always understanding, excited to hear what he thought of as courses of study, topics with walled boundaries, discussed in the context of life and philosophy. He nursed a highball and kept turning his head from one to another of the speakers.

Dr. Stafford mentioned that Charlie was well acquainted with San Leandro. Dr. Sorenson said, "Oh?" and Dr. McKee answered, "Didn't I tell you that? I meant to."

"It's fifteen years since I was there," Dr. Sorenson said, to Charlie. "Is Cruz Rael still alive?"

"No, sir, he died about five years ago."

"Then did Agapito succeed him as Turquoise Cacique?"

"Yes, sir." So this man knew that.

Dr. Sorenson put a number of further questions—about various individuals, about how well the dances were being kept up—and flattered Charlie by asking whether he saw a connection between the San Leandro Basket Dance and the Hopi Niman Kachina Ceremony. He told some pleasant anecdotes of his experiences at San Leandro. At about this point, Dr. McKee, having freshened Dr. Stafford's drink, refilled Charlie's.

Dr. Sorenson said, "There was one lead I never had time to follow up. I'm interested in the distribution of anthropomorphic figures from the Hopi country eastward. Partly, it's their scarcity that interests me, considering how eminently capable the Pueblos have been at modelling and carving for the last couple of thousand years. Old Tomás Pérez said something one time about a 'little stone man' who relates to the Thunderstone Society. Have you heard anything about it?"

Charlie sipped his drink to gain time. To be able to tell the great

Albert Sorenson something. . . . He said, "I've heard of it. It's a small stone figurine."

"Male?"

"Yes."

"They don't keep it in the pueblo, do they?"

"No. It's in a shrine to the north."

"Oh. On Chompi Mountain, I suppose."

Charlie nodded faintly. He felt uneasy.

"And it does relate to thunder?"

"I think so, sir. Really, I don't know much about it—almost nothing. You know how they are."

Dr. Sorenson laughed. "I know."

He changed the subject. The gathering broke up at eleven. On his way to his room, Charlie was thankful that the scientist had, apparently, taken it for granted that he had not actually seen the figure. If he'd asked whether he had seen it, Charlie would have had to lie.

He returned to Castellano late on a June afternoon. As he was getting out of the car, three men from San Leandro went by on the other side of the street, but he was too busy greeting his mother to hail them. He took his things up to his room. On his desk there was a brown manila envelope with "Educational Materials" stamped on it. He would see what was inside later.

There was, always, so much to talk about. There was the pleasure, which never staled, of rediscovering what fun his parents were. It was a pleasant evening, and they had claret with dinner to celebrate.

The next morning he slept rather late. After breakfast, he got into his old car and set out for San Leandro. His studies had given a new depth to his understanding, had linked isolated items of knowledge in a pattern. He knew he would see his friends with new eyes.

He parked his car at the edge of the village and went in along a narrow street, past the back of the church and the square kiva, onto the plaza. He started across it diagonally, heading for Eddie Sota's house. Four men came out of a house on the far side of the plaza. The two in the middle, who wore their hair in queues, he recognized as the War Captains; the other two were younger and were carrying short staffs. Staffs were carried on certain special occasions by young men acting as a sort of ceremonial police. Charlie wondered what was going on.

Then he saw they were coming to meet him, so he stood and

waited. As they came near, he greeted them in Piro, smiling. They did not answer. He knew them all, but their faces were the faces of strangers.

They stopped, facing him, and the younger of the War Captains said, "You get out of here. You not come back. Not any time. You are our enemy. Now go."

"But—But—What on earth? What?"

The young men stepped closer, holding their staffs horizontally towards him. "You get out, Bond, or we put you out. We beat the hell out of you."

The hostility was a force in itself. He felt dizzy. Nothing made sense. He could not, in fact, take it in. He drove home, bewildered, and went straight to his room. His eye lit on the envelope on his desk. It had the return address of the university where Dr. Sorenson taught. An idea came to him that made him almost sick. He opened the envelope. It was a reprint from the April issue of the *Southwestern Anthropologist*, which he had not read. At the top was written, in ink, "With the author's compliments, Albert Sorenson." The title of the article was "Anthropomorphic Fetishes at Modern Pueblos."

Two boys from San Leandro, Charlie knew, were going to the University of New Mexico. He had been standing, holding the reprint in his hand; now he had to sit down. Unsteadily, he turned the document over. The footnotes were printed at the end, in small type, just ahead of the bibliography. The type was black, and bright against the white paper, and his name showed clear, even in the small characters. "Personal information of Mr. Charles S. Bond, of Talvert University." Without looking at the text itself, he could well imagine what a man of Dr. Sorenson's vast knowledge could build out of the little that he had let slip.

THE ANCIENT STRENGTH

The big Pueblo Indian dances—the "line dances," with many dancers in formation, a chorus of men's voices, and a powerful, big drum, or sometimes two—have a quality of surge and ebb that fills the whole village and slowly takes possession of you if you will give it time and yield yourself to it. You don't even have to pay attention all the time, any more than the Indians do. Like them, you meet friends, talk a little, you eat at this house and that, you stand or sit to watch the dance again—nothing too much—and let the ceremony surround you and fill you.

It was while this was happening in the heat and dust at San Leandro, and I was sitting in the shade of the low adobe bench that runs along the foot of the wall of my friend Juan Rael's house, and a corner of my mind was considering the captive eagles on the housetops, and the sense of antiquity colored all my thinking, that I seriously thought for the first time that my mission might really be blocked by the very nature of these Indians, and I had a new understanding of why old Sorenson, who knows the Pueblos better than anyone else now living, had told me that if I wanted to dig in the San Leandro rubbish heap I should be sure I completed negotiations for permission before the people get involved in the big July ceremony, commonly and erroneously called the Eagle Home Dance, the one I was now absorbing.

What I was up to requires some explaining. San Leandro is a Piro-

*Originally published in the *New Yorker,* August 31, 1963.

speaking pueblo on the Rio Grande, not far from Santa Fe, New Mexico, that has been right where it is since at least Coronado's time. Some years ago, it filed a claim against the United States under the Indian Claims Act, for which purpose it is represented by a firm of attorneys. The claim is opposed by the Department of Justice. The evidence on both sides in Indian claims cases may involve history, ethnology, and archeology. Both sides commission all sorts of research, some of which has resulted in data of anthropological importance. It was in such a connection that I came in on the San Leandro case. Archeological evidence was needed to support the pueblo's claim, and the lawyers thought that perhaps I would be able to find it. Pueblo-Anasazi archeology is my field—my name, by the way, is Hendricks, and I am an assistant professor in the anthropology department at the University of Northern California. I have worked in Pueblo country for more than a dozen seasons, mostly in the Tewa and Piro sections. I was, I suppose, as well qualified as anyone for what they wanted, and I would be in the neighborhood anyhow, digging in the Rio Azulito site, the ruin of an ancient pueblo ten miles away.

The tribe was asking compensation for the loss of some twenty thousand acres of good grazing land south of its grant. It claimed that it had occupied and used this tract, commonly known as El Cajón, continuously and notoriously since time immemorial and, in historic times, with the knowledge and at least the tacit consent of the Spanish crown, the Mexican Republic, and then the United States. In the turmoil of the Confederate invasion of New Mexico in 1862 and the increased Apache and Navajo raiding that followed, a group of white men had wrongfully and by force seized El Cajón and converted it to their use. The land has a perennial stream on it, fed by three springs, and even today, when conditions are drier than they were a century ago, supports some four hundred head of cattle without overgrazing.

I'm no lawyer, but I agreed with the pueblo's lawyers that it looked as if El Cajón really had belonged to the pueblo by right of aboriginal use and occupancy, in which case the U.S. failed in its duty to protect the Indians and they had compensation coming to them. The lawyers thought it might run to as much as a hundred thousand dollars. Proof that would stand up in court, however, was not as strong as it ought to be. It was possible that I, by archeological means, could provide the additional quantum that would win the case.

A short distance downstream from the largest of the El Cajón springs are the ruins of a settlement of five houses, and near them you can see where some fields were dry-farmed. The San Leandros state that the houses were used as summer lodgings by members of the pueblo who worked that land up to the time of the Civil War, and also served as shelters for shepherds. A field study group from the museum in Santa Fe had worked there one season a few years ago. Their findings confirmed that it was probably an Indian rather than a Spanish-American settlement, that it had been occupied or visited in the mid-nineteenth century, and that sheep had been penned nearby over a long period of time. The crucial period for our case was after 1846, for Uncle Sam could not be held responsible for land lost under Mexican or Spanish sovereignty. We needed to prove that it was definitely San Leandro Indians, and not people from any one of several neighboring pueblos, who had lived in those houses, and that they were living there up to the period of the Civil War.

Pieces of Indian pottery had been found, but they were Picuris and Tewa wares that were being widely traded in the mid-nineteenth century. Anybody could have had them. There were also some pieces of a curious pottery, marked by delicate floral designs in black on white, that did not connect with anything known but was plainly of Indian manufacture. Chemical analysis showed that the clay was a compound of earths from sources still used by several pueblos, including San Leandro. These shards, the remains of not more than three smallish bowls, could be diagnostic and conclusive.

The lawyers found several old men and women who stated that the shards were indeed from a type of pottery made in San Leandro by their own grandmothers, and that there used to be examples of it around in their time. Unfortunately, Barnes, the director of the museum's dig (and the Department of Justice boys will make the most of his testimony, don't worry), stated that at the time that he unearthed those shards he showed them to San Leandro Indians and drew nothing but blank looks. The point could be made that when Barnes questioned the Indians, neither he nor they had any axe to grind, whereas later the San Leandros had a strong reason to claim the pottery.

The thing was more pro-and-connish than that. I looked Barnes up as soon as I got to Santa Fe. He's a good man, with a sound field technique. His scratching around that little settlement had been a hasty thing, although there was no question about the finding of the shards, and he had had no time to make careful inquiries about them. He had simply shown them to Indians from various pueblos when opportunity offered, then shoved them into a tray, to be dealt with at some future time. He and I had a drink together after his office hours. Over the drink, he remarked that the government's failure to protect the Indians' use of El Cajón was due to the confusion caused by the Confederate, or Texan, invasion. The Department of Justice ought to concede the point, he said, and the pueblo should accept compensation in Confederate money. I passed this suggestion on to one of the lawyers when he was out here. He did not think it funny.

Obviously, what was needed was archeological evidence that the floral pottery was a San Leandro ware of the crucial period. The place to look for that was in the San Leandro trash heap, which brings me to the matter of trash heaps in general and San Leandro's in particular.

Ever since the days of the Anasazi cliff dwellers—nay, before that, back into the Basket Maker II period at least, two thousand years ago—the ancestors of the present Indians were in the habit of throwing their trash out of their settlements, preferably where there was a drop. (I know, the basket makers were longheaded and the Pueblos are brachy, but let's not get into labile cephalic indexes, the dolicho remains at Pecos, and all that; it's too complicated.) We do not know when they adopted the present Pueblo custom of an annual village cleaning, but it was probably long ago, and we know that the Indians have been doing it for hundreds of years. San Leandro's trash heap is typical. The village lies on an old alluvial terrace of the Rio Grande that falls off sharply to the east and north. The annual dumping takes place over the terrace's northern edge; through the centuries, this has created a sort of talus slope that should make very juicy digging. There, below the level of bottles and broken phonograph records, and the red-on-black pottery now made at San Leandro, mostly for sale, one might find the floral black-on-white.

One might, if one could get permission to dig there. It was thoughtful of the Old People to dump their rubbish once each year in the same place, for thereby they have provided archeologists with quite beautiful and exact stratifications. (For example, if the floral ware was what we hoped, it would turn up in association with American-made articles of various kinds, and that would be sufficient.) It was not thoughtful, however, of the Old People to provide their descendants with a set of religious beliefs that makes it extremely difficult—in many cases, impossible—to get permission to dig in their rubbish. You run into remarks about Dust Boy (whoever he is), references to the spirit of the past, and vague remarks about ancestors, and what you are likely to get in the end is a rather convoluted negative answer.

Yet, when they approached me, the lawyers seemed to think I would have little trouble getting permission. They had already met several times over the past year with the tribal council to go over the ins and outs of the case. The Indians understood that evidence from the trash heap could be crucial, the lawyers said, and were ready to talk with me. I had been working around San Leandro for several seasons and had used some San Leandro workmen. Several members of the council knew me, or had heard of me, and they would be prepared for my coming. I would be preceded by a lengthy letter from the lawyers, introducing me and setting forth, once more, the reasons evidence from the trash heap was essential. I was offered forty dollars a day for time spent in actual work, including a few days, if needed, for negotiations. Then, if the results justified it, I would be in line for what looked to an assistant professor like a very nice sum indeed for appearing as an expert witness.

When the offer was made to me, I went to old Sorenson, who, as I have said, knows the Pueblos better than any of us, and asked his advice. He said "It can't do any harm. You know those people well enough to know you can't push them; all you can do is ask nicely and hope. Anyone in the academic line who doesn't pick up a little extra money when he can do so properly and legitimately should have his head examined."

I said, "I'm going on with my work at Rio Azulito, which is only ten miles away. If they'll give me permission, I can bring a couple of good students, and if we go in from the bottom I trust we can get into some older stuff while we're at it. It would be nice to get some contact material." (Contact material means from when the Spanish were first settling in.)

"You'll have to feel your way. Two helpers might look too big to them, but take your opportunities as they come, just so you don't get the Indians angry and foul things up for others."

I answered politely, but not without betraying some annoyance. "I hope I'm not utterly irresponsible."

Sorenson laughed. "One can't take anything for granted. But one thing—get out there as early as you can, right after exams end, and try to get permission firmly granted and work started before that July wingding of theirs comes up, the ceremony that ends with the Eagles Return Rite."

"The Eagle Home Dance? When they sacrifice eagles at the end?"

"Yes. Only you know that's a thoroughly incorrect name. You'll hear some of them speak of it as the Pueblo Houses Dance. That's still not the real name, I'm quite sure, but it's suggestive. Considering that the principal chief or head priest of a Hopi pueblo is called Houses Chief, and that you have the idea of corporate power, which is created or amassed . . ." He was talking to himself at that point. I listened, trying to follow his thoughts; then the big bell rang for the first afternoon class and I had to hurry off.

I wasn't able to follow Sorenson's advice. One overcomes the obstacles one thinks are important, and I didn't know enough, and he didn't explain enough, for me to think I should take what he said seriously. The main thing I had gone to him for, after all, was his approval of my having a try at the work, and with that in hand I forgot much of the rest. Then, that year I had only one experienced man and three new undergraduates, one of whom had had one field season. On top of that, the Rio Azulito site is on private land, the ranch of a Spanish-American named Robles, and Mr. Robles had got it into his head, for the second time, that we were going to extract a fortune from the ruin. That meant that when we got there he was all braced to demand a new contract, with an enormous fee, and after that was smoothed over he, or members of his family, were always hanging around watching to see what we took out of the ground. They got in the way, and I was worried that they'd fall into a trench and mess up the strata, or be seized by an urge to dig themselves, or something like that. Give me a site on Indian or federal land any day, where everyone understands the rules and you have a binding permit.

Under the circumstances, I did not feel too free about leaving the site. I finally made it to San Leandro on a Sunday morning at the end of June, to find that the governor—the official head of the tribe—was away. The lieutenant governor was in the room they keep for an office, with a sign over the door that says "GOVERNOR" in large letters and under that, smaller, "GET PHOTO PERMITS HERE." San Leandro is what you might call a progressive-traditional tribe. The people keep up their ceremonies and other ancient practices with vigor, and at the same time they have TV, piped water, and things like that. They have a conscious program for hanging on to the old, Indian values while adapting to the modern world; it will be a neat trick if they can make it work. Part of the plan is to select each year's governor from among the older men, the lieutenant governor from among the younger ones—preferably a veteran—and let the two generations learn from each other. This year's lieutenant governor was Juan Rael, a Navy veteran. He had worked for me on Tsepo Ruin three years before, and he had read the lawyers' letter about me.

Juan was cordial. He explained the governor's absence and told me, somewhat apologetically, that the council had not formally discussed my business. It would require a regular council meeting, he said. Now that so many of the San Leandros were working away from home for wages, there was sometimes trouble getting a full council together. He said that one man, Anastacio Pérez, was in Denver, remarking, "He's kind of on the young side, but he has his specialty, you might say, so there are things you can't settle unless he's here."

I thought it worth taking time to strengthen my relationship with this man and to indoctrinate him as well as I could. He had made it clear that he considered the claim important, and he described the pueblo's plan for using the money—scholarships for young people going to college, a revolving system for purchasing registered bulls and renting them to tribal cattlemen, things like that. Twice while we were talking, tourists came in for permits to take pictures. Then another youngish Indian, named Eddie Ortiz, turned up. He wore an Indian Service police badge on his shirt, and Juan explained that he was the sheriff. They talked together briefly in Piro, then Juan said to me, "Suppose you show me where you want to dig. Eddie'll tend store for a while and we can have dinner."

We walked to the edge of the village and I showed him the place that looked best to me. It was simply a question of where the grade looked good and the trash was thick. He thought for a time, then he said, "Yeah. That ought to be all right. Here or this way"—he gestured to the east. "Not that way"—he moved his hand west. "There's something underneath over there; they won't want you to go near it."

I said, "Fine," looking down the slope. There was a twinkle of broken glass here and there over the surface, fragments of glazed, mass-produced ceramics, and tin cans, all more abundant toward the top. I saw a brass cartridge case, farther down the half-buried remnant of an old shoe, and near my feet a phonograph record and a plastic hairbrush without bristles. Over to the left, where I was to stay away, I saw the main parts of the transmission of a car. It was hard to believe that not far under such drab, familiar leavings were the evidences of antiquity.

Juan renewed his invitation to dinner and I accepted. It was noon, I was hungry, and Pueblo food is good. We started back. On the way we passed the square kiva, a big, high-looming windowless cere-monial building. Most people don't look above eye level unless some-thing attracts their interest, and I guess archeologists are even more inclined than most to watch the ground. It was looking at the high wall of the kiva that led my eye to where a young eagle was perched, tethered, on the edge of the roof of a two-story house. The bird looked ruffled and untamed.

I said, nodding my head toward the eagle, "I haven't seen that since I was in the Hopi country."

Juan said, "Yeah. Other pueblos used to keep them, but they've forgotten."

Asking anything about Pueblo ceremonies is tricky business, but, remembering Sorenson, I let curiosity out so far as to ask, "You need them for the dance you people put on next month? Like at the end of that dance the Hopis have about then?"

"Something like that. You seen that Hopi dance?"

"Yes. It—it had power."

The Ancient Strength

The Hopis dance publicly in the masks that all the Rio Grande Pueblos keep secret. Sometimes you can talk about it, sometimes not.

Juan said, "It's a rainmaker. Hope we make rain." Then he led the talk to harmless topics.

Altogether, I counted six eagles on housetops. They are revered by the Indians, but to a white man they are simply wild creatures made captive, and it rather relieved me to think that in less than a month the birds would be sacrificed and so set free. You would not want one of these creatures to be kept tethered for very long. While my eyes were still directed upward, I saw in the west the rounded, dark green peak of Chompi Mountain, from which most of the eagles had come, and I wondered if they ever looked toward it.

The last thing Juan said to me before I left that day was to be sure and return the following Sunday, the first in July, which I did. The governor, who spoke pretty good English, was there and prepared for me. He was most friendly. He told me to come back for a full council meeting Wednesday morning. I wanted to put it over until Sunday, so as not to interfere with my work at Rio Azulito, but he said that would not do. "Everybody's comin' in now for the work we do around this time. Everybody be here by Wednesday. Couple days later, some of 'em too busy with that work." (The word "work" in such a context means ceremonial. Once they have a ceremony in hand, everything else has to give way.)

I had never before attended a tribal council. In the case of San Leandro, I would be encountering the ages-old theocracy, for which the lay officials are a front. I was curious and a trifle excited, and more than ordinarily aware of impressions, as I entered the village Wednesday morning and came into the large rectangular plaza, entering at the northwest corner, by the Catholic church, which, with its two low towers, rises a little above the other buildings. The plaza is an expanse of hard-trampled, clayey earth, dusty in dry weather, with nothing growing in it but one splendid cottonwood near the middle of the south side. The flat-roofed houses—some one story, some two stories high, some with porches—form a nearly solid enclosure. The native adobe is a warm brown with a slight sparkle to it, and under the porches—in New Mexico they are called by the Spanish name, *"portales"*—the walls are usually whitewashed. There is

201

variation in the size of the houses, in the arrangement of doors, and in the windows, which range from tiny prehistoric apertures to modern metal casements. The whole, though uniformly composed of rectangles, is not at all monotonous. Adobe weathers into softness and the Indians build largely by eye, so that angles are not quite true and the most regular construction achieves naturally the irregularity that the Greeks used to plan for.

In front of the houses and close to them there are altogether eight *hornos,* the beehive-shaped ovens, standing about four feet high, that the Spanish introduced. They are the only curved surfaces; there are no arches. One of the much touted charms of adobe is how it takes sunlight and shadow, the sunlight absorbed and softened, the shadow luminous. The play of light and shadow around a plaza such as this is its principal beauty. On the *hornos,* the light blending into shade over the curves is a delicate and wonderful thing.

An Indian plaza is bare, harmonious, and snug. On an off afternoon such as that Wednesday, there will be some children playing in it, a few mongrels taking the sun, and in front of one or two houses pottery and other wares, usually tended by a girl, set out in the hope of tourists. Even with the children and dogs, the village seems empty. Tourists are disappointed not to see Indians in costume all over the place. On ordinary days, the men are busy in the fields—unless they are in the kiva working up a ceremony—and the women are at their housework or pottery-making. There's no reason why anybody should be around, and when you come to think of it, how is it that even in quite small non-Indian settlements so many people seem to have business on the streets? What keeps them going to and fro? Hanged if I know.

I said that a Pueblo plaza is snug. You could also say contained, almost fortified. When you work in the ruins the Old People left, you keep trying to project yourself, and one of the things you feel is this enclosed, self-contained quality, whether it's in a cliff dwelling jammed onto a high ledge of rock in the Navajo country or a little, open site near the Rio Grande. The same thing is present in the pueblos of today, and it goes back at least to Basket Maker III, a dozen centuries or so ago; we don't know how they placed their dwellings before that. The houses and the people, few or many, stand close together, and perhaps that's why they are still here after a couple of thousand years of droughts and crop failures, of Navajos, Apaches, Comanches, Utes, and the white man.

Juan met me and led me to a building on what you could call a back street, obviously a structure of some age, containing a large, bare room. There were somewhat more than twenty men, most of them elderly, sitting along the walls, some on a *banco,* an adobe bench built out from the long back wall, the others on an assortment of chairs. I was given a comfortable chair placed near the door, facing the assemblage. At a plain table in the middle of the room sat the secretary, a youngish man, and there Juan joined him. As it turned out, Juan was the interpreter, and the secretary took copious notes on a lined pad. The governor was inconspicuous in the corner. Most of the men wore their hair long, done in a *chongo,* a queue wrapped in a narrow red strip of native weave. There was a good deal of jewelry in evidence—turquoise or Navajo-silver earrings, necklaces of shell, turquoise, coral, or silver, and rings and bracelets. Several men wore moccasins. The rest of their costume consisted of ordinary work clothes, except in the case of one man—whom I took to be the man from Denver—in a business suit and bow tie, and the secretary, who wore lightweight slacks and a T shirt. Their expressions were friendly. The governor spoke a polite greeting in Piro and stated that all the proper people were here and ready to hear what I had to say. Juan interpreted, and added, after explaining that he was speaking on his own, that they all knew I wanted to do something to help them.

This group had met numerous times with its attorneys, the question of the El Cajón site had been fully discussed, and my mission had been set forth in a lengthy letter. With these people, however, you don't count on any of that. You begin at the beginning and tell it all. I don't know whether they require that procedure just because they like to hear familiar tales, or as a way of having a chance to think about a matter over again, or from a canny desire to see whether everyone tells the same story, but, in any case, you review the whole question.

I would say a few sentences, then wait to be interpreted. I was brief about the claim in general, but skipped no details on the potsherds and the conflicting evidence, and presented a full, careful statement of what stratigraphy can show and how something turned up in the rubbish could be tied to something more than ten miles away. While the interpretation went on, I planned what to say next and looked around. Once you adjust yourself to it, talking through an interpreter becomes a restful mode of operation. After a few minutes, I hardly noticed the jewelry or other exotic trimmings as the dark faces of the councilmen seemed to emerge and ceased to be the faces of Indians, of another race, and became the faces of individuals, some of them wonderfully lined, all of them full of character. These were men of authority, whose minds were stored with ancient knowledge, and they were healthy outdoor men, men of their hands—farmers, stockmen, and, in season, hunters. Physical condition, age, and knowledge joined to make their faces most impressive.

When I was through, a very old man spoke in Piro. Juan made no effort to translate but sat half turned, listening. Another man spoke. They did not seem to be speaking to anyone but to be thinking aloud and letting their thoughts fall into the room. It was quiet talk and I could tell nothing from it. I listened and looked at the faces, and dreamed away the modern clothing and wondered how many centuries back the ancestors of these characters were meeting in similar councils. Piro is a language of the Tanoan subfamily. How old was it? Had these sounds once filled council rooms—kivas, mostly— at Pueblo Bonito, at Spruce Tree House, or Chetro Ketl?

Perhaps half a dozen of them had expressed an opinion when a medium-old man with a strong, broad face and a square jaw spoke at some length. When he finished, people all over the room made a humming sound that means assent. He spoke again, directly to Juan.

Juan said, "That's Crescencio Rael." (I estimate that over half of the San Leandro are either "Rael" or "Pérez." Having the same last name does not seem to mean relationship.) Juan went on, "He's high up in what we're getting ready for now, what they call Eagle Home Dance, and he's one of the *principales.* He says this is a hard thing you have brought up. We want to win our claim, and now, the way you tell it, I think we all understand about digging for those potteries. Only it ain't easy to say you can dig in there. It's kinda hard for me to tell it so you'll understand, what these old men been talking about just now. It's the old times, you might say, that are in the rubbish heap. Not the big things, like this dance we're bringing out next week, but—well, like the pottery. One time they made that kind

<del>204</del>

for a while, right here in this pueblo, then they quit. So it's in the dirt there, along with what they used to eat, and, like the stuff they used to weave in old times, and all like that. It's part of what we're made of, and it's what the old-time people, the ones that are gone now, they used to know. What was familiar to them."

I have discussed Juan's words with several Pueblo ethnographers, who found them interesting. Note that he did not say anything about the Old People coming back or ancestral spirits hovering around. In fact, he did a nice job of getting an idea across without giving away any beliefs.

Juan said a few words to Crescencio, who answered in a few sentences.

"Right now," Juan said, "they are thinking about this dance. That's what's in their minds, and this ain't no time for deciding what you're asking for. They say, let it go over until we're through with that work."

Crescencio added something more. I decided that he could follow English pretty well.

Juan said, "We're sorry to make you wait. We all know you come to help us. And he says, you come to the dance next week. You will see something good. Come and eat dinner at my house, and you can bring those boys you got working with you. Like at fiesta, we got plenty grub."

I could only accept the postponement. I tried to get a firm date for another meeting, but was put off. Then I got up and so did everybody else. Many of them, including Crescencio Rael, came up to shake hands with me, or touch hands—they do not actually shake. They said pleasant, noncommittal things, the older men in Spanish.

My attitude toward this job had originally been somewhat casual, but it had changed. The possible money would be very nice to have, and, beyond that, I was affected by the tendency in all of us to become partisan. I liked these Indians, the material the lawyers had sent me had convinced me that their cause was just, and I really wanted to see them win. In addition, there was the possibility of turning up scientifically valuable material, the desire to be one of the very few who had ever poked into the rubbish heap of an occupied pueblo. I imagined the tribe grateful to me, accepting me as a special friend, if I turned the trick. The postponement disturbed me more than I had expected, and I was worried enough to wonder if, in the end, old beliefs would make them refuse me permission. Until then, I had had little apprehension.

The dance was on Sunday week. As I understand it, this is one of the most purely Indian ceremonies that a white man can get to see among the Rio Grande Pueblos. O'Neil, a Pueblo ethnographer with whom I discussed it later, has a theory that the public part is an unmasked version of an older, masked ceremony. Yet it is held on a Sunday—one of those recent adaptations to their changing world that are a sign of the strength and viability of Pueblo culture. Wage work away from home has become important, and for the benefit of the wage workers they hold their affairs as much as possible on weekends. I had told Juan I'd plan on coming, and he had said, "All right. You stay and watch it all along, and maybe you'll understand better why these old men are having trouble making up their minds to let you dig."

The dance was performed by two teams of at least eighty men and women each, one of the people of the Turquoise moiety, the other of the Calabash moiety. Each team was accompanied by a chorus with two drummers and about twenty male singers. Their performances alternated throughout the day. Juan was not in the dance, whether because his civil office required him to be on hand for secular matters (but no photographing was allowed that day) or because he did not belong to the right society I did not know. There were all sorts of visitors dropping in at his house, and for at least two hours his wife and several other women were busy serving table after table of guests with good, hearty food—mutton stew, chili, the bread pudding called *sopa,* and the necessary quantities of weak coffee and Kool-Aid. On the table was a large plate that was kept always piled high with bread baked in the *hornos* I've described. It is European peasant bread, the pure tradition out of Spain, and it's hard to find better bread anywhere these days. Everything was as clean as you could ask for. My boys got a big poke out of it and ate very well indeed. They got a lot out of the dance, too, having enough background to approach it seriously and to imagine the antiquity of the thing, projecting it, or something like it, into the plaza of the Rio Azulito ruin.

Wherever you were in the village, the drums followed you. The sound travelled through the earth. Often it seemed to come from almost any direction. In the open, or at an open window, even away from the plaza, you would hear the voice of the chorus rise at the strong parts of a song, and then it would fade again. In the plaza, actually attending the dance, you followed all of the singing and the sound of gourd rattles in the men's hands and the turtle-shell and deer-hoof rattles on their right legs, marking a time that usually went along with the drum but sometimes separated from it. If you watched, all of these rhythmic elements were interwoven with the visual ones—the men's feet, their emphatic steps and the general movement of their bodies and heads, the women's much gentler placement of their feet, even in passages of fast time, and, weaving over and through all these effects, the maneuvers of the dancers, in this particular dance very simple but occasionally marking a larger, slower rhythm that embraced the rest.

You listen, you stop listening; you look, you stop looking. You chat. You go in and eat. Except for a period of about two hours in the middle of the day, the dance is continuously with you. If you stick around, it increasingly binds you and the other people there together—the San Leandros and the visitors from other pueblos especially, to a lesser degree the occasional Navajos and Apaches who turn up, and least of all the whites, a few of whom stay for more than an hour or two. A dance of this kind is a sophisticated, evolved form of art, which uses repetition and duration as essential elements. If you don't expose yourself to the repetition, you cannot get the impact of it.

We were there to spend the day. I visited several houses, Juan telling me what men would be at home. I felt that he wanted to help me advance my cause. I entered into no discussions of it, but I thought that the more these people knew me as a person, the easier it would be for them to let me pry into the repository of their past. I was well received wherever I went.

All the time, I was conscious of the half-dozen eagles on the rooftops, waiting to be sacrificed in the Eagles Return Rite. So then the prisoners are set free, I thought, studying the one on the top of the two-story house next to Juan's. He looked wild and hostile, not at all Puebloan. Another, farther away, was tearing at a gobbet of meat. It occurred to me that I had seen captive eagles flap their wings occasionally, but neither here nor in the Hopi country had I ever seen one seriously try to fly or break away. I wondered whether their wings were clipped. More likely, I thought, some of their pinions had been pulled.

I thought about the probable age of this dance and of eagle catching and sacrificing, and hence came again to the time-depth of the inward-turned, castellated quality of Pueblo life down the ages that I have already described. It was in the course of thinking thus, sitting on the low bench in front of Juan's house, soaked in the dance, relaxed, that it occurred to me that Sorenson might have meant that I should get my business settled with the leaders before their entering into all the complex of this ceremony carried them deep into their ancient psychological heritage, and that it really was quite possible that they would refuse to let me, one might say, make a crack in even a tiny edge of the pattern.

All day these people had been concentrating themselves, concentrating their power, building it up here within the village. You could feel it—a dynamic substance. I thought that the heart of Pueblo existence was retention, holding it all in, and that in this there was something almost morbid. There had to be a letting out, a spending, too, and in some sleepiness in the latter part of the afternoon, what with the heat and much eating and a slight lack of sleep from having gone into town with the boys Saturday night and sat up late talking shop over beer, it occurred to me that one outlet would come when the spirits of the eagles were set free at sundown to soar and wander as eagles should. This random thought comforted me and made me more hopeful of getting the permission I sought. As you can see, I had managed to get those birds on my mind.

A sharp change in the arrangement of sound jerked me into attention. The group that was dancing, the people of the Turquoise moiety, was not leaving the plaza, but the Calabash moiety dancers were coming in, their chorus singing its own song, drumming and dancing their own time. The enclosed place, the Piro center, became jammed with noise and people, with a new excitement of sight and sound. There really was not room for both teams of dancers, but somehow they worked it all out and managed to blend. A couple of my boys joined me and one of them said, "Wow! There isn't anything to say about this except 'Wow!,' is there, Doc?"

I said, "I see what you mean."

The sun was near setting and we seemed to be the only white people still there. I don't know how long that finale lasted, perhaps twenty minutes; then the two teams went off in separate directions toward their respective kivas.

Juan told me, "That's all now. It's over."

It was a dismissal. I had heard that the Eagles Return business and whatever else they did at the edge of the village after the dance was not for the public. I gathered the boys and we drove back to camp.

I wondered how soon I should return to San Leandro and see about stirring up another meeting. Not right away, I knew, as they had to have time to rest and to perform follow-up rites. They would need a little time. Next Sunday would be about right, and if things went well I could take as much as two or three weeks to work in, if I needed them.

To my surprise, Juan came to get me at the Rio Azulito site on Friday morning. We had just broken into what looked like a circular pit house dating from Basket Maker III, though I knew of no Basket Maker material from anywhere near there. I was all wrapped up in the engineering problems and the possibilities when Juan came climbing over the ruin and told me that the council was in session and wanted to see me. I had a moment's impulse to object that I could not go right then, but I thought better of it and climbed out of the hole I was working in and dusted myself off.

Juan, it turned out, had not come in his own car but had bummed a ride with a friend who was on his way to the Apache reservation up north. He remarked that his own car was a pickup and that the seat was in bad condition, so he thought I'd be more comfortable in my sedan.

Once we got going, I naturally wanted to get an idea of what awaited me, whether the council had come to a decision, and if so what. I said I hoped they'd let me dig for the evidence they needed, and he said, "You know how these old men are. They talk it over and talk it over."

The Pueblos—most Indians, for that matter, I believe—are not satisfied until they reach unanimous agreement. They could still be working on that, or Juan could be being evasive. I'd have to wait to learn the answer, and hoped I was not in for a series of indecisive palavers. We drove on in silence for quite a while, then Juan began singing quietly and beating time with his open hand on the top of the car door.

I said, "That's one of the songs they sang last Sunday, isn't it?"

"Yeah. My uncle made it. He's the one that mostly makes up songs for our side. How'd you like the dance?"

"It was beautiful."

When we had gone a good bit farther, I came out with a question I could not help asking. "Now those eagles are all turned loose, aren't they?"

"Hunh? Turned loose?"

"I mean, when they were sacrificed, that turned them loose."

He thought that over for a while. "Well, no. You know how the Hopis do when they sacrifice them?"

"Yes."

"We do kinda the same thing. So their spirits stay in, they stay with us, until we send them back to go into little eagles. They're part of the pueblo, kind of, their nests and our houses. It goes round and round."

"Oh."

He started singing again. I was depressed. It's all part of the same pattern, or configuration; everything is kept in. The eagles never get free. Their spirits are sent back into the nests, which are all well known to the San Leandro and tied to the Piro center with all the strands of ritual, and there they hatch and become eaglets again, and are taken back to San Leandro to sit on those perches until the time comes to start them around yet once more. I glanced at Juan's profile. I didn't think I'd better ask any more questions; he'd gone pretty far answering that last one. You keep it in. Once more my mind reached back across the centuries, back to the close-packed cliff dwellings. I thought of the ruin we were working on and the yet older Basket Maker site below it. Always the corn growing and the need of all the power men could gather in from every source to insure its growth, and always, you could be sure, roving hunters ready to swoop and steal. The fields were safe now. The Indians had machines with which to clear or improve their irrigation ditches, the modern tools of farming, and there were no more raiding enemies, but their way of life was under siege as it had never been before. Television aerials marred the antique lines of the flat-topped roofs . . . Against all the white man's destroying array of non-essentials they hoarded and massed the strength, and even this quite up-to-date young man beside me had behind him the captive souls of eagles. The eagles' forebears and his own had handed the strength down. We hit a chuckhole and I decided to pay attention to my driving. Shortly the pueblo came in sight, the clustered, low buildings that matched the soil around them and the slight, centralizing accent of the facade of the church, with its little towers.

When we parked the car and walked on in, I thought that one ought to be conscious of breaking through a barrier of some sort, of breasting the strength of the people. I encountered nothing except the usual restful quiet. Although it was unnecessary, as we went along I glanced to see that there were now no eagles on the roofs.

We entered the old council room. I was prepared to make a circuit shaking hands, but Juan pushed the chair toward me, saying, "Make yourself comfortable," so I did. A very old man was talking, a shrunken old man wearing a bright, large-patterned factory blanket around his body. I supposed he had reached an age at which any ordinary room is chill. His voice was thin, his speech halting. God knows what he was talking about. Crescencio Rael, who had the final say before, interrupted him pleasantly and he fell silent. Then the governor welcomed me as courteously as before, expressing appreciation that I had dropped my work to come to the council without advance notice. After that, there was rather a long pause. Not knowing what else to do, I lit a cigarette.

Juan said something to the councilmen. The very old man said a few words. Then Crescencio spoke for not more than two minutes.

Juan said, "They have talked it all over, and they are all agreed. They are sorry, because you have taken trouble and they want to help our lawyers, but they can't let you dig in the trash heap. Not any part of it. Maybe we won't win that money. That's too bad, but we been getting on all right for a long time without it. It's like what I told you the other day, and Crescencio says maybe you understand better now that you were here all day for the dance. We sure thank you and we hope you come visit us often."

As he finished speaking, I was conscious of a change occurring in

211

the gathering. Now, as I turned my eyes from him, I saw an expression of happiness and relief on the men's faces. They were all looking right at me, and I knew they wanted to see how I would react.

I guess my reaction had been building up in me, subconsciously, for some little time. I heard myself saying, "I think you are exactly right. I think the important thing is for you to keep everything whole." I rose, still surprised at what I had said, and knowing that I meant exactly that.

Everyone had to shake hands with me. It was as if we had accomplished something difficult and good together. We said friendly things to each other in English and Spanish, and one elderly gentleman with a face remarkably like a sack of potatoes taught me a Piro phrase that, Juan explained later, meant "All is well. Many thanks, friend." I was invited to stay for lunch in a dozen houses, but there was plenty of morning left and I had that site to play with, so I thanked them and drove on back to Rio Azulito. My little session with the San Leandro council had been, strictly speaking, a venture in ethnography, I told myself on the way. Sorenson might say I had muffed it, but if I had, by so doing I had uncovered a bit of simon-pure archeology that no ruin, no matter how complete, would ever yield up.